An Eng

Gabriel Stein

An English Revenge

Gabriel Stein

First published in 2018 by Rhomphaia Books

For Zoë, who wanted ‘stories’

Contents

CHAPTER 1

Battle

It was still dark when the order came to prepare for battle. Why do you always have to get ready in the dark? It only means more confusion as soldiers who are barely awake look for their arms and armour and try to put them on; and then attempt to form ranks. In the daylight, getting ready is never a problem, but in the dark, it is always almost impossible. For one thing, it's always cold, so even though you wear thick linen clothes under your armour, the morning mist will seep through them and therefore the metal will chill you to the bone. However well your armour fits, it will chafe you anyway. Also, you know that this time it's for real, which makes it even more important to get everything right. Helmets need to be tightened so that a blow doesn't make them fall off, but not so that your beard gets caught in the strap. If you wear a sword you have to belt it on properly. A thousand things can go wrong and usually they will. Someone stumbles over a sword or an axe and manages to get wounded and all of a sudden you're one man short even before the fighting starts. You are supposed to be quiet, but at night every sound travels much further, so you constantly worry about that too. But finally, we were ready and from the sounds around us, we could hear that the rest of the army was more or less prepared too. The confusion let up and instead, there was a feeling of readiness. Then our commander began to speak.

'Right lads, he said. 'You know why we are here. A bunch of stuck-up Normans and their leader – sorry, their Duke – have decided that they want our land. They show good taste, I'll give them that. But why should we let them take it? You know what that will mean; just look across the narrow seas here and you will see what Norman rule is. Free men enslaved, wives and daughters raped, farms seized, goods stolen. They've done it before and now they are trying to do it again. Well, not this time. Let them try! We won't even give them enough land for their graves. Burial is too good for them anyway. Let the dogs feed on their bodies!'

That brought some laughter and some cheers. He continued, 'we are not the helpless serfs they've met in other lands. We are fighters. Look at you!'

That was a bit difficult as it was still quite dark, although the darkness was beginning to lift. As yet, I could only the see those nearest to me. Some of them were hefting heavy battle-axes, others were loosening one-edged swords from the scabbard or trying to make their mail-shirts rest more comfortably on their shoulders. A few were stamping their feet on the hard ground, trying to get some warmth into their legs. Others were chewing on a piece of bread or meat or gulping from their leather flasks. Yes, you are told to go to battle on an empty stomach, but there are always those who need food – or drink – before battle, just to calm down.

Most of us were already peering into the distance, trying to see the enemy camp or their line-up. Not that there was anything to see. Even on a normal day it would have been a while before anything could be seen. Today, though, it was worse, since it promised to be a misty morning. Anyway, the enemy camp was too far off to be seen. With half an ear I continued to listen.

'These Normans are in for a big surprise,' the commander was saying. 'They are used to chasing peasants or fighting lightly armed opponents, cowards who will run away after the first clash. They don't know what it's like to meet foot soldiers whose axes can shear through a man in armour and his horse with one swing. If their charge doesn't break the enemy, they panic and flee. Remember that, lads – they can never beat you as long as the shield wall stands firm. Never break the shield wall! Now let's go and spill some Norman blood!'

We all cheered and began to move forward. But after I had cheered, I started to think about what he had said. How much of it was really true? Most of it sounded like the usual thing soldiers are told before a battle. No doubt the Normans were just being told by their Duke how we had never met anyone like them. How we would run before the charge of their armoured knights. How no one could stand against them. They had certainly proven that often enough – even against us. Yes, despite what we had just heard, we had met them and they had met us. But the bit about the shield wall was true too. We all knew that as long as the housecarls stood firm together, no enemy – mounted or not – would be able to break us. The Normans would soon find out that they were no exception. And if these particular Normans had never met anyone like us, we had at least met enough like them and that should give us another advantage.

It was late morning before the darkness had finally lifted. But since it was October – and wet – the mist hung on, so we still couldn't see very well. We had been told that the original plan had been for us to attack the Normans from two sides. Part of our army had left during the night to circle their position. But now we seemed to be forming up for a frontal attack instead. That meant that something had already gone wrong on our side. Vagaries of war. I had been fighting battles and skirmishes for fifteen years by now and never known one to turn out exactly as planned. What was worse was that noises reaching us from the other side told us that the Normans were alert and getting ready as well. That meant there would be no surprise attack, although I suppose that had never really been likely either.

The morning dragged on and we still hadn't started. Finally, the mist began to clear a little and we could see that the Normans were indeed forming up in front of us. We had been told that they would probably be in three groups, with a reserve of heavy cavalry behind the centre. I wondered where the Duke was. It would be nice to land a blow on him – preferably more than one. That would certainly break the Normans. He would probably be with the heavy cavalry, so I would almost certainly not even see him – unless we lost, of course, when they would ride us down. But we were not going to lose. We were going to win, beat the Normans and chase them right back home across the narrow sea. Maybe that would finally cure them of this idea that they could just wander around seizing every kingdom and every piece of land that they fancied.

We were still waiting, but at last the order came to begin. We had been told that the plan was for the shield wall to advance, followed by archers to help clear away the Normans, but it seemed that the

Normans were not going to wait for us. As we came closer, we heard them shouting and then the thrumming sound of heavy cavalry riding steadily towards us, slowly first, gathering speed as they came closer.

We gripped our axes and advanced slowly towards the enemy, looking at the men next to us. It's all very well to say, 'don't break the shield wall, nothing can harm you if you don't break the shield wall'. When you're in the heat of battle and people are screaming and dying and filled with rage, you are tired and sweaty and can't think about anything except lifting your axe for the next blow. Even that feels impossible and you don't have much time to think about the shield wall. All you can hope is that that the men beside you won't advance too far – or drop behind – or die – so that the enemy will still see an unbroken line. And that they will tire and break before you do.

Now we could see the horses and their riders coming closer, but before they were upon us, there was a whistling sound from behind. The archers had fired their arrows. Some of the horses and riders went down before us, but the rest came on. Swords clashed on our shields and spears were thrust wherever there was a gap between shields or men. But our swords were hitting back and so, more importantly, were our axes. A Norman on a bay horse was hacking towards me with his sword, yelling something. I managed to get my axe up to fend him off. The force of his blow forced my arms down again. Then I turned his sword away and lifted the axe for a downward stroke, which cut through his leg and into his horse. The horse screamed and fell, Norman below him. Godric, the man on my left, killed him with his sword. More Normans were coming up behind him and for a short while the air was full of steel and noise and dust. The enemy horsemen were pressing us so close that sometimes it was difficult to raise axe or sword and knives were used to rip up horses' unprotected bellies and then finish off their riders. Then, all of a sudden, the Normans disappeared – and I noticed that I was bleeding from a cut above my left eye, just below the helmet. Looking around, I saw that although I wasn't the only one bleeding, the shield wall had held. Only one or two of our men were actually down, but there were a number of Norman knights and horses that had not made it back to their own lines. There was a smell of blood from some of the dead horses and the ground was getting slippery where their guts had spilled out.

I turned to look towards the Norman lines. All we could see were some horses disappearing into the distance. I wasn't sure if they were fleeing or regrouping, but in either case, I was pleased to see the back of them. The important thing was now to hold the shield wall together and be lured into pursuit.

Sure enough, a few minutes later the Normans returned for another charge, shouting and yelling. But they were no more successful this time. Some – not many – fell to the arrows. The rest came up to the shield wall and tried to batter their way through. Once again, my world shrank to a small space of screaming and hacking, blood spurting from horses and sometimes from men, followed by a deafening silence as the Normans rode off. I knew I had fought with two more Normans but I don't know if I killed them. The only thing I really cared about was that they hadn't killed me.

Once the Normans had disappeared into the distance, the order came to close ranks and stand and rest for a few minutes. By now were really feeling the weight of the armour and our mouths were dry with dust. Most of us had small wounds. None seemed serious, but the loss of blood would weaken us so we helped each other to bind the wounds with rags. Those who had skins of water or wine drank and passed them around to the others. I drank some and used some more water to wipe off the drying blood from my eye. Then I looked around through the dust, trying to see what else was happening. On the right, everything seemed quiet. We couldn't see anything, nor was there any sound of battle. Presumably, this meant that our right wing and the Norman left wing had not met up yet – or else that they were too far away for us to know.

The left was different. We could hear sounds of battle and screaming and it was clear that there was some heavy fighting going on. At first, we couldn't see anything, then suddenly there was a brief gust of wind and the dust cleared. And it cleared on a beautiful sight. For now we could see that the

Normans were breaking and fleeing. All those 'invincible' horsemen were panicking and rushing back as fast as they could towards their camp, with our left wing in hot pursuit.

This was no feigned flight – this was the real thing. Our men were among them, cutting down horsemen and footsoldiers alike as they tried to escape. Some of the Normans ran into the sea in panic and were pulled down by their heavy armour. The sight of the scattering Normans changed the mood among the housecarls. We were given the order to advance again, but some of the men were infected by the sight. They began to cheer and on either side I could see I individual men begin to run. When those on either side of me began to run ahead, I tried to call out:

'Don't! Don't break the shield wall!' But I was already hoarse from shouting and the dust in my mouth and my voice was only a croak. Some of our commanders were trying to hold back their men, but others were running ahead themselves, eager to take part in the slaughter. The only thing to do was to try to keep up with the runners and hope that we wouldn't be too disorganised – or tired – when we reached the fight. As we ran, I found myself getting caught up in the excitement and rage of battle as well. Maybe this would really see my dreams come true. If the Normans were truly broken, the shield wall no longer mattered!

At first, everything went well. We reached the Normans some distance before their camp by the shore and joined in the fight. Except, it wasn't really a fight. They didn't even seem to be trying to defend themselves, just running away from us. I didn't stop to think about it, by now I was just looking for targets for my axe. At last, we were getting our revenge. This was too good to be true.

It *was* too good to be true. As we approached the Norman camp, we heard a noise above the shouting and sounds of fighting. It was a voice – and what a voice! A woman had appeared on the Norman side, wearing full armour and looking like a giantess. I couldn't hear what she was saying, but I didn't need to. She was clearly trying to shame the fleeing soldiers into standing and fighting.

And it worked! Wherever she went, the Normans rallied and closed ranks. Then two things happened at once. First, the rallied Normans returned to the attack. At the same time, we suddenly heard shouts from our right, followed by the sounds of battle and almost immediately afterwards we were under attack from that side as well. This was why we had heard nothing earlier from our right and the Norman left. Now we knew where the Norman left wing was. Some of us managed to turn towards them while others still faced the front. But there were too few of us now. Our archers were well behind us and where was our right? Not that I spent much time thinking about grand strategy right then; other things were more urgent.

A mounted Norman thrust at me with his spear. He looked familiar and suddenly I recognised the young noble I had seen the previous evening. I hacked with my axe at this spear and pushed it away, then managed to get my axe around in a blow that shattered his shield. He looked startled and angry. He dropped his spear and tried to draw his sword and I taunted him. 'How do you like that for a strong hand, filthy dog?' I yelled – well, meant to yell, actually. It came out as something between a whisper and a croak. I don't know if he could understand me, but he certainly heard me say something because he looked closer at me and his eyes widened, so maybe he recognised me too. I don't know – it all happened so quickly, but retelling it makes it seem like an eternity.

In any case, my axe missed him, his sword came out and he was hacking at me. I avoided the thrust and tried to get back at him with my axe again, but now a second Norman appeared on my left. I had to turn towards him to fend off his attack, which meant I could not concentrate on the first one. As I was trying to fight both of them off, a sword cut from above broke my axe. I dropped the haft and drew my dagger, but now there was a noise behind me. I had no time to turn around and the last thing I knew was a heavy blow to the head.

I wasn't unconscious for long – I think. The Normans must have thought me dead, for when I opened my eyes and could sit up and look around me, the fighting was still going on not much further on. But even as I watched, it began to end. I saw the housecarls beginning to break and run. I tried to get to my feet, but couldn't get up. My head was aching and my legs refused to carry me. That – and my helmet – saved my life.

For in the distance, I now saw the housecarls fleeing towards a small church. Some of them got inside and barred the doors – others climbed up on the roof. I don't know if they were planning to make stand there or if they hoped that the Normans would respect the sanctity of the church and let them negotiate their surrender. Maybe they didn't have a plan and just fled to what looked like safety. It didn't matter. When the Normans caught up with them, they didn't even stop to think. At first, I couldn't see anything, but then I saw flames beginning to lick the roof and walls. The Normans had set fire to the church! I was too far away to hear the screams from the men getting roasted inside, but I didn't have to – I could imagine them very easily.

Finally, I managed to get up. Wherever I looked, I could see that the tables had been turned on us and the battle was lost. The Normans were rampaging all over the plain, killing our soldiers wherever they saw them. Ours were running away as fast as they could, towards our own camp and beyond.

A rider-less horse came trotting by. I managed to stop him and crawl into the saddle. No time to stay and die. I pointed the horse away from the battlefield and kicked him into speed. He didn't seem too tired, so I hoped he would last enough to get me off.

By now the Normans had reached our camp. Many of them stopped there, no doubt drawn by the chance of looting. Too bad for some, but at least it meant that I could get away. I wasn't the only one; there weren't many, but all around me I could see men trying to flee, some on horseback, more on foot. Most of them with the sort of blank face that you see on soldiers who've been badly beaten – sort of what the Normans had looked like so short a time ago. But the Normans had been rallied – these men didn't look as if anything was going to make them rally for another stand. Not that anyone seemed to be attempting to do that either. I couldn't see any of our commanders, so I supposed they were already dead – or fled.

There were some Normans still pursuing us, but not many. It was easy to avoid most of them. In any case, they tended to concentrate on the higher ranks. Up ahead I saw a group of them forming up and resting their horses, facing me, but it wasn't me they were interested in. Halfway between me and them was someone who must have been one of our officers. He was wearing expensive-looking, if dusty and muddy, armour and was riding a real warhorse, not the usual smaller kind. His helmet had fallen off and I could see his bright red hair. As I watched, I saw him spur his horse and charge one of the Normans, who left their line and rode towards him. I was too near to pass unseen, so I urged my horse forward. If it came to a fight, it was better to be two than one, although with only a dagger, I wasn't sure what I could do. But even as I approached the two riders clashed. At least this was good news; the officer's spear drove straight into the Norman's breast and he toppled off his horse. Instead of pausing, the officer galloped through the gap in the Norman line. They didn't make a move to stop him, riding up to their fallen comrade instead, picking up his body and riding off towards their own lines. Fortunately, they didn't seem to want to bother with me either, so I rode around them and continued.

By nightfall, I was far enough from the battle to be able to relax. Also, I didn't want to tire the horse too much, since I had a feeling I would need him the next day. I got off and began to walk through the darkness. After an hour or so I was getting too tired, so I stopped by a stream and made camp. Some camp: I watered the horse, drank some water myself and sat down, too weary to move or even to remove my armour, which by now was getting rather smelly, dirty and uncomfortable. I didn't really want to think about today. First things first. That meant survive and get away. Time enough to start planning for the future once I knew I was going to get through the next few days. Then I could start to think about revenge.

Revenge! Suddenly I buried my head in my hands. Wasn't that what this had all been about for us? And what had we done? The Normans flee, we break the shield wall and pursue, and then they slaughter us. I could have wept. Fifteen years after Hastings and we hadn't learned a thing!

CHAPTER 2

Joining the Guard

I have spent a lot of my life fighting, mostly against Normans. Sometimes, I wonder if it will ever end. The first time I fought them was at Hastings, fifteen years ago. I was in the fyrd of Leofwine, brother of our King Harold Godwineson. My family had long lived in Essex. My great-great grandfather died next to Beorthnoth in the Battle of Maldon, long before I was born. My father owned a large farm in the county. He was not among the richest or most powerful men in the area, but he was a respected man. When he asked Earl Leofwine to take me into his household the Earl was happy to agree. There was little or no future for me at home, since my eldest brother would inherit our father's lands. I enjoyed my time with Leofwine, but it was very brief. Shortly after I had entered his service, when I was fourteen years old, our King Edward died. Earl Leofwine's brother Harold became our new King, but the Normans with their Duke William the Bastard crossed the narrow waters and invaded England, claiming that William was our rightful king. I think everyone, even here, must know the story. As long as the shield wall had held, we managed to fight them off and victory was in our grasp. Then they pretended to flee and we broke the shield wall in our pursuit. Leofwine died and so did King Harold. We lost the battle and the Bastard William made himself King of England.

But at least some of us continued to fight. We refused to accept the Bastard and took as our King Edgar. He was the son of Edward, second son of King Edmund Ironside and last of the Cerdicingas, the old kings of England. Two years after Hastings we rose in Northumbria. We took York, but the Bastard's new castle held out. We were supposed to get help from King Swein of Denmark, but he let himself be bribed and the Danes betrayed us. So the Normans defeated us again and ravaged the north for good measure.

After the defeat in York I returned to my own country and joined Hereward, who was still fighting the Normans from Ely in the south-east. There, we managed to hold off the Normans, but never more than that. When Swein of Denmark sent messages offering to help us, we accepted again. Of course, Swein's idea was that he would become our King instead of Edgar. But at least he wasn't a Norman and his mother was the sister of Canute. Canute had died many years before I was born, but everyone said that he had been a good king – probably the last really good and strong king we had had. We thought Swein had to be better than William, although the way he had treated us before made us wonder if that was really true.

Two years after leaving us in the lurch at York, Swein came back with another fleet. But he didn't stay to help us. All the Danes did when they came, was loot Peterborough and then sail for home again, leaving us to face the Bastard alone. He, at least, took us more seriously this time. After all, we had managed to get the Danes to invade England twice. But that only made the outcome more certain. Once the Danes had disappeared, we were lost again. A few of us had managed to slip away to the forests with Hereward, but by now the fighting had gone out of us. It was clear that the Bastard was firmly seated on the throne of England – at least for now. I didn't want to stay in an England ruled by the Normans. I could have gone to Wales, I suppose, or to Scotland. But the Welsh still hated us for what Harold and his brothers had done when they harried Gwynedd before the Normans came, although I was too young to have taken part in those wars. And Scotland was too far away. So I left England and sailed to France. I wish I hadn't. They say it's only a short journey over the narrows, but that must be for those that don't get seasick. If you think you are going to die, I can promise you that it seems like a year and a day.

I could have stayed in France. King Philippe was fighting the Bastard on and off and probably would have been happy to employ another fighting man. But defeating William in Normandy would probably just have made him even more determined to keep his hold on England, so it didn't really feel as if it would change anything at home. Not that it mattered very much. Of course, I wanted to fight the Normans, but not in a way that would keep them in England. I wanted them out of there. But right then I had no idea how to do that. Also, for a while I was tired of fighting. It's a lot to be nineteen years old and to have fought on and off for five of those years, even more so if you keep losing.

I didn't have much money, but my needs weren't great either. A bed if I could have it at night, preferably not alone. Something to eat and even more something to drink. Ale or beer if I could, wine if I must. I moved around in France, usually near the coast, doing odd jobs for people. At first it was mainly for farmers or inn-keepers and none of it fighting. But sometimes a merchant needed a bodyguard or a guard for his goods when he moved from town to town and I was happy to move around the country and do that too. I managed to save one or two of them from scrapes – enough so that the word got around that Edmond l'Anglois – Edmund the Englishman – was a good fellow to have around. In this way, I got to see many parts of northern France.

To my surprise, I also picked up the language. I had always wondered why foreigners couldn't learn to speak English properly – after all, the Danes did. But the Normans spoke French and the priests spoke some Latin and that had always seemed strange to me, since English was so much easier to understand.

But now I found that by listening and trying I could learn to speak French. That made me valuable to the people I worked for. I was asked to do more and they paid more – well, a little more – for my services. And if there was a group of us English, I was usually the only one who spoke French, which meant that I ended up in command of the group.

That's when I met Godric.

I had been part of a group guarding a caravan from Paris who was taking wares all the way south to Marseille. There were twelve of us: eight were English, more or less in the same situation as myself. When we came to Marseille and were paid off by the merchants – and I'll say this for merchants, they usually did pay what they had promised, little though it was – all the English moved to an inn for something to drink.

This was the first time I had been outside France since I came over from England, but I found I rather liked it. The weather was nice and warm, even though we were getting into the autumn. I had silver in my pocket. True, the people spoke strangely, but I found that if I listened carefully, I could make out some of what they said. And if I spoke slowly, it seemed that they could make out most of what I said.

When we had all settled down, the inn-keeper came to ask what we wanted. I managed to make him understand that we wanted and something to eat. He brought the wine and suggested we try something to eat, which I couldn't understand. But he smacked his lips and showed that whatever it was, he certainly liked it, so I nodded to show that he could go ahead. The wine was certainly good – much better than in the north, although I think we all still would have preferred ale or mead. But by this time I knew that the further south you went, even in France, it became less and less possible to find beer. In any case, I was beginning to find that I liked wine.

Eventually there was a really wonderful smell of something – fish definitely, but something else as well, and certainly onions and garlic and other spices, and the inn-keeper came out bearing a huge pot. When he took off the lid, the smell was almost overpowering. This really was one special fish soup. It tasted almost better than it smelled, and the bread that came with it was nice too. All in all, this was the kind of meal that made you feel that everything is suddenly all right with the world and I really found myself liking this place. 'Nice town', I told the others. 'I could stay here if they need someone who's handy with a weapon.' No-one replied – they were all too busy eating.

While we were sitting there, eating, drinking and talking, someone came over to us. He looked strange; he had the hair and moustache of an Englishman, but his clothes were different. Richer and brighter, for one. And his sword didn't look English either. It looked odd, but I couldn't say why.

He stood and looked at us for a moment, listening to our conversation. Then he smiled and said, 'Can I join you?' We were so used to hearing French that at first we didn't realise that he had spoken English. Nobody replied, so he tried again: 'Can I join you? Maybe you will let me buy you some more wine?'

'What do you want?' I asked, none too kindly. We didn't really want anyone else at our table.

'It is some time since I have heard English spoken,' he replied. 'I would welcome the chance to speak it for a while. Also, I may be able to suggest some work for you that you might like.'

None of the others spoke, but we looked at each other. Some of them nodded, so I turned to the stranger again.

'Sit down. You mentioned some wine?'

'That I did.' He sat down and ordered more wine for our table from the inn-keeper. That by itself made him welcome. He waited until the wine had come in, made sure we all had more to drink and then drank our health. 'Let me introduce myself. My name is Godric.'

'Edmund,' I said. The other said their names.

There was a brief period of quiet while we drank. This wine was even better than the previous one. When the servants had disappeared, the stranger began to speak again:

'I think I can take it that you are all English,' he said, looking around the table. When no-one disagreed, he continued. 'But you have all left England in the last few years. Can I guess that this has something to do with your new king?'

‘He’s not *our* king,’ muttered Alf, one of the others.

‘Possibly,’ Godric replied. ‘But he *is* the King of England and there doesn’t seem to be very much anyone can do about that. Quite a lot of Englishmen have left their country as a result.’

‘Get on with it,’ said Oswy, another of the group, curtly.

‘Well,’ said Godric, ‘it seems to me that the situation is this. William – ‘

‘The Bastard,’ Alf interjected.

‘Whatever. William the Bastard, if you want, is King of England. You tried to fight him at Hastings and lost. You then tried to get rid of him a few times and it failed. Not, I should say, through your fault. As a result, he is firmly in the saddle. Meanwhile you – who fought for your true king and for what you believed in – are exiled from your country and forced to work as the servants of fat moneybags or greedy farmers. You get to fight, but it’s not real fighting – a band of robbers, perhaps, but not against other soldiers. And when you lose – or you are done – or you get old – they throw you out, maybe with much thanks but with little enough pay. Am I right?'

'We're not old yet,' I said. 'But leaving that aside, yes, you are right. Now, if that was all you were going to tell us, then thank you very much for the wine and good-bye.'

So far, we had not been very nice, I admit. But he didn't seem to mind. On the contrary, he smiled even more.

'As I said, I may be able to offer you something more. A position where you will be with others – many others – of your own kind. Where you will have dignity and where other people respect you. And where you get well paid and taken care of. You will get to fight real wars. You may even get to fight the Normans again – on equal terms.'

That certainly caught our interest. He sensed it and continued.

'Have any of you ever thought of taking service with the Emperor?'

'The Emperor!' 'There aren't any English working for the German!' 'Why would he hire us? He's got men enough of his own!' 'Since when is

Henry fighting the Normans?' The questions rained down on Godric.

'Ah. It seems I am not being quite clear. I do not mean Emperor Henry. You are quite right. He has few Englishmen working for him and he is not fighting the Normans. He's got enough trouble fighting his own Germans, it seems. No, I mean the real Emperor. I work for His Sacred Majesty Michael, seventh of that name and Emperor of the Romans.'

'The what?' asked Alf.

'The Romans', he repeated. 'Surely you have heard of the Romans? Why, even England was once part of the Roman Empire.'

'But that must have been long ago', I said. 'Hundreds of years, probably. Before King Arthur, even. Surely they don't exist any more?'

'Oh, they exist all right. And you are right. Their rule in England was very long ago. But they did rule there and elsewhere – France and Spain and lots of other places as well. Egypt and Africa and so on. The Holy Land too. Well, that was long ago and they have lost a lot of it, of course. But they are still around and theirs is still a mighty Empire. Constantinopolis, the

Emperor's city in Greece, is the greatest city in the world. Of course, the Roman Emperor used to be in Rome. But they lost Rome long ago, although they continued to rule parts of Italy until about a year ago. Italy isn't so far away from here either; just along the coast to your east or a short sea-journey. So they're still near enough.'

'But what does that have to do with us?' This came from Oswy.

'A number of things. First, the people who chased the Romans out of Italy are Normans. Cousins of the people you fought in England and just as greedy. Not long ago they were just a bunch of poor adventurers, but now their Duke – recognise that title? – rules most of southern Italy and is casting his greedy eyes around for more land. Second, the Emperor may be a Sacred Majesty, but that just makes a lot of people eager to partake of that holiness. After all, if you succeed, you become a Sacred Majesty in turn. Therefore, the Emperors keep a large guard of foreigners, who are beholden to them alone.'

‘I think I know of those,’ I suddenly said. ‘From one of the Danes who came to help us in Ely. He told me of an Emperor of Miklagård, a huge city in the south. This Emperor relied on Vikings to guard him from his own people, he said, because he trusted the Vikings more than anyone else. This Dane had never been there himself, but he said he had met people at home who had been to Miklagård. Is this what you are talking about?’

‘Yes, in a way. Miklagård is what the Vikings call Constantinopolis. But most of the guardsmen are no longer Vikings, although there are still some of those. Many of them are, in fact, English nowadays. And that is the third reason why this concerns you. Last year there was a great battle in a faraway place called Armenia. The Emperor – not the current one, the previous one called Romanos – was fighting the infidel Turks. He lost, and lost a large part of his army as well. As a result, I have been sent west to recruit new soldiers for the Emperor’s Guard. As I said, the pay is good and people look up to us. What do you say?’

I looked at the others. Their faces showed various reactions, ranging from curiosity to hostility to indifference. Godric kept talking, but I wasn't listening to him anymore. Instead, I was thinking about what he had already said. I didn't know if we could trust him. Even if he was honest, it meant going to another strange land – where people no doubt spoke yet a different language and food and drink would taste even less English than it did here. Did they even have ale, for instance? Back in France I could at least feel close to home and if – through some miracle – the Bastard would be killed or overthrown, I could quickly get back, maybe even take part in that joyous event. I didn't know how far away this Emperor lived, but it clearly further away than even Marseille.

But some of the things he said were certainly true. I had seen enough old fighting men, too old or crippled to be of use to anyone, begging their food in the streets of Paris, Tours or other French cities – even in London, before the Normans came, for that matter. Few paid them any heed, fewer gave them anything. I was still young and – of course –

invincible, but the sight of a legless man, wallowing in his own dirt had stayed with me. It could happen, even to me – and it wasn't a pleasant future. Also, my current life was never going to give me any chance to settle down in one place, if ever I wanted that. And I *had* just thought of staying here, hadn't I? Now I was already thinking of going back to France – like an animal, to scared to try anything new. All in all, Godric's words certainly bore thinking about.

As my thoughts reached this point, I noticed that he had stopped talking. No-one else was saying anything either and we all looked at teach other. I made up my mind. 'I don't know about the rest of you,' I said, 'but it certainly beats guarding trade caravans.'

'Weather is probably better in the East,' Alf added. 'Warmer, most likely.' The others nodded agreement.

'Good,' said Godric. 'You are the last group I need to recruit. We set sail for Constantinopolis tomorrow.'

That was how I joined the Varangian Guard.

* * *

When we met Godric the next morning, we found that his total group of recruits was almost fifty strong – all of them English, all of them, as I was to find out during the sea voyage, with stories like ours.

It was a beautiful day when we left Marseille. I had forgotten all about my seasickness when I left England. Now I remembered – I was sick as a dog! When I asked Godric how long the journey would last and he told me at least two months, maybe three, I really thought about jumping overboard.

My seasickness eventually went away. I was not sure if that was good or bad. After two or three days at sea, I'd get better. Then we'd go into port, take on fresh water and provisions and as soon as we set sail again I'd be just as seasick again.

In my less bad moments, I became quite friendly with Godric He was only three or four years older than I, but he had spent six years in the Emperor's service – including fighting the Normans in Italy. He told me about the ports and countries we stopped in – Genoa, Gaeta, Amalfi and Messina, all of them different – and he also taught me a lot about life in the Empire. There were many foreigners there, he said –

English, French, Normans too apparently, Turks and even stranger people, all serving the Emperor. Although there were four Guards units, the Varangians were the Emperor's elite footsoldiers, his personal guards, and the most respected. 'The Greeks are strange,' he said. 'They respect us for our fighting skill. But they don't really think highly of fighters – or of foreigners. Unless you speak Greek, you are a barbarian. If you do speak Greek – even more if you can read and write it and do it beautifully – you are one of them. If you want to get ahead, you should learn Greek. As for fighters, they now prefer educated courtiers, but they have enough enemies to appreciate the need for fighters too. It's just that if they can achieve their goals without fighting, they prefer to do so.'

That I couldn't understand. If you had enemies, you fought them. If your enemies came to kill you or steal your land, you fought them off or even better, killed them. And as far as I was concerned, it was far better to fight them off before they came than when they were already burning your farms and looting your cities.

Godric tried to explain why the Greeks had other views. 'They think it's Christian to spare lives,' he said. 'Even their enemies. Who knows, today's enemy may become tomorrow's friend. Where would you then be if you had killed him?'

'An enemy is an enemy', I replied.

'Not necessarily. Look at me,' he said. 'I have fought the Normans in Italy and the Turks in Armenia. But in Constantinopolis I know both Normans and Turks who serve the. Emperor and with whom I get along. Mind you, you can't drink with a Turk, that's a problem.'

'Why not?'

'They don't drink. Their false faith bans them from drinking. Though some of them do drink anyway – quite a lot, too. But the point is they do serve the Emperor too. You may not love them – but unless you want to learn about Imperial justice, you will at least pretend to be friends with them.'

'I'll never be friends with a Norman', I muttered. 'Anyway, you can't trust them.'

Godric just laughed. 'You'll learn', he said. Then he changed subjects. 'I heard you speak French. You should learn to speak Greek.'

I was still annoyed with him. 'Why bother? And anyway, I thought they were Romans? Why do I need to learn speak Greek? Don't they speak Roman?'

'Don't be stupid!' he snapped. 'Haven't you heard a word of what I've said? I thought you wanted to leave France because you wanted to make something more of yourself. I already told you that if you want to get ahead in Constantinopolis, you have to speak their language. The speak Greek, because even though they are Romans, Greek is now their language. Anyway, I saw you in Marseille: you were the youngest of the group and yet you were clearly in command. So you must be quite a bit smarter than the others. Maybe I was wrong about you!'

And with that he stalked off. But I knew he was right – at least about the Greek. So I went up to him and apologised and asked if he would help me to learn Greek. When I told him I didn't know how to read and write he said he'd get me started on that as well. I managed to get started on speaking during the voyage, but reading and writing was more difficult. Although I couldn't read English or French, I could recognise some of the letters. The Greeks, it seemed, wrote with different letters. So not only could they not speak English like normal people, they didn't write with proper letters either. When I complained to Godric, he laughed at me. Much later, when I had seen how many other peoples wrote with even stranger letters, I laughed at myself as well.

In the event, the journey lasted slightly less than two months. Our last port of call was Piraeus in Greece. That was our first glimpse of the Empire and of how the Varangians were treated. The local garrison was commanded by a Frenchman, not a Greek. Once Godric had visited him, we were invited to a feast with his men. The food was strange, but good, the wine was strange and not so good – much thinner and sourer than the French wines – but above all, it felt good to be with fighters of your own side again.

I should not have had so much to eat. The next day, when we sailed around what Godric called Attica and into the Greek islands, I was sick again.

CHAPTER 3

Constantinopolis

When we finally landed in Constantinopolis, I swore to myself that I would never go to sea again – although at first, the land seemed to make me just as sick as the sea had done. It just didn't seem to stop swaying.

But I soon forgot that when I began to look around. Constantinopolis was amazing. Most of the cities I had seen in England and France looked like villages next to it and their churches, even the cathedral in Canterbury or in Troyes seemed mere parish churches. The others felt the same way. Godric laughed at us, but then told us that everyone reacted in the same way. He said that there was no city in Christendom that was as big or as beautiful and that at least a two hundred thousand people lived in her, maybe more. In time, we would get used to her. Meanwhile, there were more important things to do.

That meant first taking us to the barracks of the Varangian Guard, which were on the grounds of the Imperial Palace itself.

There we were inscribed on long lists and outfitted with our new armour and arms. The battleaxes were similar to those we had used in England, but the sword was different. It was the same sword that Godric had worn the first day we met – a single-edged, heavy sword the Greeks called a *romphaia*. We were also given mail-shirts and three-cornered shields. And we were paid, too – in gold. I had seen gold coins of course, on more than one occasion, but neither I, nor the others in my group had ever owned one. Now we were all given golden solidi coins. Godric told us that all our needs would be provided for, so that the money was just spending money. I was suddenly richer than ever before.

Later, Godric told me that it was unusual for people to be allowed to join the Varangian Guard immediately. Being a Guardsman was an envied and sought-after position, and before you joined, you normally had to pay a large sum as an entrance fee. Many had done so anyway, since they would be able to get their money back and more from loot gained in fighting. But the loss of the army at the Battle of Manzikert the previous year had meant that there was a great need of new soldiers for all units. For us, that meant that we were accepted into the Guard without payment. Once we did start to get some loot of our own, we were apparently supposed to 'contribute' to common funds managed by those who were already Guard veterans. But for the time being, that was not necessary and we could enjoy our new wealth.

That was good news, but there was not much time to reflect on them. The next few days were full of activity. We were billeted in the Guards barracks, which were in an upper floor of the Imperial Palace compound. Then we were inspected by the commander of the Varangian Guard, who was known as the Akolothous, and eventually paraded before the Emperor himself. That was something of a letdown. He did not seem particularly impressive, even dressed in what I later learned was the Imperial purple, the colour that only he was allowed to wear.

* * *

The unimpressive Emperor was a sign of what was to follow during the next eight years. In some ways, I could not complain. We were getting paid, fed and generally taken well care of. We stood guard around the Emperor in his palace and when he moved around in the city. We followed him to Mass in the Church of St Sophia. Some of my fellow guardsmen found this boring, but I was overwhelmed by the splendour of the Greek service. It was so different from anything I had seen in England or France. Even the Cathedral in Canterbury seemed like a mere parish church by comparison with St Sophia. When the Patriarch celebrated Mass in St Sophia, amidst the incense and the singing, with the glorious golden mosaics all around you, you could truly feel the presence of Christ Pantocrator – Ruler of the World – giving his blessing to his vicar on Earth, the Holy Emperor.

There was something else too. At first, it was strange to hear the Mass sung in Greek instead of in Latin, but as I understood neither, it didn't matter very much to me. But eventually I began to understand the Greek. And then I began to wonder why the we didn't do what the Greeks did and sing the Mass in a language that everyone could understand, not just the priests (who like as not didn't understand it either, but read it off by heart).

Although we Guardsmen had our own church, dedicated to St Nicholas, I soon took to going to St Sophia for Mass whenever I had the time. I particularly liked to go if I was feeling downcast for some reason or had had an unusually bad day. Listening to Mass would make all my worries drain away and leave me feeling that everything was well with the world. But my preferred saint was neither St Nicholas, nor the Holy Virgin, for all that I liked her church. I was a soldier so I prayed to soldiers: Saint Michael or Saint George or Saint Demetrios.

I enjoyed living in Constantinopolis. Until I came there, I didn't really have much time for city-dwellers. They had mainly seemed to be merchants and inn-keepers, all too concerned with their own money, not to mention getting their hands on everyone else's. Obviously, kings and earls needed people around them to run their courts, but somehow, those who lived in cities didn't seem to be *real* people. But once I had lived a few years in Constantinopolis, I realised that I had been wrong, just as city-peoples' views of those who lived in the countryside as stupid plodding peasants was wrong.

I began to enjoy walking around the city when I was off-duty. Although Constantinopolis was overwhelming when you first got there, you soon realised that it was possible to get to know the city if you did it a little at a time. And since different groups of people tended to live together, it was more like a great number of small cities in one place, making up one huge city. I loved seeing the different people, learning not only about the Greeks, but also about Armenians – who both provided the Empire with soldiers and with merchants – and Jews – who were mainly merchants and traders or physicians. There were English, Flemish, German, French and Italians of various kinds, merchants, priests and soldiers, Slavs from the European provinces and Bulgarians. There were Normans as well, although these were mainly soldiers like myself. I did not get on very well with them, but I avoided them and they avoided the Varangians and that suited everyone. Even among the Varangians there were all sorts of people – lots of Englishmen, but also Russians and some Vikings from the far North, Swedes, Danes and Norwegians. Some of them had probably not even been Christian until they came to Constantinopolis. There were other infidels too – Turks, mainly, who worship the false prophet Mahomet. All these lived cheek by jowl in the city, trading, arguing, sometimes in three or four different languages at once, drinking and not least worshipping next to each other. There were certainly all sorts of drink there: wine, good and bad but usually vinegary and often mixed with water, ale and mead and stronger draughts made of fruit. We English held our own against most of the others, but we had to accept that not even we could out-drink the Vikings.

Once I went to a Turkish mosque to watch them at prayers. I knew that the Emperor's Turkish soldiers were good fighters, but I could not understand how grown men could prostrate themselves like that in front of their God. As I mentioned, we Guardsmen had our own church and there were other churches for westerners where Mass was said in Latin and churches for the Armenians as well. I liked visiting them all and listening, but best of all I still liked the Greek churches where I could understand what the priests and monks said and where I felt God spoke directly to me.

I also loved walking around in the different merchants' quarters, going to the different markets, gazing at the wares from all corners of the word and smelling strange spices. Or even just to the harbours on the south side of the city. If you got there early enough, there would still be a fresh smell of the sea, mingled with that of newly caught fish, making you hungry even if you had just eaten.

But, as I said, all this was when I was off duty and most of my time, obviously, I was on duty.

That duty did involve some fighting, but not very much and most of it against the Emperor's internal enemies. Strangely enough, I probably fought more during my two years in France than during this period in the Guard. But one or two things did happen. I advanced in the ranks and became a dekarch, a senior of ten men and eventually pentekontarch – senior of 50. My Greek improved until I became quite fluent and I learned to read and write it as well. In addition, I picked up a smattering of Latin and various phrases from the other languages one encountered in

Constantinopolis, Armenian, Russian, Turkish and even stranger ones, each of them – so it seemed – with their own letters as well. It helped when buying drinks or playing tables with other soldiers. It helped even more when making up after the fights that soldiers always seem to have with each other when they are off duty. Apologising to a tavern-keeper in his own language for the ruin of his taproom would also go down well, although paying him for the daamge was even more welcome. But our main purpose was to fight for the Emperor and for his Empire, and there, things did not go so well.

By all accounts the previous Emperor, Romanos Diogenes, had been a good ruler and a good soldier. He lost to the Turks in a battle in Manzikert the year before I joined the Guard, but Godric told us that they had been betrayed by the Emperor's Greek foes. In any case he was deposed after the battle and replaced by Michael, our current lord. But Michael was not a strong ruler and he was unpopular. The price of wheat rose so that one nomisma only bought three-quarters of what it had bought before, and the people had begun to call him Parapinakes, which meant minus-a-quarter.

He was also unpopular because he couldn't keep the peace. Two of the Emperor's vassals, princes of the Slavs in the Balkans, began to call themselves Kings and were supported by foreign enemies. We thought we'd be sent out to show them who their master was, but nothing happened.

And then one of the Normans serving the Emperor, Roussel of Bailleul suddenly rebelled and proclaimed himself ruler of a new realm centred on the city of Amaseia in the Armenian theme in the east. Apparently, he was hoping to repeat there what the Bastard had done in England and what other Normans had done in southern Italy. We were sent to bring him to heel and here was a first chance for us to fight the Normans again. It should have been an easy matter: Roussel only had 300 Normans with him, although he had apparently allied himself with a local Turkish chieftain and had received troops from him. We were commanded by the Caesar John Doukas, whose brother had been Emperor for some years before the Emperor Romanos. The Caesar was a good general and our army outnumbered the Normans. Apart from us Varangians, there was a troop of Normans loyal to the Emperor and some native units.

At first, everything seemed to go well. We encountered Roussel at the Sangarios River, by the bridge of Zompos. Roussel had set up his camp on one side and we were on the other. I had thought that we would try to rush the bridge and then give battle on the other side. But Godric told me that this was not the way the Greeks fought.

'In the first place', he said, 'they will have fortified the bridge already. It won't be easy to take it. But more importantly, there will be negotiations first. The Caesar John will try to get them to surrender without a battle.'

'But why? They won't surrender. In any case, you've already told me that this is not the first time Roussel has shown himself to be unreliable! How can they trust him in the future?'

'They can't. But they may have to. He is a good soldier and the Emperor needs every good soldier he has. Maybe there is something that can return him to his loyalty. Not that I believe it myself, of course. I am sure you'll get your fighting after all.'

I suppose that was meant to make me feel better. In any case, Godric was right. The Caesar did offer to negotiate first, but whatever was said, Roussel and his men did not give up. So now we did cross the bridge. But it was hardly a rush. The bridge was slippery and more than one of our men fell and blocked the advance for a few seconds until he could get up again. But although the going was slow, it turned out that Godric was wrong. The bridge had not been fortified and we managed to cross it without much trouble. Once on the other side, we formed up for battle. The Varangians were at the front and centre, where we were led by the Caesar John himself. The Normans were behind us and the Greek units at the rear and on both sides.

Once we had formed up we began to advance. You can't rush very fast for very long, but even a slow advance can be terrifying for your enemy, unless he has archers to stop you. So we charged Roussel's men and almost immediately began to push them back. It helped that there were more of us, but much more importantly, they couldn't stand against our axes and we cut through them like butter. We were pushing ahead now, with the Caesar in the van and our shield wall began to break up. But it didn't matter. Roussel's Normans – and his Turkish allies – were already breaking. In truth, they didn't really fight much, almost as if they melted away in front of us. But it wasn't a ruse. You could see the fear in their eyes when you came close enough. I came up against a mounted warrior, who was being pressed on all sides by footsoldiers – ours and theirs. He tried to batter my axe aside but I felled his horse and then cut him down as he was trapped underneath it and begged for mercy. Soon enough their fighting seemed slower - the kind of pause that comes before an army suddenly decides that it has lost the battle and begins to retreat or to flee.

And then there was a sudden noise behind us and a clash of steel and suddenly we were being pushed forward – and none too gently at that. The Normans behind us, supposedly loyal to the Emperor turned out not to be quite so loyal after all. Instead, they charged us in the back. Apparently – but I only found this out later – the negotiations before the battle had not only been between the Caesar and Roussel. Roussel had had his own talks with our Norman officers as well. Those seem to have been more successful. Now it was our turn to realise that the battle was lost, as Roussel's men regained their confidence and began to press us from the front. We tried to re-form our shield wall, but by now we were too spread out and it wasn't possible. A few of us formed a circle around the Caesar John who kept encouraging us to fight. But soon we were being slowly squeezed together. We were still willing to fight. But there comes a point when you are so crowded on all sides that you cannot even lift your arms with your axe or your sword. And so the Caesar John ordered us to surrender. Even when fighting in England, I had always managed to keep my weapons. But now, Roussel's Turks came up to us and began to take our weapons from us and there was nothing we could do about it.

I thought they were going to kill us there and then. But when I spoke with Godric – who was trying to stem the blood flowing from a gash in his hand – he shook his head. 'No, they won't kill us. Roussel needs money much more than dead soldiers. My guess is that he will sell us as slaves to the Turks.' That almost made me hope to get killed instead!

But it turned out that Godric was wrong again – or at least it seemed so. For Roussel did not sell us to the Turks. Instead, he formed up the remnants of our army on a plain – unarmed, of course, and surrounded by his men, who were armed. There was a hastily built platform on the field, and there Roussel himself appeared, together with a few other Normans, some Turks – and the Caesar John. I was standing near the front, so I could both see and hear quite well.

The Roussel began to speak. He spoke in French, but someone repeated everything he said in Greek and some of the Varangians quickly translated the words into English and Norse as well so that everyone could understand. It certainly was a strange speech.

'Soldiers of the Emperor', he began. 'Today you have fought bravely. It is true that you did not win. But this was not your fault. Saint Michael, captain of the hosts of Heaven, did not fight with you today. You did everything you could. But you were betrayed.' Well, he certainly was right about that.

'You were betrayed, not on the field of battle, but at home. You were told that you were fighting for the Emperor. But who is your Emperor? Was he with you in battle today? Did he even lead you on the march to war? Or did he stay behind, in a warm palace, surrounded by his eunuchs and his women, while you marched out in the cold? Is that a true Emperor for warriors like you?'

There he paused and looked out at us, probably expecting some form of answer. But it took time for everyone to understand what he had said, so there was only some muttering, which quickly died away.

'Warriors need a warrior Emperor', he continued. 'Someone who shares their life, someone who knows how they feel. Someone who leads them into battle and who then rewards them afterwards. Not someone who only makes bread dearer!' That raised some laughs once it had been translated.

'The Emperor who skulks in the palace kitchen of Constantinopolis is no true Emperor. Your true Emperor is here!' This was a surprise. Was he going to proclaim himself Roman Emperor? That would certainly put the Bastard and his English Kingdom in the shade.

'Your true Emperor should be someone of Imperial blood. And who better than your own commander? Was not his brother emperor some time ago? Why should he not have succeeded to his birthright, rather than see the Imperial dignity go to strangers? Join me, and we will march to Constantinopolis and let the true Emperor, Emperor John, ascend his rightful throne!' And he and his men turned to the Caesar John and hailed him as Emperor!

I don't know if Roussel had told the Caesar John that he intended to proclaim him Emperor. Certainly, from where I stood I could see the Caesar look very startled when he realised where Roussel was headed. He turned to his son who had been captured with us, and started talking rapidly to him. But when Roussel and his men acclaimed him Emperor, he turned back to face them and looked as if he accepted it.

Roussel's acclamation was also a signal to his own men, because now all of them loudly cheered and hailed the new Emperor. And not only they, for the cheering spread and some of the Greeks that had been with us and all of our Normans also joined in. The only ones who were quiet were the Varangians.

This lasted for a few moments and then it began to feel uncomfortable as we were the only ones not to cheer. But now Roussel began to speak again.

First, he thanked everyone for showing their loyalty to the true Emperor. Then he announced that he would come and speak with every unit later on. Finally, he dismissed us. We were led away, again under guard – and not just the Varangians. I noticed that even the Greeks who had been cheering were still guarded.

We were taken to an enclosure in Roussel's camp, where we were once again guarded by his Turkish allies. For the first time since the battle we had some time to think. I turned to Godric.

'What now?'

'What do you think? Are we following this new Emperor of his?'

'I didn't hear you cheering him.'

'Nor I you.'

By now quite a few of the others had joined us and were talking it over. But there wasn't much to say. Everyone agreed that we had sworn an oath to the Emperor and as long as he was Emperor, we would remain true to him.

And so, when Roussel came to try to enlist us to his cause, we told him that we stood by our oath. He tried to talk us out of it by pointing out that Emperors had been both proclaimed and deposed before. But Godric, who was the senior Varangian present, replied that our oath was to the Emperor and that only he could absolve us from it. Roussel said that the Emperor John was a far better man and soldier than Michael. But we said that this was not important. As long as Michael was Emperor, we would remain loyal. Finally, he gave up.

'Very good', he said as he left. 'You are wrong, but I admire your stubborn loyalty. And when the Emperor John is enthroned in Constantinopolis, I am sure you will be as loyal to him. But until then, you will have to remain prisoners.'

And with that, he left us. The next day, Roussel and his army marched off, presumably towards Constantinopolis. We were marched in another direction, accompanied by some of his troops as well as our guard of Turkish archers. But to me, the strangest thing was that the further east we marched, the more people in the cities and towns we marched through, cheered Roussel's men. They really seemed to like him. But when we came past, they either turned away or scowled at us. At first, I couldn't understand it. We were soldiers in the service of their Emperor. Roussel was a rebel. They should have been cheering us, not him – not that we were much to cheer, tagging along as prisoners.

At first, I couldn't believe it and didn't want to understand it. But later, speaking with Godric and others, I began to understand what was going on. We were perilously close to the Empire's border. Here, the Turks were raiding at will and there wasn't much of an imperial army to stop them. So, when Roussel – or someone like him – appeared and began to protect the local inhabitants against the Turks, whether by force or – as seemed to be the case – by allying with them and making sure they raided elsewhere, they were grateful to him.

But knowing this did not improve matters, for me or for the other Varangians. When we came to

Roussel's main seat, the city of Ankyra, his army stopped there. We were marched further off with our Turkish guards. Eventually we came to a village, overlooked by a castle on a hill – don't ask me where it was, because I would not have the slightest idea – and there we were kept prisoners.

We were not badly treated. We could move about in the village and talk to the people who lived there. Most of them were Greeks and still hoped to be delivered from their new Turkish overlords. Some of them were Armenians, who were, of course, also Christians. But wherever we walked, there would always be one or more Turks on horseback in the vicinity.

After some days, we began to relax and settle in the village. It helped that some of the Armenian girls were very beautiful – and very impressed with the handsome soldiers from the large city. I don't think their parents were happy about that. In fact, I knew they weren't. Godric had to deal with more than one irate father or master who complained that soldiers had behaved improperly towards a daughter or servant. The fact that these advances were usually more than welcome, was not important.

But even the attentions of a beautiful dark-eyed girl eventually palled. Getting bored with the village – and also getting bored with the same food all the time – coarse bread, honey and black olives – I began to approach the Turkish guards. I had learnt a few words of Turkish in Constantinopolis and I thought I could take the opportunity to learn a few more. I also wanted to try out their food.

The food wasn't much, although they did occasionally have some very nice pastries made with honey and nuts. But I did learn quite a bit of the language, which helped me to while away some of the time. And I also spent much time talking with Godric and thinking through what had happened.

It was not our fault that we were betrayed. But for the future, it made me swear never more to trust a Norman. Roussel had been a servant of the Emperor and he had betrayed his master. The Normans in our army were supposed to be loyal to the Emperor and they had also betrayed him. From now on, I would never believe a Norman, however friendly or loyal he was supposed to be.

The next thing I learned was never to break the shield wall. Actually, I had learned that at Hastings. But it did no harm to have the lesson repeated, as long as I lived to remember. As long as the shield wall stood firm, nobody could ever destroy it. But if we broke it up ourselves, we were much more vulnerable. And there was another lesson too. The reason we had lost the battle was partly because we were attacked by our oh-so-loyal Norman allies. But it was also because we had advanced too far ahead of the other Greek troops. If we had been closer to them, they would have hit the Normans in the rear in turn, and we could have won the battle. Only later did I find out that the Greek rearguard had also betrayed us. But not getting too far ahead of the rest of the army was still good advice.

But talking about why we had lost also deepened the shame of the loss. Nor were we happy doing nothing in a village in the middle of nowhere, when we should have been fighting for our Emperor. So, my getting acquainted with the Turkish guards was not just because of boredom. I was trying to see if we could escape. We had been divided into groups, so that there were about thirty of us in this village, but I had only mentioned my escape plans to Godric. He agreed that we should try, but only if all of us could get away. Otherwise, the risk that the Turks would kill those who remained behind – even if it meant foregoing any ransom for them – was too great. In any case, the others were no doubt thinking of escape as well.

At first, I wasn't sure how we would all be able to escape. We would all need horses, that was clear, otherwise we would quickly be rounded up and brought back as prisoners. But where could we get thirty horses?

That, it turned out, was not so difficult. The Turks that I had befriended were eager to boast about the wealth of their local Emir, as they called their chieftain. That wealth was measured in cattle and in horses. It turned out that this wealth – sheep and horses – were all grazing in close vicinity to the Emir's castle. Unfortunately, the animals were all well guarded – apparently mainly against raids from neighbouring Emirs. In fact, as I reported back to Godric, there were more guards over the animals than over us.

'So we need to get rid of our own guards first; and then of the herdsmen and guards over the horses.' He frowned.

'I may have an idea', I replied.

'Go on.'

'As I said, there are more guards over the animals. But not terribly many. A dozen, perhaps. But they are not expecting an attack from the village – all their vigilance is towards the outside. If we can fool them into thinking that there is an outside attack, they are likely to move the animals between themselves and the village. If we can only get rid of our own guards, the horses will then be between us and the rest.'

'True. There are only two small problems. How do we get rid of our own guards and how do we convince the others that there is an attack?'

'I have thought of that too.' I probably sounded rather smug as I said it. Godric was my commander – but I had already thought of a plan.

'Well?'

'Once when I went to Mass –' Godric snorted. He did not tend to go to church and had occasionally made fun of me when I began to do so, calling me the Priest. I started again. 'When I went to Mass, I once heard the priest talking about how someone scared off his enemies by tying firebrands to foxes' tails and then stampeding them though the enemy lines at night. I thought we could do something similar here.'

'You may have noticed that we are fresh out of foxes.'

'True. But we don't need the foxes. What I suggest is this. Get the others to gather material for use as torches. As soon as it gets dark, let them gather near the outskirts of the village. You and I will go out of the village in the afternoon. As usual, one of the guards will follow us. Once we are out of sight, we should be able to overpower him, as long as he is alone. I will then disguise myself in his clothes, take his horse, circle around to where the herds are kept and shout for help, as if there is an attack on the village. The guards will gather on the far side of the herd. You must return to the village. Get the others to set fire to their torches and panic the sheep and the horses so that they run towards the herdsmen. Grab enough horse for all of us and we should be able to get away before they know what is going on.'

As I was talking, I looked at Godric's face. At first, he seemed sceptical of my idea. But as he listened, he gradually seemed to change. When I had finished, he thought for a while.

'It could work. But there are a lot of things that could go wrong.'

'Well, if you would prefer to stay here for the rest of your life, just say so.'

'No, we will give it a try. Not tonight though. We need to prepare the others. And there is a full moon.'

I hadn't thought of that. This meant that we would have to wait for almost two weeks for a moonless night.

I thought the next two weeks would never pass. I tried to spend more time with our Turkish guards to get them used to me and also to learn a few more Turkish words. But every time one of them turned to me, I was convinced that he could see our plans clearly written out in my face.

But at last we were getting to darker nights – not dark enough, I worried, as we were in the middle of summer.

Towards the evening, Godric and I began to walk outside the village. This was on the opposite side from where the rest of the Varangians would gather. We walked slowly, apparently deep in talk but mainly to make sure that we were seen. Sure enough, the soft sound of hooves padding on grass told us that we had a Turkish rider coming up behind us. We didn't look back towards him, but soon enough he had overtaken us and was riding to one side, a short distance away. A short distance beyond the village there was another small hill. Godric and I continued beyond the hill, the Turk trotting along next to us. Once we had crossed the hill we could no longer be seen from the village. At the same time, the sun was rapidly setting.

Now Godric and turned towards each other and began to shout at each other. What we said didn't matter – no Turkish guard was likely to understand English. Then we began to wrestle each other. At first, the Turk simply sat and watched and laughed at us. But when Godric drew a knife, he suddenly gave a shout and moved his horse towards us. As he came closer, he tried to separate us with his spear, shouting all the time. Godric and I continued to struggle, but gradually the Turk forced his horse between us. 'Now!' Godric shouted and grabbed the horse's reins. At the same time, I jumped up behind the Turk, knocked off his helmet and began to strangle him. He tried to fight back, but Godric kept hold of the horse and I was too strong for him. It didn't help him that he was taken by surprise and at first didn't know which was the best way to defend himself. He should have dropped his spear and tried to stab me with his dagger. But by the time he had thought of that, it was already too late. I squeezed his throat with one hand and grabbed his dagger with the other. As he tried to twist around, Godric stabbed him in the leg with his knife. He shifted again, trying to protect himself against this new threat, but as he did so I managed to draw his dagger and plunged it in his throat. He made a gurgling sound and blood spurted out over my hand but I kept the dagger steady until he stopped struggling and slumped.

Godric was still holding the horse, trying to calm it as is smelled the blood. As soon as the horse was standing still, I slid off it and dragged the dead Turk out of the saddle. We quickly stripped him of his cloak and took his weapons. Godric kept the curved sword, while I took his spear and dagger. Then Godric started running back towards the village, while I looked frantically for the Turk's helmet. As soon as I found it and put it on, I mounted the horse and began the ride that would take me in a long arc around the village and castle and towards the Turkish herdsmen. Once I got closer to them I dismounted and made sure to keep out of sight while I peered through the dark towards the village. It seemed to take an eternity, but suddenly I saw a light flickering – the signal agreed with Godric.

But I had to wait further, until I knew that the animals had been stampeded and the Turks were already confused. My horse was fidgeting under me, but I kept a tight rein on him. Then I saw another light flickering, and suddenly the whole field seemed to be ablaze – and rushing towards the guards. I could hear them shouting to each other, wondering what was going on and trying to deal with it. In the light I could now see that the animals had reached close to the guards. Now it was my turn. I spurred the horse and rode towards the Turks. As soon as I was within earshot, I started waving my spear and shouting – words that I had carefully learned over the past two weeks.

'Enemies! Raiders! Quick! There!'

I rode closer to the guards for another few seconds, then turned the horse around and began to ride off. I could hear shouting behind me as the Turkish guards began to follow.

Getting the guards away was easy. Now the difficult part came. I had to make sure that they followed me, but not closely enough so that they could recognise me (or try to speak with me to find out what was going on). Then I had to make sure I lost them and finally find Godric and the others. I began by riding off in the direction from which I had come, drawing them with me. I could hear them calling out to me, but I just bawled something vague in reply, waved my spear – I wasn't sure if they could even see it – and rode on. Once I judged that we were far away enough from the village, I began to weave in and out of the little hills and gullies that surrounded the village. For a while, I could hear the guards shouting to each other and riding around, but gradually their noise died. Carefully and quietly I began to guide the horse towards the south of the village – the direction Godric and I had agreed was the least likely for the Turks to search for us.

I had no idea what had happened with Godric and the others. I had to hope that their part of the plan had worked as well. But as I rode on through the night, neither hearing nor seeing them I was beginning to worry that I alone had managed to escape. What should I do then? Return to the village? Probably not a good idea. Return to Constantinopolis? Sure – just tell me where it was and I would go there.

At one stage my horse waded through a brook. When I heard him splashing through the water, I froze, fearing that the noise would travel everywhere. Sure enough, when I was on the other side of the brook, a shadow suddenly rose from the ground and grabbed the horse. I dropped the spear and drew the dagger in one move when the shadow spoke up.

‘You took your time.’ It was Godric.

‘I had some company. I could have brought them if you wanted.’

‘Not this time, if it’s all the same to you. I think this excursion is only for Englishmen.’

He whistled and a group of riders appeared. One of them brought a spare horse for Godric. He sat up and we began to move out a trot. As we rode on, Godric told me how they had all fared. Apparently, everything had gone according to plan. The guards had been taken completely by surprise by the stampeding animals. He doubted if there had even been anyone around to see them steal horses for themselves, chase away the rest and then disappear. After all that, the ride to Constantinopolis was almost wholly uneventful. That was lucky, since we didn’t have much in the way of weapons. We marched by night and kept hidden during the day until we had reached Roman territory. Then we could move much faster, but it was still many weeks before we finally reached the city.

When we had reported for duty, we found out what had happened while we were away. Roussel had indeed marched on Constantinopolis and encamped outside the city, the Caesar John in tow. But now it was the Emperor's turn to call on a Turkish ally. With his help, Roussel was defeated. The Turks took over his prisoners which eventually were ransomed by the Emperor. Unfortunately, Roussel was also ransomed (by his wife) and continued to make war on the Emperor.

Eventually, Roussel was defeated and captured by Alexios Komnenos, a young soldier whose uncle had been Emperor some years earlier and who was now the best general the Greeks had. As for us, we were rewarded for having escaped. My reward was a promotion. Godric told the Akolothous that our escape plan had been my idea. I was promoted to dekarch – senior of ten men and commanding the other nine. It meant better pay – but above all, it showed me how efforts could be rewarded. But overall, we still felt bad about the whole episode. Although our defeat had not been our fault, we were burning with shame and eager to redeem ourselves by taking on the Normans again.

Meanwhile, Michael's reign was not destined to last long. In late 1077, Nikeforos Bryennios, *dux* or governor of Dyrrachion in the far west of Greece, rebelled together with his brother John. So, too, did another Nikeforos, this one called Botaneiates, a general based in Anatolia, east of the capital. The most immediate threat however was Bryennios. He also concerned us Varangians more, because Bryennios and his brother had managed to lure some of the Varangians stationed in the provinces to join them. Although things had not yet come to a fight, the stain of Varangians betraying their oath to the Emperor was felt by all of us. Godric, who by now was a Komes, or commander of a bandon of one hundred men, sent two men, a Swede named Olof and myself to the city of Adrianopolis, where Bryennios had established his headquarters. Our mission was to talk his Varangian supporters into returning to their proper allegiance. Now, there are some missions where things start out all right, but then begin to go wrong. There are others, where things begin wrong, but turn out all right. This was not either of those.

This was one when everything went wrong from the start and then simply got worse.

For one thing, Olof was clearly unhappy to have me along and did not take long to tell me. The moment we were out of Constantinopolis, he turned to me and 'explained how things were'.

'I will talk to my comrades', he announced. 'They know me. You are very new.' By this time I had been in the Guard for six years, but there were quite a few who had been there longer. Olof had at least six years more behind him, maybe even more. Even so, his manner grated on me.

'These men, I know them. They are Vikings, some from Sweden, some from Denmark, Norway and the islands. They raid England at will. They think the English are weak. They will not listen to you, only to me. They know me. I am a great warrior. What have you done? I will persuade them. You will just stand aside and do as you are told.'

'Maybe', I replied. 'But first we have to get there and get through to Bryennios's Varangians. That may not be so easy.'

'Don't worry, Edmund. There will be an inn. Where there is an inn, there will be drink. Where there is drink, there will be Vikings. And now, I need a drink.' At which point he brought out a leather bottle and took a deep draught. He took a few more and soon after that he began to sing in a loud voice as we rode along.

I have nothing against drinking. Yet when I noticed how Olof took every opportunity to fortify himself, morning noon and night and at all times in-between, I was getting worried. In addition, the man seemed unable to keep quiet. His singing was bad enough, but what was worse was that he took to telling everyone who we were and what we were about. So much for hoping to reach the rebel camp quickly and in secret and weakening Bryennios by getting his Varangians to abandon him. In addition, he continued to annoy me by treating me as inferior to him – not even as a subordinate, more like a servant. I was more than once tempted to take the stupid drunken Swede by the neck and shake some sense into him. I could have done it easily – I was bigger and stronger and the fact that he was usually drunk would only have made it easier. But I was worried that I would have to kill him – not a brilliant way to succeed on a mission.

On our fifth day out from Constantinopolis we were in a small village where we had spent the night. Olof was coming out of an inn where we had spent the night. Looking around, he didn't see me and started bawling for me.

'Boy! Bring the horses! Hurry up, Englishman!

That did it! I was in fact standing behind him. Without stopping to think, I grabbed him around the waist and threw him into the water trough outside the inn. As he splashed around I grabbed his neck and pushed his head under water. Then I held it there for a few moments before letting him up to draw breath – and promptly pushed him under again. When I had repeated this a few times, he gradually stopped struggling. Then I hauled him up again and – still holding him in a tight grip around the neck so that he could just breathe – I pushed my face close to his.

'My name is Edmund! Not 'Englishman'. And I am not your servant. We have an important mission, so I will let you live. But you will now start to behave like a soldier instead of like a drunken Swede. Is that clear?'

He just looked at me, so I repeated the question, squeezing his neck a little extra. This time he nodded. I shook him a little more to make my point and then let him go. The first thing he did was to be sick in the trough – before even getting out of it. It stank.

He still stank when he stopped being sick and came out of the trough. He didn't say anything, just shot a wary glance at me. For the next day or two, he actually behaved himself. That is to say, he drank less and he didn't treat me like a servant. But he insisted on singing. With all this, the ride to Adrianopolis, that should only have taken at most five or six days, took eight.

In one matter, however, Olof was right. When we finally reached Adrianopolis, there was indeed an inn – several, in fact. And most of them were full of bored soldiers having a drink. We stopped outside one of them. Olof slid off his horse and handed me the reins.

'Here boy. Stable our horses. I will scout out this inn.'

I was tempted to remind him of the water trough, but he probably realised that there was little risk of me fighting him here. By now I just hoped we would be able to accomplish what we had to do and disappear. So I let it pass. ‘Very well. Try not to drink too much before I am back.’ But I was wasting my breath. Olof had already disappeared inside the inn.

When I walked into the inn, I was not surprised to see Olof sitting near a fire, a large tankard of beer in his hand, talking to a group of soldiers, but no Varangians. He was not quite drunk – yet – but he was well on his way to getting there. I decided to seat myself away from him and see what happened.

‘Yes’, he was saying, slurring slightly, ‘it was a long ride to come here. But I wanted to join you. Get a good Emperor. Save th’Empire. Good fighting and looting, eh?’

‘We should get that, all right’, one of the others said and they all nodded. ‘Mind, the Emperor doesn’t want us to loot Constantinopolis, he’s said. He wants the people there to support him. But there is plenty on the way.’

A man near me shuddered as he heard this. I turned and looked at him for the first time. He was not a soldier, that was clear, looked more like a merchant. I recognised the type from my time in France. I was quite surprised to see him there. His clothes showed that he was quite wealthy, yet here he was, sitting in an inn frequented by common soldiers. He noticed my look.

'It's very well for soldiers to talk about the joys of looting', he said. 'But for those of us who get looted, it's a much less joyful experience, I can assure you. No wonder the Bard only talks about the heroes and their fighting and never about the people who are fought against or about or around.'

By the Bard I knew he meant Homer, an old Greek poet whom all Greeks thought had written the most perfect poem ever. It was an old story of warfare but I had never heard more than short pieces of it. 'Yes, I think I can see that', I replied. 'But you'd better stay out of the way of the looters then.'

'That is easier said than done. Sometimes you can't stay out of the way, because sometimes the trouble seeks you out. And then the only way out of it is to get in even deeper.'

This was beginning to interest me. I hadn't given much thought to merchants and their troubles since leaving France. But I thought I recognised what was going on. This was a pattern I had seen before.

'Forgive me for intruding on your problems. But let me guess: you are a merchant and have come to recover goods that were stolen from you by some of these soldiers?'

'An all too common occurrence', he said. 'The *dynatoi* – the great lords – fight about who is to be Emperor. But they always need money to pay their supporters and they are rarely particular about how that money – or whatever else they use – is obtained. In my case trade goods that I was sending from Thessaloniki to Naissus was 'requisitioned'. I am here to try to obtain compensation – although I very much doubt if your commander has either the time or the inclination to see me, much less pay me.'

He clearly assumed I was with the rebels. I did not bother to correct his error. If he believed me to be one of them, then so, presumably, did everyone else.

Talking to him would also help keeping me unobtrusive. Meanwhile, Olof was being far from unobtrusive: at the moment, he was singing what I presumed was a Viking song and demanding more to drink.

I turned back to the merchant. ‘And if Bryennios loses?’

‘Then I have even less chance of seeing my money’, he replied. ‘The Emperor will just say that I was helping Bryennios and I’d be lucky to avoid punishment, assuming I was foolish enough to complain. So however I do, I probably lose out. It won’t destroy me – but it is a loss all the same and I’d rather it didn’t happen. Still, did not the writer once say that maybe one day we shall be glad to remember even these things?’

I didn’t understand that last thing. But as for the rest, I could see his point and told him so.

‘But I am being discourteous. My name is Georgios Kassandrenos, merchant of cloth and fabrics from Thessaloniki. And you are?’

‘My name is Edmund.’

‘Are you perchance also a Tauro-Scythian?’

'No, I am English' I replied, 'and England is part of Greater Britain, an island in the west.' I had been long enough in Constantinopolis to know that educated Greeks believed that the world still was peopled by the same tribes that their ancient writers had written about. Westerners were either Franks – which covered all of us – or, if distinctions were needed, Kelts, Iberians or other such fanciful names. Vikings, for instance, were referred to as Tauro-Scythians'.

'Oh. The far islands so eloquently described by Pytheas, the renowned geographer of old, no? I apologise. It was your fair hair and grey eyes that misled me. You are, therefore, a Kelt. And you are here as a soldier?'

'Yes.'

'So you are one of our new Emperor's Varangians. Will you, perchance, be able to tell me if I will be able to see him – or at least someone who has his ear? After all, he will need money when he is firmly shod with the purple boots. Maybe he will feel that compensating a merchant is not a bad idea.'

‘It isn’t quite that easy’, I began, when my attention suddenly was distracted. Three Varangians stepped inside and immediately noticed Olof. That was not so difficult. He never stopped drinking and was easily the loudest person in the room.

‘Olof! When came you here? Has anyone else come to join us? What news from the capital?’ I did not recognise any of them, but they clearly knew him, which was as he had said.

But his reply was not quite according to plan. Once he had focused on them, he suddenly turned red with rage and started shouting. ‘Join you, Björn? Never, you oath-breaker. You have betrayed your friends. ‘m here to take you back to Constantinopolis and punish you!’ He began to stand up and reach for his sword, but at this stage he was so much the worse for drink that he hardly managed to scramble to his feet. He might have been able to get up if he had been all alone in the room. But he was surrounded by a number of soldiers who until now had believed him to be one of them and who suddenly realised that he was an enemy. It was amazing that they managed to get to him since they all tried to at the same time, but the outcome was never in doubt. As for myself, I realised that I now had only one chance. I turned to merchant.

'Get out of here, now! Leave! I'm coming with you. If anyone asks, I am your bodyguard and I've been with you all the way from Thessaloniki.'

When he hesitated, I added, 'Do it! I guarantee that you will get compensation for your goods!'

He looked at me. Then he suddenly nodded and slipped out through a back door, with me hard on his heels. As we came outside, he straightened up and began to walk away slowly – much too slowly, I thought, for the noise of the brawling behind us remained loud, but I knew walking was better than running. Eventually, the noise died away behind us. I stole a glance backward and could see Olof, trussed like a chicken, being dragged out by some of the rebel soldiers.

I suddenly realised that Georgios was talking very quietly to me. '… I said, I assume that you know the loud Tauro-Scythian?'

'Yes.'

'And I now find that although you are a Varangian, you do not, in fact, support Bryennios?'

‘Yes. I mean, no. I mean, that’s right. We were sent here to remind his Varangians of their oath. But – ‘

‘But your friend picked a rather peculiar way of doing it, I must say. No matter. Time, in its flow, produces all sorts of men. But Cythera conceives new schemes, new plans in her breast. Come with me.’ And he went off again.

‘You won’t regret this. I promise you that you will receive compensation for your goods.’

‘Yes, so you already said. It would come in handy. But I think it’s more important to get you away. Having already seen how Bryennios runs a camp, I don’t really think he would make a good Emperor. I think I’d rather stay with Parapinakes and it will do me no harm to have saved one of his guardsmen.’

As we walked on we were approaching a house guarded by two armed men without uniform. Georgios stepped by them and – as they looked suspiciously at me – told them to let me past as well. When we came in, he turned to me again.

‘I think you had better return with me to Thessaloniki.’ As I opened my mouth, he held up a hand. ‘Bryennios’s men don’t yet know that your friend was not alone. But they soon will know. You are unlikely to be able to get back to Constantinopolis safely. However, from Thessaloniki you can get a ship. Also, by the time we are back there, we will know who is Emperor. And on the way, you can tell me about your country. Maybe I can trade with your countrymen? Do they have anything to sell?’

The thought of another journey by sea wasn’t quite calculated to cheer me up. But he was right, of course. Not to mention that I could not figure out another way of getting out of the camp. Finally, Olof’s captors would soon enough find his horse and be told that a Varangian had stabled two horses – a Varangian who was not Olof! So I decided to go along with his plan. When I told him, he called in the two guards, introduced us to each other, told them that as far as anyone else was to know, I had worked for him for years and to get the horses ready for departure. I was given a long cloak to hide my armour and as soon as possible we set off. We were challenged as we left Adrianopolis, but Georgios explained to the guards that he had achieved what he set out to do and was now returning to Thessaloniki to spread the word of Bryennios's generosity. A thin story, but it worked.

The journey back to Thessaloniki took 13 days. But although longer than the ride to Adrianopolis with Olof, it seemed much shorter. For one thing, Georgios was a pleasant and interesting man. As a Greek and an educated one at that, he automatically looked down on foreigners. But, as Godric had told me, my ability to speak Greek reasonably well – even if I did not have the education, which meant that I missed most of his literary allusions once he left Homer behind – put me somewhat above the ordinary barbarian. In addition, he had travelled widely. He had been to Egypt and to Italy and to most of the Slav principalities on the Empire's north-western border. He had even been to Georgia at the far east of the Euxine Sea. He knew about foreign countries and knew that the barbarians, although generally uneducated, weren't necessarily the uncivilised brutes many Greeks took them for. He was sharp too, always on the lookout for new ways of expanding his business. I had to tell him everything I could about England and about the trade there, including how people dressed and in what fabrics. That wasn't very much, but he seemed interested in hearing that there were many sheep in the country and wondered aloud if there could be a market for Keltic wool. He was quite upset to hear that I had no friends or relatives back in England that I could write to. (I didn't bother telling him that even if I had had anyone to write to in England, they wouldn't be able to read my letter. That would have been altogether incomprehensible to him.) I had to promise that if I ever went back to England, I would keep a look-out for a trading partner for him. Since it was likely to be a long time before I got back to England, it was an easy promise.

Meanwhile, I told him about my past and about the Norman invasion of England – interestingly, the Normans were not Franks or Kelts to him, as they would have been to most Greeks, but he actually called them Normans. He was doing some business with them in Italy, apparently.

When we came to Thessaloniki, Georgios took me to his house. This was my first glimpse of how wealthy he must be and the first time I saw the private house of a rich Greek. He lived in the south-eastern corner of the city, between the church of St Sophia and the hippodrome, with the Via Egnatia just to the north. The house itself was much smaller than the palaces of the greatest nobles of Constantinopolis, but it was still big enough to be almost a palace in itself. Georgios had already told me that he had two daughters, but no son. Needless to say, I did not meet the daughters, but he introduced me to his wife, who deigned to notice my presence with a nod. Then I made my way to the Acropolis and asked to speak to the garrison commander. Once I had identified myself as a soldier of the Varangian Guard, I was let in. It wasn't just a courtesy visit; I wanted to find out what had happened with the Bryennios brothers and their rebellion. On that score, at least, everything was well, since the rebellion had already collapsed. But he didn't know any details and I was unable to find out what had happened to Olof, or to any of the Varangians who had supported Bryennios.

Meanwhile, I managed to surprise him when I told him how I had managed to get away and come to Thessaloniki. It seemed that Georgios was one of the richest and most important merchants in the city. Although that didn't carry much weight with most of the Greeks – any educated courtier automatically looked down on a mere trader, the same way he looked down on a foreigner – his wealth still made him an important citizen. That would explain both why he thought he stood a chance of getting compensation for his seized goods and why he felt that even if he didn't receive it, his business would survive.

When I returned to Georgios, I told him the news. He, meanwhile, had some news for me. It turned out that his cousin, who worked in the same business in Constantinopolis, had a son who was shortly getting married. The marriage was also a union of two business families and so would be celebrated with more than usual opulence. Hence, he was going to Constantinopolis himself, and bringing his family as well. Since he was going to travel on one of his own ships, I was welcome to come along.

Being in Constantinopolis would also enable him to pursue the case of compensation for the goods seized by Bryennios's men, as I had promised him (however I was going to arrange that).

It shouldn't have taken long to sail from Thessaloniki to Constantinopolis – barely four days – and the ship was large and comfortable. Unfortunately, the weather was bad and the voyage stretched out over more than two weeks. Not that it mattered for me – I would have become seasick if it had been half an hour in the harbour. As it was, I barely lasted until we had cleared the port. But for once, I was not alone in my misery. As I was standing by the railing, being sick, I suddenly noticed someone else beside me, who seemed to try to compete with me in the violence of his seasickness. It looked like one of the younger sailors, which surprised me, since I had assumed that people didn't become sailors unless they were immune to seasickness. When we both had a moment of recovery, I turned to him and was surprised to see that it was, in fact, a girl. Or, rather, a young woman. And a beautiful one too. She had black curly hair, but – unusually for a Greek lady

– blue eyes. She was shorter than I – say five feet and five inches tall – and quite slim and she couldn't have been more than 18 years old. It says a lot about my state that I couldn't understand who she was or what she was doing on board. But she seemed to know who I was, because she smiled bleakly at me. Her words confirmed it.

'You must be Edmund, the Kelt. You came with father. I didn't think men could be seasick.'

So she was one of Georgios's daughters. 'Oh yes, some of us can, lady. May I ask your name?'

'I am Irene. My sister and I saw you when you – ' here she had to stop again, to be sick.

When she had stopped, I tried to explain how her father had saved me in Adrianopolis, but this time I had to break off. Eventually, we just gave up trying to talk and laughed weakly at each other whenever we were not staring down the side of the ship.

The next day I was surprised to receive an invitation from Georgios to join him and his family for a meal. One of the many ways in which the Greeks differed from us, was that you never met their womenfolk. If they walked outdoors, they were veiled

– and guarded – and if you came to their houses, women would be in a different part and would not meet strange men. Oh, some of them could be different. Obviously, guarding the Emperor meant that you occasionally saw the Empress and her ladies-in-waiting or other ladies at the court (although never without their own retinue of eunuchs). And there were women in the shops and in the markets, and, of course, there were always ladies – or at least women – available for soldiers with wages to spend. Some of those could be very nice indeed – as long as you had money. But that wasn't the same thing as actually meeting an important and wealthy family in private. I wondered what lay behind the invitation.

The cabin had obviously been refurbished for the owner's family. Despite what I had been told by the Thessaloniki garrison commander and even after having seen some of Georgios' house, I had not realised how wealthy Georgios must be. There were expensive carpets on the deck and valuable plates and crystal on the table. And the man himself was dressed in silk, as was his family. Although all three women were veiled, it was not difficult to recognise Irene.

Her sister was rather taller and had straight hair. It was difficult to see more and I knew it would be rude to stare.

Georgios welcomed me, mentioned that I had already met his wife, to whom I bowed. Then he turned to his daughters. 'The apples of my eye', he said. 'Theodora –' apparently the elder '- and I believe you already have met Irene.' I bowed again.

It wasn't only the surroundings that were luxurious. The meal was easily the best I had ever had – or was likely to have, unless I became Emperor myself. There was white bread, baked with oil to make it softer and moister. There was plenty of fish – grey mullet, tuna and bass – roasted and fried and fish soup as well, spiced with coriander and anise. There was beef and lamb and chicken, a mountain of vegetables, olives, asparagus and others which I had never seen or tasted, and peaches and apples and other fruits and those little pastries dripping with honey that I had learned to like when I was held captive by the Turks. There was enough food to feed a company of hungry Varangians. And with all that, Georgios apologised for the paucity of his table and said that had we stayed in Thessaloniki he could have offered me a proper dinner.

In fact, I wondered why he had invited me. It was quite clear by now that his kind of people did not have to invite poor soldiers to eat with them. But the reason quickly became clear. Even a short sea voyage quickly became tedious. Georgios thought it would amuse his family to hear me tell about the strange countries – well, England and France – that I had seen. He also had the Greek respect for learning and tried to impart it to his daughters. So I talked about my home, about my childhood and youth in England. About how first the Vikings and then the Normans came and how we had defeated the one and been beaten by the other. I talked about what England looked like, the countryside and the weather – I think it came across as mostly rainy. I talked about our cities, although I had to confess that even London was a mere village compared with Constantinopolis or Thessaloniki and York was even smaller. Then I talked about France, of the cities I had seen there and of the difference between the north – which was more like England – and the south – which was more like Greece.

Georgios was friendly and the rest of the family was polite. But I still felt as if they regarded me somehow like a tame animal, brought in to entertain them with its amusing tricks. I don't know how much they really believed – or understood – about the rest of the world, although given the extent of Georgios's own travel, they must surely have some awareness of it. Nevertheless, it was a pleasant enough way to pass the time, and when Georgios asked me if I would join them at their next meal, I was happy to accept – subject to my not being seasick!

As I spent more time with the Kassandrenos family, it seemed that I was making the transition from tame-and-amusing-animal to a person in my own right. Both Theodora and Irene started to ask me questions, and even their mother, who was much more reserved, condescended to speak to me – once. By the time we entered the Bosporos, Theodora was flirting slightly with me, although Irene was quieter. On the other hand, I had seen more of Irene, as we had spent much time being seasick together.

When we anchored beneath the city walls in the Golden Horn, I asked Georgios to let me know where he could be reached. He seemed puzzled at the request, but I explained that I wanted to know where the compensation for his stolen goods should be sent. That surprised him. Apparently, he had been convinced that this was only something I had promised to enlist his help in getting out of Adrianopolis. He was partly right – but I was going to make an effort to fulfil my promise.

I did not see the ladies of the family when I left the ship, even though I had prepared a short speech with some feeble literary allusions of my own. I might not actually have *read* Homer, but I had heard enough people talking about him to be able to borrow a few lines from others.

As soon as I arrived at the Imperial Palace, I went to our barracks and reported to Godric. He was pleased to see me. Once he had heard about the failure of Olof's mission, he had assumed that I was dead. When I had finished my report, I asked about the compensation for Georgios. He was surprised that I raised the point. Yes, he said, Georgios had saved my life. But that was no reason why we should be involved in paying him compensation for goods stolen by rebels against the Emperor. In any case, this was not a decision for him to make. I would have to put my request to the Akolothous, who in any case wanted to hear my report for himself.

The Akolothous listened to my story. Then he asked me a few questions about Georgios, his business and the family he had in the capital. I suppose it was to consider whether he was important enough to be favoured. While he was thinking, I asked Godric what had happened to Olof.

'Your drinking friend made a real mess of things', he replied. 'His reward was equally messy. When John Bryennios found out what he was up to, he had Olof's nose cut off.'

I knew that the Greeks were given to blinding and mutilating people as punishments and considered it milder than killing. But the thought of how close I had been to losing my own nose made me feel ill in a way that fears of a battle wound never had.

'He didn't gain much by it', he continued. 'Once they knew that the Emperor was prepared to act against them, the brothers proclaimed Nikeforos Bryennios Emperor and marched towards Constantinopolis. The Emperor sent out Alexios Komnenos against them with an army, including a unit of Varangians, who had been told what John Bryennios had done to Olof. The Varangians arrived by sea at Bryennios's camp. Although the other troops had not yet come up, we stormed ashore and put him to flight.'

'And the Bryennios brothers?'

'Still at large – '

But at this stage the Akolothous interrupted us. 'Regarding your merchant, his dreams of compensation are never going to be fulfilled. Even if for some reason he was considered important enough – and he isn't – the Emperor is not going to spend money trying to placate a tradesman. He would never hear the end of it, since every little petty dealer in what-have-you would insist on being paid back for some imagined loss. Useless lot anyway. If they are so keen on their money, they should never go into trade in the first place. What do they do for the Empire?'

I was a little taken aback by this. I agreed that merchants were a pretty useless lot. But Georgios had saved my life and I had promised him compensation. Now I would have to explain why he couldn't get it. I began to argue, but I was cut off. 'It is not going to happen. If you feel so bad about it, go tell your merchant that he must come to se me to ask about his compensation. I will enquire further up, but I can already tell you the answer. And now we need everyone back on duty. Bryennios may be defeated, but we still have Botaneiates to deal with.'

So before going back to duty, I looked up Georgios. He seemed mildly surprised, if pleased to see me. 'You have come to tell me that, regrettably, my request for compensation has been rejected?' he smiled.

'Yes. No. That is... If you go to the Akolothous in the Imperial Palace, I believe that there may at least some hope that your request may be granted.' Even as I said it, I could feel that he saw right through me.

Still, he smiled again. 'It seems I am in your debt. As the blessed Apostle says, I am debtor both to the Greeks and to the Barbarians. Is there anything I could do for you?'

I was going to decline and take my leave, when, to my horror, I heard my voice say, 'Yes, as a matter of fact, there is. I would like to marry your daughter Irene.'

If Georgios had seemed surprised before, it was as nothing compared with his expression when he heard this. His smile disappeared and he slowly sat down in a chair. Meanwhile, I noticed a curtain behind his chair billowing although there was no draft in the room.

'Does my daughter know of this?'

'Er – no, sir. At least, I don't think so. I mean, I haven't asked her or spoken to her about this. That is to say – 'I stopped, realising that I sounded like a complete fool. I began again: 'I would not have said anything to your daughter before I had spoken to you.' That, at least sounded right.

'So, do you have any reason to suppose that she would want to marry you? Assuming, of course, that I even gave my permission to such a ludicrous idea? How much do you actually know her, in fact?'

'I – don't know, sir. If she would marry me, I mean. But I have spoken to her – about other things – on the ship.'

'On the ship! When in the name of all the gods did you have time to speak with her on the ship?'

'When – when we were seasick, sir.'

That actually made him laugh.

'I didn't think you managed to say very much when you were seasick. But enough of that. Let me ask you something else. You are a landless, poor soldier, is that not so?'

'Yes, Kyr.'

'Are you, perchance, of noble background? Many noblemen have found themselves reduced to penury and served as common soldiers. There was even a Tauro-Scythian king, so they say, who served the Empresses Zoë and Theodora before he went back to his dark north, so I have been told.'

'No, Kyr. My family were farmers in England. But this is a very respected trade.'

'No doubt. Now, forgive me for being blunt, but you are, presumably, aware of my wealth?'

‘Yes, Kyr.’ This was going badly and I was feeling more miserable by the minute. I couldn’t understand what had caused me to blurt out those words. Until I did, I hadn’t even realised that I loved Irene.

‘My daughter will receive a large share of my wealth. Has this played any part in your strange request?’

My astonished face must have told him the answer even before I spoke. ‘No, Kyr, not the slightest.’

He sighed. ‘Edmund, you are a nice man. I am sure you are a good man and honest. And you may have done me a good turn, although – if I may remind you – I have also done you one. But we move in different circles. My daughter will marry someone who can carry on my business and expand it. Surely you understand that. And even though I like you, I have to think of her first. Not to mention my wife, who I am sure would have a lot to say about this.’ At this stage, there was a distinct noise behind the curtain. ‘You are not even an officer. What can you offer her – or me?’

'Nothing – I suppose. But I love her and the love of an honest man surely counts for something?'

'Not much, I'm afraid. The satirist tells us that honesty is praised and left to shiver. I thank you for your help and I admire your taste in women. But the answer is no. Good-bye Edmund. I very much doubt if I shall see you again.'

I was not feeling very happy when I left. Once I was back in the barracks, however, there was no time to think about that. It was clear that Nikeforos Botaneiates was moving towards the city. Everyone expected that we would be sent against him. But things never got that far. By now, Michael Parapinakes was thoroughly unpopular and apart from us, there was no one prepared to defend him. Even before Botaneiates reached the city, there was a revolt inside the walls. We were preparing to put it down, when we were told that Michael had abdicated and become a monk.

That took care of the politics as far as we were concerned. Our oath was to the Emperor. If there was no Emperor, the oath was in abeyance until someone else had been proclaimed. But the city didn't calm down. Riots broke out in different quarters. As always happens in these cases, the mob decided to go to where the loot was and started to attack the houses of the rich. So we, together with the other guards were called out to maintain order.

Stopping a riot is not that difficult. The rioters are usually less well armed and not particularly disciplined. But there are two problems. The first is that they frequently start fires. Sometimes this is intentional (they particularly like to burn any place where there is likely to be any record of a debt, either taxes or to a merchant) and sometimes because they are careless or because accidents happen. The second is to find them. Oh, you can always hear them and move towards them. But unless you manage to corner them and charge, they are as likely to melt away and then form another mob some blocks away. As a result, I spent a number of hours on patrol, moving around the city, sometimes fighting, sometimes just chasing people off. It was hot and it was thirsty work.

An hour or so before midnight we heard more shouting and yelling a street off or so and set off at a trot around the corner. I hadn't paid much attention to where we were for the last little while, only that we were somewhere on the southern side of the Golden Horn and in a part of the city inhabited by merchants. But this street I recognised. It was the street leading down to Georgios' cousin's house. But we couldn't see the house itself, because the street leading up to it was blocked by a heaving mass of people. Some of them were carrying knives or swords, some were carrying torches. All of them were yelling. Some houses along the street were already burning and had clearly been broken into and looted.

I shouted to Alf and Oswy, who were both with me, to close up and then we and the rest of the patrol charged. Although we were outnumbered by the mob, the fighting was easy enough. We came upon them from the rear and we weren't expected. Flailing swords and axes opened a route through them, but their mere numbers meant that the going was slower than I had hoped. As we approached the Kassandrenos house, I could see that the mob had not yet managed to gain entry. Both Georgios and his cousin employed watchmen and the house – like the others in this part of the city – was surrounded by a wall. But even as we came closer, the mob pushed through the gate. I could see one or two watchmen retreating towards the house, closely pursued by attackers.

'Come on!' I yelled to the others. Then we hit the back of the mob. There were screams of fright, but there, in the narrow street, they had little scope for running away. Now we were not trying to chase them out of the way, but aimed to kill and quite a few of them went down. As we approached the gate, their resistance lessened and we could advance faster. It wasn't entirely one-sided – one man managed to pierce my arm with a spear before Oswy cut him down. But now we were through the gate and in the court-yard. Here, there were only a few rioters. The Kassandrenos guards, who had seen our approach, were now pushing forward again and between these two forces, the last of our opponents were driven off. I left five Varangians to hold the gate with Georgios's men and entered the house. Inside, there was noise and confusion. Part of the roof was on fire and two armed figures, one I recognised as Georgios and the other presumably his cousin, were trying to organise the servants to extinguish the fire. I told the other Varangians to help them, removed my helmet and walked up towards Georgios.

Before I had time to reach him, a door burst open from the side and a group of women rushed out. Most of them were running towards Georgios and his cousin, but one of them looked around and then rushed up to me and threw her arms around me. 'Edmund, oh Edmund' she cried. 'I knew you were going to save us! I knew you wouldn't let those people harm us!' Then she began to cry.

I put my arms around Irene and tried to pat her hair. 'Don't cry', I said. 'It's over. You are safe now.' But she continued to cry and then she suddenly turned her face towards me and began to kiss me.

At this moment, a hand touched my shoulder. I couldn't turn around, but I stopped kissing Irene and turned my face. It was Georgios. He held out his hand and I took it.

'Thank you', he said. Then he looked at Irene in my arms, turned around, looked at his wife and shrugged. Then he turned back to us.

'It seems as if you still would like me to grant your request', he said to me. I just nodded.

'Irene, do you really wish to marry this man?'

'More than anything else.'

'Very well. Had it not been for you, I recognize that we would all be dead. I will no longer oppose your marriage.' There was a strange sound behind him. 'Neither will my wife.' There was another sound. 'But you will not be allowed to marry yet. My daughter will not marry a common soldier. When you have been promoted, you can come to me again. If then you still wish to marry each other, you will be allowed to do so. And now, I must ask you to return my daughter to her mother.'

Now it was my turn to hold out my hand and thank him. Then I collected the other Varangians and stepped out into the street. There was not a living soul to see – but there were the remains of quite a few recently departed ones. Satisfied that things were quiet, we returned to the Imperial Palace.

Within a few days, Botaneiates was proclaimed Emperor. I was told he was the third Emperor to be called Nikeforos. But the other Nikeforos, Bryennios, refused to accept this and still claimed the throne for himself. Botaneiates made Alexios Komnenos Domestic of the Schools – that is to say, commander of all his armies – and sent him against Bryennios, who was defeated and blinded. Once again, we were left out of the fighting.

*　　*　　*

Botaneiates's victory should have improved things. He had been a good soldier when he was younger and that was exactly what it seemed the Empire needed right now. There was certainly no shortage of enemies. In the west, the Slavs had rebelled as I have already mentioned. In the east, the Turks were flooding the country after their victory over the Emperor Romanos. From what I had seen when I was Roussel's prisoner, I could easily imagine what was going on. The Turks would be taking over the countryside even as the cities remained in the hands of the Empire. There were certainly enough refugees coming to Constantinopolis. And there were also many more Turks coming to serve the Emperor, even though there was a lot of muttering about using the infidels to fight other Christians. So, all in all, we could have done with a fighting Emperor.

Unfortunately, by now Botaneiates was old and tired and not much better than Michael had been. There was no attempt to lead us against the enemies of the Empire, whether foreign or home-grown. Worse, he forgave his enemies – which the priests say is a very Christian thing to do, but not good if you are the Emperor – and didn't reward his friends. Nikeforos Bryennios had been blinded, but was soon restored to Imperial favour. So, too, was his brother John. But he didn't have long to enjoy it. Shortly after he had been pardoned, he was given an Imperial audience. As luck would have it, one of the Varangians standing guard outside the Sigma, the hall, where the Emperor gave audiences, was the nose-less Olof. When John Bryennios came out of the hall, Olof recognised the man who had ordered his nose cut off. He raised his axe and killed him in one blow.

Needless to say, Olof was condemned to death and executed. But this created much ill will among the Varangians. Why should the rebel be pardoned, while the man who had been mutilated in his Emperor's service and had avenged his slight, was made to suffer?

So the unrest continued. And worse was to come. One afternoon, when I was on guard duty inside the Imperial chambers, there was suddenly a clamour from the courtyard below. People were calling the Emperor's name – and none too kindly, it seemed. Botaneiates had been talking to some of his clerks on a balcony. Suddenly arrows began to fly. Luckily, we were on the top floor of the palace, so the arrows didn't have much force. Nor was the aim the best – we later found out that the men had been drinking and cursing the Emperor. But even so, one of the Imperial scribes was hit by an arrow and later died.

Not content with that, the soldiers – Varangians all – charged up through the Palace. I don't know if they had any plan at all or if they were just drunk. Nor did I care. There were only four of us on duty, three Englishmen and a Russian called Oleg, but we formed up to defend the door to the Imperial chamber. Behind us, I could hear people trying to block the door from inside, but there wasn't much time to think about that, because now a group of Varangians burst through the outer door and charged us and everything became a desperate hand-to-hand struggle to stop them from getting through.

I really don't like to fight indoors. There is usually barely enough room to swing an axe. Instead, there are plenty of little tables, chairs or chests that you can stumble on as you move around, trying to defend yourself as well as to get your own strokes in.

The attackers, as we found out afterwards, were all Swedish Vikings. They were howling as they came through, chopping at everything and everyone in their way. I was trying to hold off a giant of a man, but it seemed that however much I wounded him, it didn't have any effect as he kept pressing me backwards. His sword cut through my shield and the force of it broke my arm so now I was without a shield. I flailed at him one-handed with my axe but he kept pushing me back towards the doors to the Imperial chamber. I was rapidly losing strength and was beginning to despair.

Suddenly the doors opened from the inside and a man rushed out, wielding a sword. He sprang at my opponent and the fury of his attack took even the giant Swede by surprise, so that he fell back. This gave me split second to recover my breath and get my axe back up. At that moment, Oleg managed to fell his attacker, who careened into my opponent. As he stumbled, the man with the sword jumped back and gave me my chance. I lifted my axe and swept it downwards. The blow sheared off his leg and he stumbled again. As he fell, Alf plunged his sword into the Swede's side and at the same time my axe came down again on his neck. By now there were Greek soldiers rushing into the room and the fight was quickly over. Most of the attackers were down and those still standing turned and ran. Some of the soldiers that had come to reinforce us pursed them back to their own quarters, where they barricaded themselves and eventually surrendered.

As for those that remained, we had one dead and three wounded on our side, though none of the wounds was deadly. It turned out that, the man I had fought was the only one of the attackers to be killed. Later, one of the other Swedes told me that the man had been a berserk – mad with battle-rage – and that it was very rare for anyone to manage to kill a berserk in a single fight.

As we looked around the chamber, we suddenly realised who the man with the sword was. It was Botaneiates himself, who had come out, fighting for his life. He may have been a weak Emperor, but he was still a brave soldier and knew how to handle a sword.

The Emperor's reaction to the attack was both good and bad. For killing the berserk – even though I had not really done it alone – I was promoted to pentekontarch, so that now I was senior of fifty men, commanding the other forty-nine. That was the good part. The bad part was that the ones who had taken part in the attack got off lightly. They were judged by their own officers and were exiled to distant garrisons. It was rumoured that this was because the Emperor didn't want to offend the Varangians. But his leniency made the wrong impression, particularly on those of his own subjects who felt that they were better fitted to rule than he was.

For me, however, the promotion was excellent news. I wrote a letter to Georgios, letting him know and asked if it would be suitable for me to visit Thessaloniki. His reply surprised me. Instead of writing back, he and his family again appeared on a ship some weeks later. And some weeks after that, Irene and I were finally married in the Church of Christ Pantocrator. This time, there were no disapproving stares when I kissed my bride. Even my mother-in-law smiled, although probably more at her daughter than at her son-in-law. But I was happy and Irene was happy and that was all that counted.

Being married changed my life in many ways. Although I remained a Guardsman, I moved out of the barracks and we – that is to say, Irene – bought a house on the southern side of the city, near the Church of Saints Sergios and Bacchus. The house was on two floors and had a small garden, where apples and pomegranates grew in the summer. Irene had the walls painted with scenes from saints' lives and we had one room with a mosaic floor. It was certainly more comfortable than the barracks. Although our lifestyle was not on Irene's father's scale, I also ate better than I had before. And my Greek improved even more.

Strangely enough, I hadn't thought much· about what being married would mean. It was unusual for Varangians to be married, but not entirely unheard of. A few had found Greek (or foreign) wives and settled. But usually, their wives were washerwomen or even prostitutes that they had fallen in love with. No one had married a rich woman like Irene. I had assumed that Irene would live in a gynaikeion, quarters of her own, and rarely venture outside the house. I knew that this was how high-born Roman women lived. But it did not take her long to disabuse me of this notion. When I asked her where the gynaikeion was in the house, she turned and looked at me and her blue eyes darkened.

'Surely you do not think that I intend to spend my life like a prisoner in a cage?' she asked, with an edge to her voice. I was surprised.

'No, I – that is to say – no. I mean.' I swallowed. 'I just assumed – I thought, '

'You thought wrong. If I had wanted that, I could have married anyone my mother picked for me. I love you and wanted to marry you because you were different. Do you really want me to sit around a house all day, doing nothing except wait for you to come back – or be told that you never will come back from some far-away battlefield?'

She still looked angry and I thought this was starting us off in a very bad way.

'Irene, I had absolutely no idea of what you wanted to do. My mother died when I was too young to remember. I just thought that you were going to live like other Roman ladies of your rank. Honestly, my love, you can do whatever you want. But I didn't know that you knew anything about trade?'

My face must have told her that I was serious, because her expression changed.

'Some women do – some women don't. But my father doesn't have any sons. He wanted to be sure that Theodora and I knew enough to make sure that whoever we married did not waste all his money. So, he trained me in his business. I will act as one of his agents here. I will also start my own weaving workshop, employing other women. Does this bother you?'

This was indeed a new side of Irene. If Theodora was as clever – and I knew she was – I don't think Georgios need ever worry about his sons-in-law.

'Not if it is what you want to do. As long as you remember one thing: I don't intend to end up on some far-away battlefield. I will always be back. I may just be late home sometimes.' She laughed and embraced me. But it was a timely warning that my wife was much more than just something pretty to look at in the day and someone to share my bed at night. It made me love her even more. But I suddenly thought of one problem. 'What will your mother say?'

'She will not approve. But it is not her decision any more. If you approve, she will have to accept it. And my father will think even more highly of you.'

Life changed even more in 1080, when Irene gave birth to a daughter, whom we gave the name Theodora after her aunt, although it quickly became just Dora.

* * *

As I said, most of us felt that Botaneiates was being too lenient and that his mercy would be misinterpreted as weakness. Sure enough, another

Nikeforos, this one called Melissenos, rebelled. And finally, so did Alexios Komnenos. He had been loyal throughout to the Emperor. But it was said that the Empress – who was much younger than her husband – was in love with him. Maybe she was and maybe she wasn't. Then it was said that the Emperor had ordered him to capture Melissenos, but the two of them were brothers-in-law and he refused. I don't know. But there were always enough people ready to fan the Emperor's jealousy against a young and popular rival. Botaneiates had two friends in particular, Borilos and Germanos, who tried to turn him against Komnenos. In any case, both Komnenos and Melissenos proclaimed themselves Emperors and marched on Constantinopolis.

And as if that wasn't enough, the Normans reappeared. Emperor Michael – the one I had first served, Parapinakes – had betrothed his son Constantine to the daughter of Robert, the Norman Duke of southern Italy. Any Englishman could have told him that was a dangerous thing to do. Of course, when Michael was overthrown, the betrothal ended. But Robert was not going to be fobbed off. In many ways, he resembled the other Norman Duke, the Bastard. He found some Greek monk who he claimed was Michael and announced that he was going to restore him to the Imperial throne. More likely, he was going to repeat what his northern cousins had done and try to take over Empire for himself, with his 'Emperor' to give his blessing to Robert's rule. And we, who should have defended the Empire and were dying to fight the Normans, were cooped up in the city, guarding an old Emperor who was not going to fight. Most of us already felt that Alexios would be a better Emperor than either Botaneiates or Melissenos, but we were going to stick to our oath.

For a while, it seemed as if we would have to. Alexios Komnenos was the first of the rival rebels to reach the city, where he bribed the commander of a German troop to let him in. When his men entered the city, Borilos, whom Botaneiates had made a general, called us and some other troops out. He wasn't our Akolothous, though, so we were not sure if we should obey him, even if he did claim to speak in the Emperor's name. In the end, we didn't have to.

Before there was any fighting, Botaneiates abdicated and Melissenos agreed to stand aside.

And so we had a new Emperor, Alexios, first of that name. I had not seen him yet, but I knew that he was young – only a few years older than I – and that he was a good general. That was highly necessary. Three months after he had become Emperor, Duke Robert and his Normans crossed the narrow waters between Italy and Greece and besieged the port of Dyrrachion. As the Emperor gathered an army, it seemed that we would finally be able to face the Normans again. First, though, we had to make sure we had an army to do it with. Apart from the various guards units, there were apparently precious few armed men to fight with.

CHAPTER 4

Parley

It took some time before we were ready to march out. The Normans had landed in May and attacked Dyrrachion in June. We didn't even march out from Constantinopolis until late August. When we did, it was a strange army. There were 1,500 of us Varangians – Englishmen mostly, but some Russians and a lot of Swedes and Danes as well. There was a regiment of Franks with their own commander and a mounted guards unit, the Exkoubitors, commanded by their Domestic, Constantine Opos. Then there was a unit of Macedonian cavalry and one of Thessalian, and also the Vardariotes. These were Turks, whose ancestors had apparently been moved to the western frontier of the Empire by the Emperor Theophilos hundreds of years ago. Nowadays they also doubled as civic guards in the capital. I had had the odd run-in with them after some drinking sessions. Their commander was called Tatikios. He was the son of a Saracen prisoner of war, but he was now a good Christian. Even better, he was a very good general. There was also a 2,800 strong regiment of heretics, a group called Manicheans. They had a strange faith that I couldn't even try to understand, although they themselves claimed to be true Christians and that the rest of us were heretics. I had long since learnt that the easiest way to get into a fight with someone in Constantinopolis was to question his faith. Although I didn't mind the fighting - though Irene always seemed to mind if I came home bruised after a day off duty – and I knew that my faith was true and theirs wrong, I usually preferred to fight for other reasons. And if someone was supposed to fight on my side in a battle, I preferred not having him angry at me for having fought him a week previously.

If the army was strange, so too was its arms: short swords and long swords, double-edged and single-edged (ours), straight swords and curved. Not to mention chainmail, no mail (I didn't really want to think about how *they* would fare when they met the Norman knights!) and the Greek knights in their scale armour that they called *klibanion*. And then there was the heavy cavalry, the kataphrakts. They looked impressive, but all too few of them were mounted on proper warhorses. With the exceptions of the Thessalians, whose horses were famous, most of us were on smaller and lighter mounts. I remembered the horses I had seen in the west, in France and in Normandy. They could cause us a lot of trouble. Outside Adrianopolis we met up with further units and then we marched off towards Dyrrachion. Altogether we could have been about twenty thousand.

This was the first time I marched with the full Imperial army on a real campaign. It was certainly different from marching with the fyrd. Then, we had marched during the day and slept during the night wherever we found a place to rest. This army marched in a set order and along roads that were much better. I was told that the road westwards from Constantinopolis to Dyrrachion was called the Via Egnatia, the same road that passed through Thessaloniki. It was hundreds of years old, but it was still good. If there was a city where we stopped for the night, we were billeted in the city – and all was arranged by the time we came marching up. If not, every night we built a full fortified camp. It meant that the march was slower. But it also meant that the risk of a surprise night attack was much smaller than if we had marched in any order and camped under the stars. And throughout the march, there were scouts ahead and patrols all around us to make sure no surprises occurred during the day either.

Some time after Adrianopolis, our scouts encountered a man from Dyrrachion. He was taken to the Emperor and the commanders and asked to describe what had happened. I was not there, but Godric had been on guard duty outside the tent where they met him and later told me what he had managed to overhear.

'The main thing is that Dyrrachion is still holding out against the Normans', he said. 'That's good news, not least because it means we can catch them between our army and the city garrison, rather than having to storm a fortified city.'

'Yes', I replied 'we could do without that. But how can we be sure that the city will still hold out until we reach it?'

‘We can’t, of course. But the garrison will soon know that we are coming and that will spur them to fight until we are there. And from what I hear, the Normans have almost shot all their bolts. They built a siege tower and the Greeks sallied out and burned it down. Their siege machines are not having much effect on the walls. The Emperor has also ordered the Venetians to attack the Norman shipping. I am not sure exactly how that has gone – the man was vague and there seem to have been more than one battle – but they clearly are not receiving reinforcements. And to cap it all, they’ve had disease in the Norman camp. But we will still have to hurry up.’

That was not only Godric’s opinion. Next day, the pace of the march was increased. But it still took some time and it was only on 15th October – fifteen years and one day after Hastings – that we reached the enemy. However, Dyrrachion was still holding out.

As we camped, I asked Godric when he thought we would attack.

‘Not yet,’ he replied. ‘First, there’ll be an embassy to the Normans to try to persuade them to withdraw without a fight.’

‘Surely not!’ I exploded. With the exception of the brief fight against Roussel’s men, I had not fought the Normans for fifteen years and I had actually become – somewhat – friendly with one or two of them who were serving he Greeks. But now the old fire was burning again. This would be the revenge for Hastings! The Normans had invaded our country. Surely we were not going to let them just sail away again without punishing them?! ‘Anyway, the Normans aren’t going to withdraw without a fight, are they? I am not even sure I want them to!’

‘Probably not. But you never know. And negotiations can be helpful in many ways. We may find out more about them that could be useful to know. For one thing, some of them may be unhappy with the fact that they have been besieging a city for four months with precious little to show for it. In any case, it will gain us some time.’

‘Won’t they gain the same time?’

'Of course. But we can use this time better, for instance by getting in touch with the city garrison, or even getting reinforcements. The Normans aren't going anywhere. More to the point, no-one is going to them either. They are not getting reinforcements. Nampites says there is still a Venetian fleet in the Adriatic, making sure no more Normans cross over.' Nampites was our new Akolothous. 'And even if the Duke won't leave, maybe some of his vassals might be encouraged to withdraw or at least stand aside.'

'Bribed, you mean? That's despicable. Why won't the Greeks fight? The Emperor is a good general. You know that! The army is ready and willing to fight.'

'Bribed is such an ugly word,' Godric said. 'Why not call it a gift from the Emperor to show his respect and friendship for the Norman warriors. If they then reconsider their situation and decide that they prefer to be the Emperor's friends than his enemies, then so much better.'

'But it's cowardly,' I insisted.

'Not really. Haven't we already talked about this before, Edmund? You have to think like a Greek.

After all, you've lived here for almost ten years now. You're even married to one. Remember what I told you when we first met. They Greeks will certainly fight – and bravely – if they have to. But if the war can be decided without a fight, they feel it will save many Christian lives, which will please God. Then there is also something else. Look around you. How many are we? Fifteen thousand, maybe twenty. Despite their losses, the Normans still have a bigger army. Can you guarantee victory?'

'Of course not,' I muttered.

'Quite. We might win. If we win, we will still have lost a lot of men. The Normans have only one enemy right now and that's us. If we win, they will go back to Italy and wait for another opportunity.

'But the Empire has many enemies. There are the Turks in the east and the Pechenegs in the north. I know that may of them are fighting in our ranks today, but if the Empire is weakened, they are just as likely to turn against us. And that's even more true of Constantine Bodin, the Slav Prince of Zeta who is here with his men. He has already rebelled once and would dearly love to cease being the Emperor's vassal. And all that is if we win. Now, if we lose, the Empire has no more soldiers at all. We are the only army Alexios has. So anything that can weaken the enemy and possibly even avoid battle and still mean we win, makes sense.'

'I suppose so.' Actually, I knew that what Godric was saying made sense. Almost ten years with the Greeks had indeed taught me some of how they thought. It was just that during the last ten years, I had always thought I'd end up fighting the Normans and now, when it seemed almost certain, it might not happen anyway. I felt like a child, that been promised a treat and now doesn't know if it will get it. Godric saw that I was moping and disappeared off.

Soon afterwards, he was back. 'Dry your tears,' he said. 'You have work to do.'

'Don't be silly,' I replied. 'What work? The camp is already made.'

'The Emperor is sending an ambassador to Duke Robert. The ambassador needs a guard. Nampites says you are it. Pick three others and report to him at once.'

I chose three men from my group of ten – Oswy, Alf and the Russian Oleg whom I had become friendly with – and went to see Nampites. That wasn't his real name, by the way. He was from Sweden in the far north and Nampites was apparently the Greek pronunciation of his Swedish nickname Nábitr which meant 'corpse-biter'. I don't know what his real name was. He was about my age and had only been appointed Akolothous a few months earlier.

'Ah, Edmund,' he said. 'His Sacred Majesty is sending his brother, the Protosebastos Adrianos, to convince the Normans to leave our lands. Not that I expect them to do so, so we will fight after all – I know you are looking forward to it. As are we all. I haven't had a good fight for ages. And we will beat them, you know.'

I didn't reply.

'However, the Emperor feels we should try negotiations first. You and your men are to guard the Emperor's brother. Make sure that the honour of the Empire is upheld, but don't start the fighting all on your own. I know you don't like Normans, but this is a ceremonial duty only. Now, come with me and I'll take you the Protosebastos.'

When we reached the generals' tents, the Protosebastos Adrianos Komnenos was already mounted. I hadn't heard his title before, by the way. It was a new one. Apparently, Emperor Alexios had invented a whole new range of titles and parcelled them out to his family and allies. Protosebastos meant something like 'first of the revered'. That meant absolutely nothing to us, since it was clearly not a military rank. But as long as it meant something to someone, I suppose that was enough. Anyway, there were four horses ready for us, so we mounted up and proceeded to ride towards the Norman camp. As we approached, the Protosebastos turned to me.

'What is your name?'

'Edmund, Kyr.'

'You are a Kelt?'

'English, Kyr.'

'Yes, that is what I mean. Your island was conquered by these Normans quite recently, wasn't it?'

'Only until we drive them out again.'

'Hmmm. Well, that is for another day. Today we have other matters to concern us. But do you speak their language?'

'I speak French, Kyr, I don't speak Latin very well.'

'Don't worry about that, I speak Latin. But I want you to listen to what they say among themselves. If there is anything of importance, you will let me know. Do you understand?'

'Yes, Kyr.'

'Also, keep your eyes open as we ride through their camp, you and your men. Then, when you get back, report everything to your commander.'

'Of course, Kyr.'

And with that, he turned his attention to the approaching Normans, for we were now almost at their camp and a group of them were riding towards us. When they came nearer, the Protosebastos said his name. They were clearly expecting us and told us to follow them to the Duke's tent.

* * *

When we arrived, we were kept waiting outside Duke Robert's tent for the better part of an hour. I felt this was slighting to our leader's status, but Godric had already warned me that something like this was likely to occur. It was part of the Norman way of showing their superiority and how little they cared for our envoy or for the Emperor. Eventually, of course, we were let in.

The tent was of medium size. It contained a table, which was covered with parchments as well as jugs of what seemed to be wine and some mugs. There was also a cot and a brazier which was glowing red in its attempt to keep the tent warm. It didn't work, but it spread an acrid smoke.

It was quite clear who the Duke was. He was tall, with his hair cut short but with a long beard. Although I knew that he must have been almost 65 years old, he looked like a young man. Some of the Normans in the tent were wearing armour and – judging by the mud caked on them – must have come directly from the siege-works. The Duke himself was not, though he did wear a sword by his side. He was surrounded by Norman nobles and more came in while we were there. There were also some that did not seem like Normans, as well as a monk who seemed well out of place.

At first, everything seemed polite enough. The Protosebastos was courteously welcomed and was offered wine – although we were not – and some of the Norman nobles were introduced to him. The introductory remarks were of the usual meaningless politeness common to negotiations. But soon enough they reached the subject of the meeting. Although the Protosebastos had said that he spoke Latin, he decided to use Greek. This meant that I could understand what was going on – although I hardly thought that was why he did it. More likely, it was to gain another advantage in case something was let slip by the other side. If they did not know that he spoke Latin or that I spoke French and everything had to be translated, the Normans might talk among themselves while the translator droned on.

'His Sacred Majesty is upset to see war among Christians,' he was saying. 'He has sent me to ask why you are here and if there is no way of resolving our differences peacefully.'

It took some time for the translator to turn this into French. Some of the Normans were sniggering at the idea that the Emperor wanted to know why they were there, but their Duke silenced them.

'Surely your master knows why we are here,' he replied. 'We are not here to fight against him – we are here to right the wrongs suffered by my daughter at the hands of the Emperor Botaneiates. You know that she was betrothed to the Caesar Constantine, the son of the Emperor Michael. When Botaneiates became Emperor, my daughter was turned out of the palace. This insult must be avenged.'

'I understand,' the Protosebastos was saying. 'But Botaneiates is no longer Emperor. Whatever harm he did to your daughter or to you has been avenged and he is now spending his days repenting his misdeeds. In fact, the Caesar Constantine is again highly honoured by our Emperor and I am sure the betrothal between him and your fair daughter can again be discussed. If, as you say, you have no quarrel with the Kyr Alexios, surely there need be no war between us. The Emperor of the Romans is a mighty lord and terrible to his enemies, but he is always prepared to be generous to his friends.'

'I am pleased to hear that. And if there is peace between us, I would be your master's friend and come to his help if he was threatened. But first he would have to agree to my conditions. There is much to be discussed beyond my daughter's betrothal. For one thing, this expedition to avenge her honour has been very expensive. And my men would think little of me if I had nothing to show for it. Yon city, for instance, should be part of my daughter's morning gift. That way we would be able to protect you against the rapacious Venetians, who even now prey upon our shipping.'

'The Venetians acknowledge the sovereignty of the Holy Emperor and help him in his need. But I am sure everything is open to negotiation, even if it is not for me to pre-empt the words of my brother. Yet surely nothing can be decided while your vassals and the Emperor's men mistakenly look upon each other with hatred in the eye. After all, if relations are to be friendly between us, there is no need for an armed camp on our shore.'

'My friends are simply here to see to it that we are given our right.'

While this was going on and much more in the same vein, I could see some of the younger Norman nobles standing together and talking among themselves. One of them was a tall, pleasant-looking fellow, a few years younger than I – 25 or 28 at the most. The others seemed to defer to him as their leader. I could overhear some of his comments, although his French was different from what I knew. He was indicating us four Varangians and saying something about 'the English,' which made them all laugh. Then he started talking about something to do with the Emperor, indicating the monk, and pointing to the Protosebastos. The others laughed even more and seemed to egg him on.

I muttered to the others to keep an eye on the group and took a step nearer the Protosebastos. He was still talking with Duke Robert.

'You say that Botaneiates is no longer Emperor. We know this, of course and recognise that this changes matters. But your master cannot be the rightful Emperor as long as the Emperor Michael lives.' With these words, Robert indicated the monk, who – noticing that he was mentioned – drew himself up and tried to look impressive.

The Protosebastos laughed. 'It is true that the former Emperor Michael still lives and is indeed a monk. But surely you are not trying to pretend that this poor creature is him? I have seen him in his monastery. In fact, even the Ambassador you sent to the Emperor some time ago saw him. This fellow doesn't look anything like him.'

The Protosebastos's laugh seemed to galvanise the young Norman I was watching. Suddenly he shrugged his shoulders and moved rapidly towards the Protosebastos, while he called out in Greek (that was worse than mine):

'Show some respect to your Emperor, you low-born dog!'

I didn't know if he really intended to attack the Protosebastos or not, but I was not going to take any chances. I had already taken moved even closer to him and now I quickly stepped between them. I had one hand on my sword, while I grabbed the fellow's sword-arm with the other. He was strong, but I am no weakling either. He tried to break loose, but I tightened my grip and held tight. Out of the corner of my eye I saw Oswy, Alf and Oleg moving up between us and the young Norman's friends. The Duke and the Protosebastos were just turning to see what was going on. While the Norman was struggling to free his hand from mine, I growled at him in French, '*You* show some respect to an Ambassador – Norman!'

Now the Duke was moving. One hand gestured to the other Normans to stand back. Then he addressed the one I was holding: 'Peace, Bohemond. Don't insult our honoured guest.' Turning to the Protosebastos, he continued, 'My son Bohemond. You know how impetuous youth can be. He will apologise to you, of course. But I think we have little more to say to each other at this time. Please convey my message to the Emperor.'

I had still not let go of Bohemond, although he had stopped struggling. When the Protosebastos nodded at me, I let him go. He took one step back, turned to the Protosebastos and said 'I acted hastily and my conduct was unworthy of either of us. Please forgive me.' When the Protosebastos nodded, Bohemond turned back towards me and looked me over, while he smoothed his tunic. 'What is your name, Englishman?' he asked.

'Edmund – Domine,' I replied. He was the Duke's son and if he wasn't going to fight, there was no harm in being polite.

Suddenly he laughed. 'You have a strong grip, Edmund. Is your hand equally strong when there is a sword in it?'

'Pray you never find out, Domine.'

'I will keep an eye out for you on the battlefield,' he said. Then he suddenly stuck his hand out at me. I couldn't understand it. One moment he seemed ready to fight – the next he behaved as if we were the best of friends. But when laughed, he seemed transformed. It was impossible to remain angry with him – so I shook his hand.

Then we left and rode out of the camp. On the way out we continued to look around to gather as much information about the Normans as we could. Our escort, of course, tried to hurry us on, to make sure we saw as little as possible. Their camp certainly seemed to belong to a larger army than ours. There were plenty of siege machines and they seemed busy building more, although I could see the still smoking ruins of a siege tower. I was amazed that Dyrrachion was still resisting.

When we reached the camp, the Protosebastos turned to me. 'Well done,' he said.

'Thank you, Kyr.'

'But I think you have gained a dangerous enemy today. Don't underestimate him – or any Norman.'

'I won't, Kyr.'

'Better get back to your tents. Try to get some sleep. We will be fighting these people very soon.'

But before we went to sleep, there was a Mass, followed by the whole army chanting the trisagion. This was something we did every morning and evening when on the march, calling out to God: 'Holy God, holy mighty one, holy immortal one, have mercy on us!' When I saw the entire host, kneeling in prayer, with a forest of burning wax candles stuck on their spears and swaying in the evening, I knew God would not let us lose this battle.

On the night of 17th October, the order was given to attack.

CHAPTER 5

Back to the West

On the third day after the battle I rode into Ohrid. It seemed that most of the refugees from the battle had come the same way. I had passed quite a few on the way. Many enough to know that we had been badly beaten, too few to make up another army. Now I remembered what Godric had said about us being the only force the Emperor had and how he couldn't afford to lose us. Well, lost us – or most of us – he had. Was this just going to be a repeat of Hastings, with the Normans marching on Constantinopolis and Robert proclaiming himself Emperor? The monk he claimed was Emperor Michael would presumably disappear somewhere along the way. It certainly looked likely and I was not feeling particularly cheerful as I rode into town.

Ohrid seemed chaotic at first, with lost soldiers milling around and no one apparently in charge. But even as I tried to find other Varangians – and there were precious few of them around – a few of the senior officers were trying to bring some sort of order out of chaos. I was lucky. As I led my horse towards an inn, Nampites stepped out of a house. So he too had survived, at least. I was pleased to see someone I knew, but he seemed even more pleased to see me.

'Edmund!' he exclaimed. 'Just the man I needed to see. Come with me. Don't worry about your horse.'

He took my arm, opened the door again and pulled me inside, while he yelled for a servant to take care of my horse. Once inside, he offered me some wine and asked me to sit down. This had never happened before.

'Edmund, how much do you know of the battle?'

'I know we lost.'

'Obviously. Otherwise we would be sitting in Dyrrachion now instead of here. But we lost badly. As far as the Varangians are concerned, I doubt if there are more than a two or three hundred left.'

He paused while I thought about that. Two or three hundred left – maybe? A week earlier there had been fifteen hundred of us! As if that wasn't bad enough, he continued:

'Most were burned in the little church of St Michael on the battlefield. It seems the Normans have no respect even for the sanctity of a holy building. Your friend Godric is lost – he may have been inside the church.'

Godric too! Was there anything more that could happen?

'The Emperor urgently needs to rebuild his army,' Nampites was saying. 'Mourning the dead must wait until victory. Meanwhile, there is work to do. First, you are promoted. You were a pentekontarch – now you are a komes, with your own bandon.'

Komes? Commander of a bandon – a unit of a hundred men – and better pay. But would there even be a hundred men for me to command? Hearing about the loss of almost the entire Guard and of my best friend had made me slow on the uptake. Now I was beginning to wonder if there was something more going on here. Nampites was still talking.

'...you should be able to recruit a large number of Englishmen.'

'Huh? I mean, what? I didn't quite understand that.'

'I said you have two missions. First, you are to go to Italy with one of the Emperor's emissaries who is trying to raise rebellion among Duke Robert's vassals. Then you will continue to your own country and recruit new soldiers for the Guard. You won't be alone. Others are travelling directly to England and you should be able to recruit a large number of Englishmen. Is that clear?'

His tone had changed from friendly superior to commanding officer. I stood up and acknowledged my orders.

'It may take a day or two before we get you on your way. Find yourself lodgings. Then come back here – I will have work for all my surviving Varangians.'

The next two days I was busier than I had been for a long time. Although our losses were smaller than we had feared – maybe 5,000 all told – that was still almost a third of our army and many of the survivors were not fit for duty anymore. But those that were had to be rounded up and the neighbourhood of Ohrid scoured for supplies – everything from food to horses. Not to mention space; my lodging meant space next to my horse in a makeshift stable, and I was lucky to get that. Quite a few of the survivors had to huddle under blankets outside in the cold. Nampites was too busy to talk to me about my mission and I was too busy to grieve for my friends.

On the third day, I was rushing around a corner when I collided with someone who had been standing, talking with some friends. The other man managed to remain on his feet, but I fell into the mud, so he bent down to help me up and I grabbed his arm. At first I didn't notice his face, because everything happened so quickly, but I did recognise the flaming red hair. This was the officer I had seen unhorsing the Norman on the day of the battle.

As he helped me up, I tried to apologise and to thank him at the same time. 'Well done, Kyr, unhorsing the Norman at Dyrrachion. I think you saved not only yourself, but me as well.'

While I was talking I suddenly noticed that the group he was with consisted of very richly dressed and armoured officers. Then I saw his face and a horrible feeling began to grow inside me. I looked around to see if I could get away, but his friends were now all around me, looking none too friendly. I quickly let go of his arm, and as I did I glanced down. Sure enough – he was wearing the purple boots that only one person in the Empire would wear.

I swallowed hard and tried to say something. It did not come out well. 'Er…. Ummm… Your …..'

Suddenly a hand was laid on my shoulder and another voice spoke.

'This, brother, is the man who protected my Embassy from Count Bohemond. Now you know for yourself how strong his grip is.'

I turned around, but I already knew whose the voice was. The Protosebastos Adrianos was smiling at me.

The Emperor looked at his brother and then at me and smiled, while the nobles around us relaxed a little. 'We prefer if you try to uphold our dignity rather than drag it through the mud of Ohrid,' he said, but the smile showed that it was a joke. 'And we thank you for your services to our brother. Edmund the Kelt, isn't it?'

'Yes, Sacred Majesty.'

'We are glad that you survived. Continue to serve us well, and you will be rewarded.'

And with that, the Emperor and his entourage moved off, not waiting for my stammered word of thanks. The Protosebastos stayed behind for a moment. 'Don't worry about it,' he said, still smiling. 'My brother has more important things on his mind right now than a Varangian who failed to send him flying in the street. And he will be flattered that you saw him kill the Norman. One or two of his friends were not sure whether it really happened – although if they really were his friends, they would know that he does not exaggerate. Now off with you!' Then he went off as well, probably not hearing my 'Thank you, Kyr.' But his words had made me feel better.

The next day, Nampites called me in to meet the Emperor's emissary to the Norman counts of southern Italy. He was a Norman himself, one of those serving the Emperor and his name was Richard of Matera. A week later we set off for the Adriatic coast. Nampites had told us that a Venetian ship would meet us at a specific beach about a day's ride north of Dyrrachion and sail us over to Bari in Italy.

Needless to say, I was seasick the whole journey.

CHAPTER 6

Italy

At least the trip was a short one, barely more than a night and a morning. Before we entered Bari, Richard came up to me as I was leaning over the ship's side, feeling miserable, but at least not being sick.

'Are you well enough to talk?' he enquired. I nodded, not quite sure if I really was.

'Good. I just wanted to make sure that you know why we are here. Our task is to travel around the country and convince the Norman counts that they are better off as the Emperor's friends than as his enemies. They may not care very much about that, but what they do care about is the imperial gold which we will promise them and the fact that they don't like their Duke. Most of them think that he is only waiting for a chance to clip their wings. After all, it is not so long ago that all Norman lords here were equal. Now Robert, whom they call Guiscard, the Cunning, has raised himself over them as Duke. There are a lot of men who don't like that.'

He smiled. 'I should know – I am one of them myself. I rebelled against this upstart, but was defeated. Now, rather than live under Robert's rule, I will serve the Emperor – at least for now.'

I nodded to show that I was listening.

'There are others as well who will listen to us. Before we Normans came, the land was ruled by Lombard lords. Some of them are still around and would not mind restoring their fathers' glory. Then there are the Counts of Aversa. They are another Norman family and some think they are the rightful lords of all Normans in southern Italy, not Guiscard and his Hauteville brood. And then there is the Emperor.'

By now, this was getting too complicated for me. Lombards and Norman lords, ancient rivalries and jealousy. 'What about the Emperor?' I asked.

'Not Kyr Alexios. Henry, the German Emperor. Apulia and Calabria – all of southern Italy, in fact – was once part of the western Empire, just as it was once part of the Roman Empire. He is no friend of the Greeks – but he likes the Normans even less. And the Greeks are far away, but the Normans are nearby.

While the Normans were besieging Dyrrachion, Henry was besieging Rome. The Pope supports Robert – but Henry has his own Pope, whom he dearly would like to install in Rome in exchange for a proper imperial coronation. He's been forced to retreat for now, but he'll be back – with Greek gold paying for his army. Finally, the Venetians will help us, to ensure that no one controls both sides of the Adriatic and blocks them up.'

It was complicated before – now I was really confused. 'And what are we supposed to do?' I asked.

'As I said, we travel around, meet some of my old friends and persuade them that they would be better off on our side. But, remember – I am in charge. I know the country, I know the people – you don't. I will do the talking, you will watch my back. But we are here to be friends – not to fight anyone. Do you understand?'

It seemed I had heard this before, from Olof. 'You watch, let me do the talking'. But here I supposed he was right. I certainly did not know anyone of the people we were likely to meet. And he couldn't possibly drink more or sing worse than Olof.

So I replied, 'I understand. You talk – I watch your back.' Even so, I remembered what he had said about serving the Emperor for now and decided that I would watch a bit more than just his back. Richard of Matera seemed mainly interested in serving himself.

When we landed in Bari, Richard led us off to an inn. He told me to wait, while he arranged for the next leg of our journey. I was perfectly happy to wait – for one thing, I was looking forward to some food that would actually stay in my stomach. I ordered a bowl of soup, some bread and a jug of wine and settled back as near the fireplace as I could and waited.

Bari seemed unthreatening enough. I knew that the city had only fallen to the Normans some ten years earlier and there were still plenty of Greeks left. In the inn I heard both Greek and French spoken, as well as other languages. Arabic, I thought, recognising three men for Saracens even though I did not understand their language, and another that probably was Lombard. No one looked twice at me – I had left my axe in Ohrid and was only armed with my knife and sword. I had long since adopted the

Greek style for my hair and beard instead of the English and without armour I could be taken for another vague foreigner.

I tried to listen in to other conversations. Some of them were about the war in Greece. They already knew, of course, that Guiscard had defeated the Emperor. I was surprised – and pleased – to hear that Dyrrachion was still holding out. Others were talking about the ongoing threat from the German Emperor in the north. But most of what I heard was just the usual inn talk – complaints about life, women, money, so I concentrated on my soup instead. It did stay down.

After about two hours, Richard was back, looking pleased with himself. 'I ran into an old friend,' he said. 'He will take us in for the night. And he told me some good news. Guiscard left his younger son Roger Borsa in charge when he attacked us. But he is a weak and greedy man who prefers to sit still and count his money. That's why they call him Borsa – the Purse. The other nobles despise him. So now he is sitting helpless in Apulia, while his cousin Abelard is gaining the allegiance of the Norman lords.'

I wasn't quite sure why one Norman lord was preferable to another and said so.

'Because Abelard de Hauteville serves the Emperor – at least for now. Of course, what he really wants is to be Duke himself. Believes he is entitled to it too, since his father Humphrey – Guiscard's brother – was Count of Apulia before Robert became Count and then Duke. But that is not really our concern. What we want to do is to force the Normans to leave Greece. If that means giving Abelard a helping hand, then that is what we will do.'

Yes, I thought. And I wonder if it also means giving Richard of Matera a helping hand to achieve his goals in Italy. I definitely would keep an eye on him.

* * *

Richard's friend, a Norman called Jordan, had provided horses. He had an estate south-west of Bari and that is where we spent the night. He didn't seem particularly interested in me – I don't know what Richard had told him about me – which suited me. I rode together with his men-at-arms, trying to listen to what he and Richard were saying to each other. It wasn't very interesting. Richard kept asking about mutual friends, how they were, where they were and so on. He was also boasting about his life in Constantinopolis. Instead, I spent my time looking at the countryside. It was different, both from the French and English landscapes I had left so long ago, and from the Greek lands I had recently seen. For one thing, it was more arid, even though autumn rains had filled small rivers with water. And it wasn't as thickly settled as the Empire. Instead of small farmers, there seemed to be mainly larger manors, presumably owned by Norman nobles, or maybe by some of those other peoples that Richard had mentioned – Lombards and Italians. But there seemed to be quite a lot of monasteries everywhere. I asked Richard, who told me that most of them were inhabited by Greek monks. That could prove to be useful.

Jordan's house was one of these estates, although I couldn't see very much of it as we arrived in the dark. Once we had arrived, Jordan and Richard closeted themselves together. I didn't like that at all. I couldn't complain about my bed or the food, but I didn't trust Richard very far and wanted to know what he was saying to Jordan when they were alone.

Next morning, we left Jordan's house. Richard rode in silence, while I was thinking about how to bring up the subject of sitting in on his talks with his Norman friends without letting him understand that I was wary of him. After about an hour or so, he turned to me.

'Yesterday was very interesting,' he said.

I didn't reply, just nodded.

'Jordan is none too bright a fellow,' he continued. 'But the news of Dyrrachion means that the usual methods may not be enough.' He looked at me and thought. 'I think it would be a good idea if you sat in on my talks with my friends here.'

I was taken aback, but tried not to show it. 'How so?'

'Don't worry about that, Englishman. Just agree with anything I say and we'll get along fine.'

I did not care very much for his tone of voice, but on the other hand he had just arranged what I wanted, so I let it pass.

That night we stayed at an inn in a small village, but the next day we approached another Norman lord's home. This looked rather grander than Jordan's home had done.

'I don't know this fellow,' Richard was saying. 'We will just have to make it up as we go along.' And riding up to the gate, he enquired after the name of the owner and asked for lodging for the night.

The owner turned out to be called William. He was smaller than most Normans and darker. Richard later told me that he probably had an Italian mother, which would account for his darkness. But his voice and manner rather recalled a giant from a child's story – deep, booming and even more boastful than Richard.

While we were eating our dinner, Richard tried to sound him out.

'You are clearly a great lord,' he began.

'Greatest in the neighbourhood,' William interrupted. 'My lands are richer and my wine is finer than anyone else's.'

Certainly, his wine – if it was his – was very drinkable. I had gotten so used to the Greek wine, that

I had forgotten how wine elsewhere tasted. In Constantinopolis, the wine was usually not very nice. There may have been better wine – certainly the wine Georgios had served had been excellent – but not for the Imperial guardsmen. But this was very nice, much richer and definitely not mixed with anything. The food was good too – a nice vegetable broth and some very good boiled beef. Not much in the way of vegetables or spices, though. I had become rather spoiled with spices by my wife and now found other food somewhat bland.

'But I am surprised that such a great lord is content to sit in peace when there is honour to be won on the battlefield.'

'In Greece, you mean? How much honour is there to be won fighting the Greeks? They are cowards – run at the hint of battle. No, if you want honour, go fight the Saracens in Sicily with Count Roger. I will join him again next summer and get my fill. He appreciates me – says I'm his best soldier.'

That sounded rather unlikely, whoever Count Roger was.

‘But surely your Duke could make use of such an eminent soldier,’ Richard persisted.

‘Duke? Hah! Doesn’t care for anyone but himself. Tries to set himself above us. Why should I help him make himself Emperor? That would make him even worse. And I can’t stand that son of his – too smooth, too cocksure, too ambitious.’

‘Bohemond?’ I exclaimed, surprised. That was my first contribution to the conversation.

‘Yes, him. Do you know him?’

‘We have – had an encounter.’

‘Thinks he is the greatest warrior in the world, that one. No wonder that sly Guiscard named his younger son Roger Borsa the heir and made everyone – Bohemond too – swear an oath to honour his wish. Otherwise he might find himself a dead ‘Duke’ soon enough.’

That did not seem likely, from my short encounter with Bohemond. I was sure Guiscard was smart and strong enough to withstand any attempt by his son to hasten his inheritance. But I was not going to argue. Instead, Richard broke into the conversation again.

'But don't you see, William, what a danger you are facing? As you say, there is not much honour spent fighting the Greeks. Look how they ran away at Dyrrachion.' At that I gave a startled glance at Richard and began to say something, but he continued without letting me interrupt him.

'If Guiscard continues, he is likely to defeat them before next year is out. Why do you think I left Italy? You said it yourself. All Normans used to be equal until Guiscard came along. We elected our Counts – now he calls himself Duke. What next? You think he is overbearing now – how will he be when he styles himself Emperor of the Romans? And what does Bohemond care if Roger Borsa succeeds Guiscard in Apulia? After all, does not that leave Bohemond next in line for the Empire?

'Look at England and you will see what happens when a Norman Duke gets a crown. In Normandy, nobles were also equal. But as soon as your namesake could call himself King of England, he would have no equal – not by a long shot.

'Look at my friend Edmund; he is a noble English lord, son of an Earl.' That came as a surprise to me. 'He's got nothing against Normans.' An even bigger surprise! 'He could have stayed in England and ruled a large estate. But he left England because he didn't want to be William's slave, however that was dressed up. If you let Guiscard get away with making himself Emperor, you will all soon be slaves here as well.'

'And what is your interest in this?' William asked. 'Who do you work for?' Maybe he wasn't quite as foolish as he seemed.

'My interest is in regaining my estate. And I freely acknowledge that I work for the Emperor, but he is far away. When I have my estate back and when Guiscard's wings have been clipped, I will leave his service. I care no more for an Emperor than for a Duke. But I care about my pride and my own standing and I will only work with someone who respects me'

That certainly sounded like the truth.

'But what can we do? We are all divided and Guiscard has a victorious army behind him.' For all William's boastfulness, this sounded more like a whingeing child.

'You will have to unite. Show Guiscard that he should stay in Italy and rule his realms fairly – taking note of his equals instead of spending money and men on his imperial dreams.'

'It's not as easy as all that –' William began.

'Come, William,' Richard was saying. 'Think about what I have said. Remember, where will you be when Guiscard is Emperor? And remember something else: The Emperor may have been defeated. But he is still Emperor – and the Emperor is rich. He can punish his enemies – and he can reward his friends.'

That seemed to get through to our host.

'Oh, you are right enough,' he boomed. 'We have to curb Guiscard's ambitions. I will take counsel with my friends. Will you stay and meet them? It may take a few days to bring them together.'

'Gladly.' And with that, Richard and I went off to bed.

A few days went by while different Norman nobles drifted to William's home. After three days, there were about a dozen there. I had spent time with William's men and tried to find out more about him.

He had indeed fought in Sicily and fairly bravely too – but none of them seemed to think that he could be Count Roger's most valuable soldier – except if talking was fighting.

William hadn't introduced us to them, but that evening we all had a meal together. Afterwards, William introduced us – or rather, Richard – as a 'friend of old Norman freedoms'.

Richard repeated what he had said to William on the first evening, exaggerating the wealth of the Empire that Duke Robert would be able to command if he defeated the Greeks. He had asked me about my encounter with Bohemond and now told everyone about it, but that too was rather changed. For one thing, I didn't remember Bohemond swearing to avenge every slight and insult he had encountered, as soon as his father was Emperor. But the Normans seemed ready to believe it – just as they believed that all Greeks were weak, cowardly slaves.

When he had finished, the Normans began to talk among themselves. Now and then they would ask Richard for advice.

'There are many things you can do,' he would say. 'You could make Roger Borsa recall his father from Greece. If Guiscard were forced to spend more time in Italy, he would have to take more notice of what you think. He wouldn't be able to make himself Emperor and set himself up above the rest of us. Or you could elect a new leader – maybe Abelard of Hauteville or his brother Herman. After all, their father led us before Guiscard. And then there are the Princes of Capua – were they not the first leaders of the Normans before the Hautevilles rode down into Italy? I hear Prince Jordan is talking to Emperor Henry. Or elect someone else. But whatever you do, you should make sure that your new leader is a worthy one, one who will respect ancient Norman liberties.'

The talking – and drinking – continued well into the night, without any decision being taken.

The next morning, Richard and I left William's house together with one of his friends. This now became the pattern for the coming weeks. We would stay with some Norman noble, Richard would try to incite them against Guiscard, friends and kinsmen would come over and listen and then we would ride off with someone else. Richard didn't always use the same arguments. Sometimes he would talk about how strong the Empire was, say that Duke Robert's defeat was all but certain and that the Emperor was sure to take a terrible revenge on all Normans. At other times, it was about the wealth of the Empire and of the Emperor's generosity to his friends. But always it was about the need to get Guiscard back from Greece.

One thing puzzled me as we rode. There were plenty of cities in this country. But we never ventured near them. In fact, it seemed as if we consciously stayed away from them. When we stopped to eat at an inn, I asked Richard about it.

'There are many reasons', he replied, drinking some wine. 'Some of the cities are ruled by lords already on our side, such as Capua and Aversa. Some others, like Amalfi and Naples, are as friendly as they can be with the Emperor but lack the power to oppose the Normans. In others, Guiscard's power is too strong for us. But the most important reason is that although we Normans rule this land, there aren't terribly many of us. And we tend to live in estates scattered around the countryside. So we are going where we can meet the people we need to see.'

'How can you rule the land if you are so few?'

'How can you ask? Our kin in the north rule England and are equally few. We rule because we defeated previous rulers. Because we are better fighters and because none can stand against us.' That hurt, because I recognised the truth of it.

'But in England, our king was killed and his soldiers were gone. Here, there was no king. No one person for you to kill.'

'True. As long as the king of England was alive, we could not defeat you. So, he had to die. Here, there were – still are – many different rulers. There are Lombard counts and dukes, cities that are all but independent, bishops and abbots and above them all the Pope, who claims to rule them all but doesn't. Well, the Pope is on our side now – one fight against us taught him the folly of opposing us. And as for the others, they have never been united. That makes it easier for us to rule through them. If ever they did unite, however, it would become very difficult for us Normans to rule them.'

'Why do you always have to rule? Could you not just live here among them?'

'The world isn't like that, Edmund. You must have someone who rules. And that will always be the strong, because otherwise, the weak would have no protector. Remember, we have not gone anywhere uninvited. A French King asked us to come to Normandy to protect him from the Norsemen.' That was news to me.

'I thought you were Norsemen yourselves?'

'We are – or were. We were given Normandy to stop other Norsemen from raiding France. And in England, did not your King Edward name Duke William his successor? Did not even Earl Harold swear to support William's claim?'

'That's a lie! Harold was William's captive – he would have been killed if he hadn't sworn fealty to him. But an oath given under duress is not valid!' I had heard all about the Bastard's claims on England and had fought more than once, both in France and in the Empire with those who claimed that William was the rightful successor to King Edward. But I also knew, to my shame, that Edward had favoured the

Normans. Maybe he had promised the Bastard the succession?

'Among us Normans, an oath is an oath. But that's not my point. And you can sit down again – people are staring at you.' I hadn't noticed, but I had risen to my feet and overturned my food. My face must have been red with anger. But I sat down again and tried to keep a grip on myself.

'What I am saying', he continued, 'is that what was true in France and in England is also true here. We were invited to come here and help the locals in their internal battles. Then we proved stronger and none, as I said, could stand against us. And so we rule.'

'Then why are you not on Guiscard's side?'

'I've told you that too. No Norman should set himself up above the others. Look at England. King William rules with a strong hand and none dare set themselves up against him. That's not how it was in Normandy. There, he had to listen to his vassals. Here, as long as he only ruled Italy, Guiscard had to pretend to do the same. But if he were to become Emperor, he would be just like William.'

'That's what you are telling your Norman friends here. I have already heard it. But what do you really believe?'

He sighed. 'Edmund, I am telling you the truth. I am out for myself. But my interests happen to be the same as those of the Emperor. That's all. And if you don't trust me, maybe we should part ways, or even go outside and make an end. You choose.'

I still didn't believe him. The only thing that rang true was that he was out for himself. But I had to stay with him. Killing him or leaving him would not help me in any way. For one thing, it would be difficult for me to move around Italy without him. I certainly would not be able to carry out his mission. So I swallowed my anger and rinsed it down with more wine.

'No', I said. 'We both work for the Emperor. We shouldn't quarrel. Drink some more – a toast of friendship.' And I raised my mug.

'At least to co-operation.' And he drained his own.

We drank a lot more that night. Partly I wanted him to feel safe again in my company – I did not want to be left out from any of his meetings. But I also drank to wash out my feelings of shame and dislike. Richard wasn't easy to get along with. He was not unpleasant like Olof, the Viking I had ridden with to Adrianopolis. But he was boastful and condescending. Even so, I would have to stay with him and humour him. So we settled down to an evening of drinking and singing. As usual here in Italy, the wine was much better than the ones drunk in Constantinopolis. And as it was undiluted, it could quickly go to your head. I have a dim memory of trying to teach him some English songs and he was singing away in French. He did sing better than Olof – that was at least something.

I don't know when we went to sleep, but I know that I woke up close to noon. I couldn't recognise the room and when I tried to sit up I banged my head against the table. I must have rolled to the floor and fallen asleep. Once I could sit up again – carefully – I moved away from the table and staggered out. There was a trough of water there for the horses. I stumbled over and plunged my head into it. That made me feel a little bit better.

When I came back into the room, I called for something to drink. As the inn-keeper brought me another mug of wine, a backdoor opened. Out came a good-looking servant girl I dimly remembered from the previous night. After her, looking as if he had had a good night's sleep and not a drop to drink, came Richard.

'Ah, Edmund, you are up. How good of you. Are you capable of riding or should we wait here another night?'

He sounded insufferably smug. Truth to tell, I would have preferred not to move anywhere that day. But I was not going to give him that satisfaction.

'I am fine. Ready when you are.'

'In that case, let's go.' And so we gathered our packs and rode off. I barely had time to drain my wine and there was certainly no time to eat anything. I spent a truly wretched day. To cap it all, it was warm and sunny and Richard was moved to talk at length about how beautiful the countryside was and what fantastic estates he had at Matera. I just counted the hours until we reached another inn and could settle down for the night. An early night. As I staggered off, Richard looked after me and smiled. Then he waved at one of the serving girls and told her to come over to his table.

And so it continued. We had arrived in Bari and started towards the southwest towards Taranto, skirting Matera. But Apulia was not friendly territory. It was the heartland of Guiscard's authority and the writ of Roger Borsa ran strong. Instead, we turned towards the northwest, slowly making our way towards Salerno, Nocera and even Naples. Then we turned south again, moving down into Calabria. It was clearly a rich country. But I could see what Richard had meant when he said that it was not united. The country was full of people, but they were always different. Lombards, who had ruled the land before the Normans, Saracens, who had taken some of it from the Lombards. Little Greek communities, usually clustered around monasteries, who still remained even though the Empire had been driven hence more than ten years earlier. Normans in their estates, sometimes mixed with Frenchmen. And Italians, who looked like none of the others and spoke their own language.

Everywhere, we tried to stay with Norman lords, to let Richard speak with them and try to turn them away from Guiscard. It was difficult to judge how much effect his talking had. None of the Normans we saw seemed prepare to commit themselves, always waiting for someone else to move first. We had arrived in Bari in early November. Now, as we moved across the country, November had turned to December and December into January and eventually February. And still there was very little to show for our efforts, except that it was getting cold and wet and that I was picking up the local way of speaking French. Occasionally we would run into other travellers and try to find out how the war was going, although they didn't seem to know very much. Once or twice, Richard told me that some of the travellers were people engaged in the same work as us. Occasionally we would stay the night in one of the Greek monasteries. I came to look forward to those nights. Surrounded by Greeks I felt safe – and I also felt more at home listening to the Greek. Whenever we did stay in one of the monasteries, I always went to Mass and to confession. Richard would frequently close himself up with the Abbot or with other travellers. Sometimes he would tell me what he had picked up from them, but that was little enough.

It was like travelling through a fog, cut off from everyone and everything else, and only occasionally hearing a noise from the outside world. I was getting seriously worried about what was happening in Greece, and I think Richard was as well. Certainly, he seemed to be getting moody and angry. But so far there was nothing we could do about it.

It was mid-March and we were now near a small town called Scalea on the west coast of Italy, deep into Calabria. Our current Norman host was named Geoffrey. We had met him in the house of another Norman lord. He had seemed friendly enough and invited us to stay with him for a few days. Yet he seemed less ready to listen to Richard than many of the others. Every time Richard tried to bring up the war, or Norman freedoms, he found some reason to change the subject: he had to go hunting and would we come along? It was time for Mass. His wife was poorly and he needed to see to her. And so on. Also, he had not invited any of his friends and neighbours to listen to us, although he kept saying that they were bound to come any time to meet his visitors.

The third evening we were with Geoffrey, Richard was again trying to convince him. This time, he was talking about the might of the Empire and the power of its armies and how Italy would suffer if the Emperor invaded it in revenge for the Norman attack. As he was talking, one of Geoffrey's men came in and whispered something in his ear. He apologised and went out. While he was away, I turned to Richard. 'Maybe we should leave. You don't seem to be having much luck with this one.'

'No, it will be fine. He just needs some more persuading, that's all. Leave this to me.'

When Geoffrey came back in, he turned to Richard and seemed to have a new expression on his face – half smile, half sneer.

'Go on,' he said. 'You were telling me about how strong the Greeks are.' He seemed to be savouring something.

'Yes,' Richard said, but now he sounded uncertain. 'Although Guiscard managed to defeat the Emperor outside Dyrrachion, that city still holds out against him. He cannot leave the coast, and meanwhile, the Emperor is raising new armies. Soon he will march west again and this time, all Normans will feel the force of his wrath for having supported his enemies. Not only those in Greece, but in Italy as well. The Venetians already hate us and will gladly help Alexios move an army across the narrows. What hope have we then?'

'How interesting,' Geoffrey said. 'But I have something interesting to say as well. What would you say if I told you that Dyrrachion fell to Duke Robert almost three weeks ago? It was betrayed – by another of the Emperor's loyal servants, no doubt. How about if I told you that all of Illyria is now in our hands? And that Kastoria has fallen without a fight – despite a garrison of 300 Varangians, similar to your English friend here? It seems that they show about as much fighting spirit in Greece as in England.'

I felt sick. The fall of Dyrrachion was a blow, but not really unexpected. If he had only mentioned that, it could have been a lie. But the talk about Kastoria and the Varangians guarding it rang true. Were there *any* Varangians left to fight now?

I didn't have time to think about this for long, because there was noise behind us. Geoffrey's men had come into the chamber, and we were unarmed and outnumbered.

'Seize them!' he commanded. When we were gripped tightly, he turned to Richard again.

'I know what you have been doing for these past months, Richard. Not all Normans are traitors to their Duke, nor are they willing to sell themselves too the Emperor like whores. You should have known that. Now I have something more to tell you. Roger Borsa is giving you a choice – which is more than I would do. You can renounce your allegiance to Alexios and join your kin once again. If you can prove yourself to be loyal and true to your Duke, your estate at Matera may well be returned to you. Or you can wait in a dungeon until such time as the Duke can spare some time to think about your fate.'

Richard looked at him. 'How can I trust you?' he asked.

'You can't. But I know how I can trust you. You will tell me everything about who you have met and who you have bribed with your Greek gold. When you have done that, your Imperial master is unlikely to be very pleased with you. So you might as well stay with your true master. As I said, your estates *may* be returned to you.'

Richard thought for a moment. 'And my companion?' he asked.

'His life is forfeit – he is an enemy. The only question is what you will do. But choose now. You don't have much time.'

'You are very persuasive,' Richard replied. 'You know that I am not working for my personal gain but for the good of all the Normans in Italy. It would be nice to have my own estates back, and, to tell the truth, I am getting a bit tired of the sour wine they serve you in Greece. But a man doesn't change masters as he changes horses. I would like some time to think it over.'

'You have until tomorrow. At dawn, you and your friend will be sent to Roger Borsa in Apulia. Take them away.'

I wasn't angry at Geoffrey – this was war, after all and he was the enemy. Richard was a different matter. Just as I had thought, he seemed ready to betray his – and my – master at first sign of adversity. I tried to spit at him, but my guards were holding me to tightly and in the wrong direction. 'Traitor!' I shouted. 'Scum! I knew you couldn't be trusted to stay loyal. You don't know the meaning of the word! Just like any Norman. I'd kill you myself, if I could!'

'Oh, shut your mouth,' he replied wearily. 'When the world changes, you must change with it if you want to stay ahead. That's what you stupid English never learned and that's why you were defeated in England and defeated again in Greece.'

I couldn't reply, because at a sign from Geoffrey, one of his men had gagged me. Now we were taken away separately. I was thrown into the room I had slept in the night before. My weapons had already been taken away, my hands and feet were firmly and none too gently tied up and there was a guard outside the room.

Things were not looking good.

CHAPTER 7

To England

I don't know how long I had slept when a hand suddenly clamped down over my mouth and another hand shook me by the shoulder. I tried to bite the hand – about the only thing I was capable of doing – but I couldn't get at it.

'Stop it! And be quiet! Not a sound!'

It was Richard. 'I'll remove my hand if you promise to be quiet. Nod your head.'

I nodded, unable to think of anything else to do. He took his hand away and quickly cut off the ropes binding my hands and feet. 'Can you stand? Don't say anything; just get up if you can. Rub your hands to get the blood flowing again.'

I tottered to my feet. The bindings had been firm, but not rough. I could stand and I stamped my feet to get the cramped feeling out of them.

'Quickly now' he whispered. 'We've got to get out of here before we are missed.'

I had a lot of things I wanted to say, but thought they should wait. If there was a chance of getting away, I should grab it with both hands. Richard opened the door to my room and stuck out his head. Seeing nothing to worry him, he stepped out and beckoned me after him. Outside, the guard was lying on the ground. His throat had been cut. Richard motioned to me to grab his feet while he took the arms and together we dragged him into my room. Richard took his sword and gave me his knife and spear. Then we crept out again.

Richard was still signalling to me to keep quiet and to follow him. He tiptoed around a corner and through a corridor. Apart from the guards, I assume everyone in Geoffrey's house must be asleep. It was almost pitch black. As Richard opened a door, I could barely make out the courtyard outside. But I remembered it well enough from our arrival and from seeing dozens of similar houses. The stables would be next to the house – in this case, to our right – servants' quarters to the left, a wall with a gate finishing off the square.

'What now?' I hissed, my first words since Richard had woken me up.

‘The gate,’ he whispered back. ‘There are two guards. You take the one on the left.’

We crept along the servants’ quarters. The sky must have been cloudy, because I only saw one or two stars. When we came close to the further wall, Richard tapped my shoulder and disappeared. I continued to advance as stealthily as I could. Soon I could make out two outlines in the dark – the two guards he had mentioned. The one closer to me was leaning on his spear and facing his friend, who was saying something.

I edged closer again. Suddenly there was a noise on the other side of the guards and both turned around, startled, trying to dispel the darkness. There was no time to wait. I quietly put down my spear, grabbed the knife and jumped. My left hand closed around the guard’s throat and before he had time to react, I struck him with the haft of the knife on the right side of his head. He went down like an ox, but I kept my hand on his mouth until he was down. Then I looked up to see what was happening with the other guard. He was down too. Richard was bending down over him, wiping his knife on the man’s tunic.

‘Is yours dead?’ he asked.

‘Stunned.’

‘No time for niceties – he must die.’ And with that he leaned down over my victim and stabbed him twice in the heart.

‘Quickly now, open the gate. Then help me with these two.’

I unbarred the gate and turned back. At first, I couldn’t see Richard. Then I realised that one of the dead guards was gone and I could hear Richard hissing at me. I grabbed the other one by the feet and began to drag him across the square. When I reached the stable, Richard was waiting for me.

‘Inside with these two. Hurry up.’

We opened the stable doors and dragged the dead guards inside. Once that was done, Richard grabbed saddle and reins and began to prepare a horse. I did the same. We opened the stable doors enough to lead the horses out, but when I started, Richard held me back. Before I had time to ask what was going on, he took out tinder and steel and struck a spark. Then he carefully set fire to a bale of hay in the stable. Only then did he lead his horse – which was getting skittish as it smelled the fire – through the door. Once I was out, he carefully closed the stable door and led his horse to the gate, with still following. Once we were out, he shut the gate as best he could. Then he turned to me. 'Now ride,' he said. 'Ride like the wind.' And with that he swung himself into the saddle and set off.

I rode after him, but he was ahead until – about three-quarters of a mile further off – he stopped on a ridge and looked back. We could see the light from the burning stable and it was easy to imagine the panic that must be reigning there, horses going mad with fear, Geoffrey and his men attempting to save the horses, wondering why the stable was on fire while they tried to put it out. With a bit of luck, the bodies of the dead guards would be too badly burned to show how they had died and it would be some time before they began to count the horses and thought of the prisoners.

Richard was shaking his fist towards the house. 'You thought you could capture Richard of Matera, did you, Geoffrey! Well, it takes someone with twice your brains to do that, you dung-heap! Now run to your penny-pinching master Roger and tell him you lost your catch. See how well you get rewarded for that, whore-son!'

'Shouldn't we ride on?'

'Oh yes. I have no wish to see that turd again. We ride to Scalea.'

'Won't he guess that?'

'He will. It's the obvious thing to do. Unfortunately, it is also about the only thing to do right now.'

I suddenly remembered something.

'Richard?'

'Yes?'

'How did you escape? I was trussed up like a chicken.'

'I wasn't. I dare say Geoffrey didn't trust me – how right he was – but there was a slight chance that I might really change sides. Better treatment would help. But he did leave two guards outside my room.'

'And?'

'I told them I needed to relieve myself. One of them took me to privy. I asked him to stand guard outside and leave me alone. They had taken my weapons, but I have found it a good idea always to hide a dagger underneath my clothes. As soon as he turned his back I cut his throat. Then I came to get you.'

I digested that.

'I owe you an apology. I thought you were going to betray the Emperor.'

'Yes, I know. That is because you don't know me. You think all Normans are alike and you don't like us because other Normans conquered your home country. I understand that. But you are wrong. All Normans are not alike. And you are wrong about me too. If you think back, I have told you the truth many times. Yes, I am mainly working for myself. I would like to get back my estates at Matera. The only way that is likely to happen is if Robert Guiscard and his friends are defeated. That means that my interests are the same as the Emperor's. You know of Roussel de Bailleul?'

I nodded. 'I fought against him when he betrayed the Emperor.'

'He started by serving the Emperor loyally as well. But Roussel thought he could do better and tried to set up his own Duchy. I don't. I don't what to live in Asia – I want to live here. My land is here, my friends are here. You may think it strange, but I am trying to do what is best for my people. It's just that I think we live better as equals than with an overbearing Duke – or a King, for that matter.'

'Or an Emperor?'

'If serving the Emperor is the way to achieve a free Norman Italy, then that is what I will do. As long as the Emperor keeps out of Italy, I will be loyal. And when I leave his service, I will tell him so myself. Now let's ride on towards Scalea.'

About three hours later we rode into Scalea. It was more a castle with some houses than a town and I couldn't understand how we would get away from there. But Richard did in fact have a plan. Scalea was also a fishing village. In exchange for our horses and their gear, one of the fishermen agreed to sail us up the coast all the way to Amalfi.

If I had known that our escape involved a sea journey, I think I would have stayed in Geoffrey's house. The wind was against us too, so the trip took almost two days. When I could speak I swore never to go to sea again. Richard just laughed at me.

*   *   *

When we arrived in Amalfi we said our farewells to the fisherman. Even if Geoffrey had followed us to Scalea, he would have been a few hours behind. Then the fisherman's friend would have to tell him who had taken us and why – and risk losing the horses and gear we had traded for the journey. And even then, he wouldn't know where we had gone – because we had carefully avoided telling anyone until we were safely at sea and out of sight from land – so we should be reasonably safe, at least for a few days. Eventually, of course, Geoffrey would know, but by that time we should have left Amalfi long since. And the Amalfitans were not enamoured with the Normans who ruled them, Geoffrey told me, so that would help even more.

Richard didn't intend for me to have a few days ashore. Once we had stepped ashore, he led us to the nearest inn. This was in the port area. I had seen that Amalfi was a busy port, so it was no surprise to find the place full of sailors. Richard sat me down, ordered some bread, cheese and wine and while I tried to get my stomach back in order, he circulated around the room, talking to different sailors. Then he came back to me.

'This is where our ways part, Englishman.'

'Why? Surely we still have work to do?'

'No longer. Even that lazy money-counter Roger Borsa has bestirred himself. All the Emperor's agents are being hunted across the land. But it's too late for him. The sailors here tell me that Emperor Henry is moving towards Rome again.'

'So we go back to the Greece?'

'No, my English friend. I go back to the Emperor. *You* have more work to do, remember? You need to recruit more of your country-men for the Varangian Guard. Isn't that what Nampites told you?'

The truth was, I had forgotten all about that. He was right of course. A horrible suspicion began to form in my mind.

'I didn't just get news from the sailors,' Richard was saying. 'I have also booked a passage for you. Don't get too used to *terra firma* – you sail for Marseille in the morning. Oh, and you will need this.' With those words, he took up a purse and handed it over. I looked inside; some gold, mainly silver. 'And this.' That was a parchment with a lead seal, authorising me to raise soldiers for the Empire.

'Don't waste the money. It has to last you until you get back to your commander. And now you had better get some sleep. It will be your last good night for a while, I'm afraid.'

I was too shocked at the thought of another boat journey to even protest. Next morning, Richard took me down to the quay and led me to a large trading ship. He introduced the captain as Raymond and paid him in advance for my passage. Before I went on board, I made a last attempt.

'Isn't there any way to go on land?'

'It would take too long. Now get on board. I will presumably see you back in Greece. Have a nice trip.'

Raymond's ship was the largest I had ever been on, with a crew – I found out – of 30. I had thought that a larger boat would mean less movement and maybe save me from seasickness. I was wrong. I didn't really think that it was possible to be as sick as I was on that journey. And it didn't help when the sailors told me that the weather actually was perfect for a sea journey – just enough wind to move us in the right direction. I hope I never have to sail anywhere in a storm.

* * *

The trip to Marseille took six days. I had hoped to be able to find new recruits for the Guard in Provençe or in France, so at first I stayed on in Marseille. I took lodgings in an inn – the one where I had met Godric so many years ago – and began to move around the city. I was looking for the same kind of people that Godric had recruited with me – Englishmen, working as guards or men-at-arms. But whether I had arrived at the wrong time or there were fewer Englishmen in this work nowadays, I was out of luck. So after about a week in Marseille, I began to think about travelling north. And now I had better luck. I did not fancy travelling alone to France, even though I was armed. But a merchants' caravan was going to Troyes and was happy to have an extra guard on the way. It also meant that I was able to save the money I had been given, since I was paid – badly – and fed. In late April, we set off.

It was slower than I had hoped to travel. I marvelled how much worse the roads were here than in the Empire. Compared to the Via Egnatia, the road from Marseille to Troyes seemed like a dirt track. Was there really no one who made sure the roads were kept in good condition? As it was, it took three weeks to reach Troyes. But at least nothing much happened. And the merchants provided me with news about what was happening in England. There had been another rising in England, but that was already five or six years ago and the country was apparently quiet. 'All the fighting beaten out of them', one of the merchants said with a sneer. Instead, the Bastard was having trouble with his own brood; his eldest son Robert Courthose was chafing under his father's thumb in Normandy and there was constant small-scale fighting going on there. I might be able to find willing recruits there, but I was not particularly interested in hiring Normans – whatever Richard of Matera had said. There must still be Englishmen who preferred not to be ruled by a Norman bastard.

We travelled on to Troyes and when we reached that town, I continued on my own towards the coast.

The money the merchants paid me helped to buy me a decent horse, because now speed would be more important. Two days later I rode into Paris. Although I well remembered this part of the world well, I was amazed at how much it had changed in the nine years I had been away. The cities which then had impressed me with their size and wealth, now looked like little villages, and none too prosperous at that. Oh, Marseille had been big enough and Paris, when I passed through, showed that it was a King's home. But they were small and dirty when compared with Constantinopolis or Thessaloniki, the great cities of the Empire. Not only that. There were parts of Constantinopolis that were not necessarily safe, not even for an armed soldier. But in most of the city even a woman could walk safely, at least in daylight. In Paris, I constantly found myself gripping my sword and looking around to make sure I was not being followed too closely by someone who fancied relieving me of my purse, possibly slitting my throat in the process. I couldn't wait to leave the place.

From Paris I rode northwards, avoiding Normandy. I didn't wish to get caught up in any fighting going on, since it would only serve to delay me. By now I had been gone for about six months and although I was looking forward to seeing England again, I was beginning to miss the Empire. Also, I was wondering how the war with the Normans was going. The last thing I knew was what Richard had told me in Amalfi, but that had been old news even then. For all I knew, I might be recruiting soldiers to serve an Empire that didn't even exist any more – or rather, to serve a man who was no longer Emperor!

Anyway, I rode north from Paris, as I said and then northwest from Amiens, until I arrived in Boulogne. This was really small – the area within the walls was not bigger than two or three streets in Constantinopolis. But it was a fishing-port and that meant there would be a boat ready to take me to England – in return for a small payment, naturally. And now, I had to face something that I had tried to keep out of my mind ever since I left Marseille – the only way of getting to England was by boat. I did *not* want to go to sea again.

First, though, I found myself an inn near the port in Boulogne. It was dirty, smoky and smelly. Most inns are, of course, but this was worse than most. But the land-lord agreed to stable my horse for twelve weeks, payment in advance and a promise that the horse was his if I didn't come back before the time was up. Then I went down to the quay to find myself a boat. There were plenty of those, but I was hoping somehow to be able to pick one that would not make me seasick again.

As I walked back and forth, stopping to look, now at one boat, now another, one of the fishermen stopped me.

'Where do you want to go, friend?'

'Across the narrows, to England.'

'That is easy enough – anyone will take you. I will do it myself, for a silver penny. For two pennies, we will land well away from any of the King's men.'

I doubted that that was important – I had not been in England for eleven years and I had been only nineteen when I left, so I didn't think anyone would remember me, or if they did, care particularly. However, if the fisherman thought I had any reason to hide, he was welcome to it.

'What is your boat?'

'Next to you, my Lord. The swiftest in Boulogne.'

There was indeed a boat a few feet away. The reason I hadn't noticed it was because to my eyes it looked like a pile of driftwood. It must have been painted in some colour once, but now it was just an indistinguishable grey. Three crewmen were working onboard, knitting nets and mending the sail. They looked none too pleasant and I wondered if they also did a little piracy on the side.

The owner noticed my hesitation. 'Is the boat not to your liking, noble sir?' he asked. 'What is it you are looking for?'

'If you must know, what I really am looking for is a boat that won't make me seasick' I blurted out.

He laughed. 'Oh, that!' he said. 'It's not the boat. What makes you seasick is the imbalance in your body. You are a landsman – you are not used to the wet sea. What you must do is to make your body liquid as well. In other words, drink. Go back to your house and get really drunk tonight. Drink as much as you can and then come on board. When we are at sea, your body will be in balance from the wetness outside and the wetness inside and you won't be seasick. Now, are you coming? We leave with the morning tide.'

I thought about it. Maybe he was right. It was the first sensible piece of advice against seasickness that anyone had ever given me.

'Very well. One silver penny to take me to England. Dover will do fine. I'll see you tomorrow morning. What's your name?'

'Henri. And don't forget to balance the liquids.'

And with that I went back to my inn, had a word with the innkeeper and started to drink. The local ale was not bad, but it didn't taste like the English ale I suddenly remembered. I drank and drank and I don't think I have drunk as much for a long, long time. This was worse than when I had gotten drunk with Richard in Italy.

About an hour before the tide came in, the innkeeper and one of his servants carried me to the fishing boat and helped me stagger on board. I remember the fisherman and his crew laughing at the sight – I couldn't understand why. And then we cast off.

I don't remember much from the crossing, but I do remember one thing – the seasickness I had felt before was *nothing* compared with this. On my journey from Amalfi to Marseille I had merely thought I would die – this time I was sure of it. I didn't even know that a man could vomit as much, and the fisherman and his crew just kept looking at me and laughing. I must have passed out at some stage, because I don't remember much of the crossing. But at one stage I dreamed that I saw Irene looking at me. She looked furious. 'Edmund, you are such a fool!' she said. 'I still love you. But do stop believing in what everyone tells you.'

When we landed in Dover, they had to carry me ashore. But although they looked like pirates, they didn't behave like them. They didn't let me go either, but took me to an inn and propped me up on a bench.

'Can you understand what I say?' the fisherman asked.

'Dog!' I muttered.

'Just a little joke,' he replied, laughing. 'But listen to me: this inn belongs to my brother-in-law. His name is Robert. When you need to go back

France, come here and tell him and he will get me. Don't drink so much next time. Farewell.'

And with that he disappeared and I was left, trying to get over both a hangover and my seasickness.

It took some time, but I did get over both. It might have gone faster, but when I eventually went into the inn, the air was thick with the smoke of a particularly fat lamb being cooked, which made me sick again and I had to stumble out. Once I had recovered, Robert, the innkeeper, gave me a room and I looked through my pack. Amazingly enough, it seemed as if everything was there – including my money. I had been more than half convinced that Henri and his crew would take the money and as soon throw me overboard as take me to Dover. Well, I was wrong – fortunately, because the way I had been, a kitten could have pushed me into the sea.

And so I was back in England. That felt strange – at home and away at the same time. Now I had to plan how to recruit my countrymen to the Emperor's service.

CHAPTER 8

Recruiting Varangians

The next day, I bought a horse – I was getting rather used to that by now – and set off. I had decided to avoid London and instead concentrate on the part of England I had originally come from – East Anglia. Not only because I knew the people, but also because that was where the fight against the Normans had gone on for the longest. But to get there, I would still have to ride close to London. On the other hand, no one knew why I was in England and I doubted if anyone at all in England would even know who I was.

I had a strange feeling when I rode through Kent. It was as if everything was – I don't know, *normal*, I suppose. The grass had just the right colour that grass is supposed to have, the flowers smelled the way they were supposed to do and even the people I passed looked the way I somehow felt they should. I hadn't realised how much I had missed England. In many ways, Constantinopolis was home now – I had a wife and a daughter, I spoke Greek daily and even thought in Greek – but I realised that I had always felt out-of-place there. England was home and always would be. But would I ever really come back here to live? How could I do that?

When I came to Canterbury I decided to stop. I had not heard the Mass for a long time – not since Richard and I had staid in one of the Greek monasteries in Italy, in fact – and although this normally didn't bother me, I suddenly felt I wanted to hear it here. It felt good, even though it wasn't the church I remembered. That had apparently burnt down some years after Hastings, I was told. The new church had been built by the Bastard's new Archbishop, Lanfranc. It was bigger than the old, but it still could not compare with the Great Church in Constantinopolis. There, in St Sophia, you could feel the presence of God and His Son Christ. On the other hand, Canterbury felt closer and more human. I was glad I had stopped and decided to stay there overnight and go to Mass in the morning.

Yet it was that day that I realised in how many ways I had also changed. For one thing, having heard Mass so often in a language I could understand, I was taken aback to hear priests in England celebrate in a strange language. Not that I didn't know that it was Latin, of course. After all, I had picked up some of it in Constantinopolis. But what other soldiers teach you over a game of tables or when discussing women, is not quite the same as the words in the Mass.

The second thing was when I sat down to eat. When I was in Italy or in Provençe or in France, I had just eaten what was set in front of me and not thought much about that. But now when I had ordered a meal, I suppose I was dreaming of 'home food'. Yet when I got the mutton stew, I felt that it lacked something and automatically reached for it. It took me a few short moments before I realised what my hand was grasping for – and not finding. I was looking for the fish sauce, garum, which was added to almost everything I ate in Constantinopolis. When I finally understood, I started laughing at myself – and stopped abruptly as people turned to look at me. However much I tried to explain, it was unlikely that they would understand that an Englishman wanted rotten salt fish sauce to put on his mutton. They would just think that I was mad and that would draw attention to me, something I could do without. But even as I laughed, I felt sad as well, because I knew that in some small way, I was no longer only an Englishman.

Before I rode off the next day I talked with some of the people in the inn. I wanted to hear what they thought about the Bastard who now had called himself King of England for 16 years.

The answers were disappointing. None of the men I spoke with liked the Normans and there were plenty of dark glances and mutterings about arrogant foreigners. Even so, no one seemed willing to speak ill of William. 'He's harsh, but at least he keeps order,' was the usual reply. But most of the people I spoke with were traders and merchants and they never care who rules them as long as things are quiet and they make money. I was sure I would get a different reply when I came to Ely.

Then I rode on northwest towards London. I had intended to ride around the city, but when I came close enough I decided I would ride through after all. I was glad I did. London had changed a lot since I last saw it in King Harold's reign. For one thing, the city had grown and was far busier than I remembered it. And so had the Bastard's Tower. I had heard about his new fortress even before I left England, but it hadn't sounded quite so big. He must have kept building and adding to it ever since. I stayed the night in London, but here I was careful not to talk about anything that could arouse any suspicions. I knew that no one could recognise me or know why I was there, but it was still wise not to draw attention to myself.

The next day it rained as I began to ride towards the north-east and Essex. My first goal was Colchester, which was about two days' ride off. The first night I spent in a farm halfway. The farmer took me for a Norman noble and didn't really want to have me there. I explained that I was English, despite my foreign clothes and hairstyle, and he seemed to calm down. But his worries about hosting a Norman made me feel better, so I tried to draw him out about life under the Normans.

'I couldn't say, sir,' he mumbled.

'But you were not happy about having a Norman stay overnight with you?'

'Well, a noble like yourself shouldn't stay with the likes of me.'

'Why not? I wouldn't harm you.'

‘You should be staying with others like you – not sleep on a bed of straw on the floor or eat our food.’

‘Look, I already told you that I am not a Norman, nor a noble. I just want to know how you feel about the Normans. I have been away for more than ten years and I don’t really know what life in England is like anymore.’

‘I couldn’t say, sir.’ And that was all I could get out of him. But, as I said, it did give me better hope that I would be able to recruit some of my countrymen to the Guard.

The next day it was still raining and I was wet through and through as I rode into Colchester. I found another inn, stabled the horse and got myself something to eat and to drink. This time, I didn’t even bother to feel around for the garum. I just had to accept that food in this country – in my country! – tasted bland and insipid. The inn was full of people waiting for the rain to finish and I had no trouble finding people to talk to.

Here for the first time were people who were prepared to say something against the Normans, despite the big, brand new castle that towered over the town. But even that took some time. First, I had to treat all the drinkers to a round or two of ale. Then I had to convince them that despite the way I looked, I was in fact English. And buy them more ale. And then do all the explanations again.

‘So why did you say you were dressed like a Norman?’

‘I am not ‘dressed like a Norman’. I am just dressed differently from you. Where I come from, most people dress like this.’

‘But you said you come from here!’ This from another man.

‘I *do*. But I have been away. I left England about ten years ago. I have lived most of the past ten years in Constantinopolis.’

‘Where is that? In France?’

‘No, stupid, it’s in Germany.’

‘I heard it was in Italy.’

I sighed. These people knew even less than I had done eight years ago.

‘Constantinopolis is in Greece. It’s the home of the Roman Emperor. I am a soldier serving the Emperor. He is fighting the Normans.’

That got their attention. In more ways than one. The first reaction was as I had hoped. Dark glances towards the door and mutterings of 'He can have all of ours too, if he wants' and similar. This sounded promising enough, but another reaction was more interesting. It came from a man I had at first overlooked. He had been sitting with his head down, dead to the world, but when I had said that I was serving the Emperor, he suddenly looked up startled and stared at me. I couldn't see him very well, but what I saw was worrying enough. First, he looked like a Norman – a real one, not like me – and second, he did not look like a farmhand or a merchant – rather, he looked like a nobleman. Here was a bad start to my work, I thought, but then he slumped over his table again and seemed to be fast asleep. He was certainly snoring loudly. Maybe I had been too nervous. But he had looked at me, of that I was quite sure.

I turned to the others again.

'You don't seem too happy with the Normans.'

'Neither would you if a bunch of foreigners came and took over your country.'

This was getting silly. 'This *is* my country. And I fought the Normans when they came, at Hastings and after, in York and then with Hereward.'

Mentioning Hereward's name made the locals somewhat warmer. But I still hadn't gotten very far with them. I tried again.

'You don't have to live with the Normans.'

'How are you going to get rid of them? Hereward failed – and he had the Danes to help him. Are you going to do it alone?'

'I am not telling you to rise against the Bastard. I realise his grip on England is too firm – for now. But it won't always be that way. And meanwhile, you can live like men, without having to bow down to every jumped-up Norman that rides by or tries to take your land.'

'How do we do that? They rule all England now.'

'You can leave England. The Emperor of the Romans is looking for good men, men he can trust, men who know how to fight. And he is fighting Normans. Come with me to Constantinopolis. And when we have defeated the Normans in Italy, we'll come back with an army and do the same here.' I hadn't thought about that before, but as I said it, I realised that this was what I really was hoping for – train an English army abroad and then come back and get rid of the Normans, free England from them and have an English King again. After all, where could Englishmen better learn how to beat the Normans than in Greece? Surely a grateful Emperor would help us if it weakened his Norman enemies? If we could defeat the Normans both in Italy and in England, they would once again be stuck in their own little country.

Two or three of the men I'd been talking to seemed interested. But most of them were content to complain about the Normans and leave it at that. To actually do something was less attractive. In fact, they probably felt that talking about it was dangerous enough, so while thanking me for the ale, they began to drift away. It helped that the rain was beginning to stop as well. The three who remained now wanted to know more about what I was proposing. So I told them about the Varangian Guard and that I was recruiting soldiers. They were all about ten years younger than I – barely twenty. Two of them, Wilfred and Edgar, were sons of an English landowners, whose land was being steadily whittled away by Norman neighbours. The third, Grim, was completely different. He said he was a farmhand, but I got the impression that he was a runaway serf. No matter, he seemed strong and eager.

I did not tell them that I was going to continue to East Anglia. But I did tell them that if they were interested in serving the Emperor they should meet me in Dover – and I described Robert's inn – three weeks later. And if I wasn't there, they were to wait for me for one week.

It was getting late. The three recruits (I was already thinking about them that way, pleased with at least some success) said good night and left. And I took my gear and went upstairs to sleep in my room.

As I was walking along a dark corridor, I suddenly realised that I was not alone. But before I could look around or grab a weapon, a hand seized my throat in an iron grip, while another hand held my right arm. I couldn't make a sound, but I swung my free arm around towards where I guessed my attackers body would be and drove my fist into something soft. I heard him grunt and shift to soften the blow. That made his grip around my right arm less firm and I managed to break free. But only for a moment; he clamped down again, managed to fell me to the floor and tried to weigh my body down with his. I managed to twist away but my throat was hurting and I was having difficulty breathing. I flailed away with my left hand again and hit something which I think was an eye. My foe groaned again. But just as suddenly as he had attacked, he released me and backed off. As I breathed in and crouched down, ready to defend myself or jump at him, he whispered, 'I am not here to fight you.'

The words were so surprising that I didn't shout, as I had intended to. But I backed off my back towards the wall and grabbed my knife before I whispered back, 'You certainly behave as if you do. Who are you and what do you want?'

He ignored the first question. 'Do you really serve the Emperor in Miklagård? Are you a Varangian?'

'Yes. Now answer my questions. Who are you and what do you want?'

'I want to join you.'

That certainly took me aback. 'You are going about it in a strange manner.'

'I will explain. But can we have some light?' And with that, he struck a spark on a tinder and lit a tallow candle. Until then, I had thought that this was one of the men I had spoken with earlier, although I couldn't understand why he was approaching me in this way. But as soon as I saw him, I recognised him. It was the Norman who had looked so strangely at me earlier.

'You are a Norman. Why do you want to join me?'

'I am not a Norman. I will explain.' Now that I listened to him, he didn't sound quite Norman. But he still looked like one. I waited.

'I am a Dane. My name is Erik Orm's Son. I wish to join the Varangian Guard.'

'Why? What are you doing here? And why attack me like this?'

'You have many questions. I will answer all. I wish to join the Varangian Guard because I am here on a fool's errand and I cannot go back. I also do not like the Normans. I didn't mean to attack you, but I had to be sure you would stay silent.'

'Go on.'

'I serve Knud, King of the Danes. I am one of his most trusted men and of the royal kin: my grandsire, Svarthöfde Orm's Son, was a cousin of King Knud the Great himself. And *his* uncle Are Toste's Son long ago served in the Varangian Guard. My king sent me here to spy out the land because he wishes to invade England like both his father and his namesake. He himself led his father's fleet to England six years ago. But I know now that he never will do so again. If I go back, he will try to blame me for his decision, since otherwise he will lose the respect of his men. I cannot go back and be made a fool. I do not want to serve the Normans. And I am of royal blood – I will not be someone's thrall. But the Emperor of Miklagård – him I will serve.'

I had never heard that King Canute had had any kin except his two sons who succeeded him as kings of England and Denmark. But Erik's story could still be true, since this was not something I would have known anyway. And it would certainly be helpful to have someone like him around in areas still settled by many Danes. I rubbed my throat which was still hurting and nodded at him.

'Very well, Erik. Come with me in the morning. And no more night attacks. If you wish to say something, just say it.'

'No, no, rest easy.' And he disappeared.

* * *

I was surprised that I managed to sleep the rest of the night, but I did and awoke none the worse for my experience, except that my throat was still a little tender.

I didn't see Erik anywhere, but I had collected my horse and had begun to ride out of Colchester, when he suddenly appeared, riding a sorry nag himself. Now that I could see him in daylight, I realised what a giant of a man he was. I am taller than average, but Bohemond had topped me by half a head and this fellow must have been about a head taller than that and was broad to match. I had felt his strength myself, but I was pleased to notice that he sported a huge black eye in memory of last night's encounter.

He didn't seem to mind, though. He was laughing and pointing at it as he rode up. 'I think you marked me more than I you,' he said. 'But it will go away. Now you must tell me your name and where we go.'

That was true. In all the confusion of the night, he had told me his name but I hadn't told him mine.

'I am called Edmund. And we ride north, to Ely, to find more Varangians.'

'Do you hope to find more in East Anglia than in Essex?'

'Yes. Mainly because that was where the last resistance against the Normans was. And also because I was born there and know the people.'

'Then north we ride, Edmund.'

And so we did. It wasn't raining as much today, barely a drizzle. The rain gave the late spring countryside a peculiar smell and once again I felt as if I had come home – despite the bland food.

Now I knew that one day England would be freed from the Normans and that I would return to live here. It made me look at the countryside in a different way. In a village I rode by some children playing in the street and thought of how Dora would find living in England. Would she find it strange? I was sure Irene would – but surely she would do it for me? As I thought of this, I wondered how my family was and realised that I was missing both my wife and my daughter very badly. Not that there was anything I could do about it, but I would have given a lot just then to be back in Constantinopolis, holding my wife in my arms and watching Dora grow up.

As we rode north, Erik questioned me about life in Constantinopolis and service in the Guard. I told him what it was like, in peace and in war. I said that if he wanted to get ahead he should learn Greek, but at that he looked sceptical. I also told him about Dyrrachion and why I was looking for new recruits. I hadn't wanted to mention our defeat to the others, because I thought that might discourage them. But Erik seemed different. He was trying to get away from England and he really wanted to join the Varangians. Also, he seemed friendly – and I had travelled for long without someone to talk to about the things that really mattered.

He didn't comment much on the defeat at Dyrrachion; he was more interested in how the Greeks and the Normans fought, how they were armed, if they were mainly mounted or on foot and so on.

I asked him about his life too. He was very proud of his background and happy to talk about it. It seemed that his grandfather's mother had been the daughter of King Harald Bluetooth, a great King of the Danes almost eighty years ago. Harald's son Swein Forkbeard had invaded England and he was the father of Canute the Great, who Erik called Knud. Of the current King, another Knud, he didn't say much. I gathered that he was quite unpopular among the Danes, except among the churchmen. Erik had been one of the King's advisers, but this was more due to the royal kinship and even he didn't have much to say in Knud's favour. Apparently, his idea to invade England had been an attempt to raise his standing among the leading men, which was why a failure even to set out would be even less welcome to him. Erik guessed that he would be forced to take the blame if the invasion idea was abandoned and preferred to move off elsewhere. As for his great- (or was it great-great-?) uncle who supposedly had been a Varangian, he only knew his name and that this must have been almost a hundred years ago. If true, that would place him in the time of the Emperor Basil, who had been a great warrior and had fought a large number of wars against the Bulgars, who in those days had tried to be independent of the Empire. Erik said that he had been travelling in England and in Normandy for some months and was now getting nervous lest someone in authority found out what he was doing there, which was why he had regarded my coming as a God-send. And again and again through his story he returned to something by which he apparently set almost as much store as his family – he claimed to be irresistible to women. According to him, he only had to show up to make them throw themselves at him.

Our talk meant that the day sped by. As a result of my experience in Colchester, I had decided that my best hope for recruitment was among the sons of such English landowners as still existed. They would be proud and used to weapons but they would also be used to seeing their lands of their fathers encroached upon and gradually being taken over by Normans who now ruled in their fathers' stead. Also, when we came back to free England from the Bastard and his brood, they would be able to lead the people. If they had any followers who wanted to come east too, then so much the better. So instead of looking for an inn in the villages we rode through towards the evening, we began to ask people for the most important English landowners around the area.

On our first night, we came to the farm of a man called Walter. He had seemed reluctant to have us, but eventually relented. The farm seemed prosperous enough, yet the food we were offered was what you would have expected in a poor peasant's hovel. The man himself was surly, and didn't seem interested in talking.

'It's all a man can do to keep hunger from the door,' he muttered, when I asked how he was faring.

'But you have a large farm,' I replied, 'and this is a fertile part of the England.'

'Fertile enough, unless there is a drought or a flood,' replied this sunny fellow. 'It takes a lot of work to draw anything from the ground and you have all these lazy mouths to feed.'

Despite his professed hardship, both Walter himself and his nearest family looked prosperous enough.

'Surely there is enough to feed you even in bad times?'

'Never seems to be enough,' he said – a patent lie, judging by his own well-fed state. 'And if there is, the King will have his taxes and greedy neighbours try to grab what's left.'

'You do not get along well with the Normans, then?'

'I am not saying anything against the King.' He suddenly seemed terrified.

'Nor am I asking you too,' I smiled. 'I was asking about your neighbours.'

'I am not saying anything against them either,' he muttered.

'Of course not. Bad enough that they have the ear of the King or of his Earls and use it to encroach on other peoples' lands, without being accused of talking treason. But a man also has to stand up for what is his. That's not treason – that's just right.'

'Exactly.'

'But if a man's land is taken from him, he has to try to provide for his family in another way,' I continued.

'What do you mean?'

'Take someone like yourself. You have sons. But their future is in doubt. Unless you can protect what's yours from your Norman neighbours, their lot will be to work for someone else – the same Normans, no doubt.'

'But what can a man do?'

'Your sons can have a career elsewhere. Let them come with me and serve the Emperor of the Romans. They will be honoured and rich. And in the future, they could come back – with an army of Englishmen – and assert their rights.'

'I'm not sending my sons to serve any man, King or Emperor,' he muttered. 'They will stay and take over their land after me.' I could see that his sons were interested, but there he finished the conversation and asked one of his servant girls to lead Erik and me to our room.

I woke in the middle of the night because Erik was sick. At least, that was what I thought. But before I could ask him what was wrong, I realised that the moaning wasn't his and that I recognised perfectly well what it was. He wasn't sick – nor was anyone else. And it seemed that maybe he was right about women throwing themselves at him – at least the servant girl who had taken us to our room was doing a fair bit of throwing. I turned over on the other side and tried to fall asleep again. Eventually I succeeded.

In the morning, I tried to continue the previous night's conversation with Walter, but he refused to listen to it. So, after breakfast, Erik and I rode off.

We hadn't ridden far from the farm, when Erik suddenly reined in his horse. 'Wait,' he said.

'For what?'

'You will see.'

'Is your girlfriend from last night joining us?'

But he just smiled.

We hadn't waited for long when I heard a horse coming up behind us. As it turned the corner, I recognised the rider. It wasn't Erik's bed-mate – it was one of Walter's sons. He rode up to me and said, 'I want to join you and serve your Emperor.'

'Your father won't like it.'

'I don't care what he likes – he's mean and old and spends his entire life complaining and doing nothing about the things he complains about. Anyway, my brother is staying. He will inherit the farm and there won't be anything for me. So I am going with you.'

'If that is what you want, I am happy to have you. But you are not coming with me. You are going to Dover. Do you know where that is?'

'No-o, I don't think so.'

'It's a port, south-east of London. Do you know where London is?' He shook his head. 'No? Well, ride south-west from here until you come to a big city – very big. That is London. Don't tell anyone what you are doing, but ask for the way to Dover and ride there.'

And I explained to him about Robert's inn and when to meet us there.

As he turned around to ride off, I called out, 'What's your name?'

'Edmund,' he replied, 'like yours.' Then he laughed and was gone.

'You knew this' I said to Erik.

'The girl told me. I'm surprised there was only one.'

'Well, go easy on the girls. Not all men will appreciate your bedding their servant-girls.'

'How can I help it?' And he smiled broadly.

Our next host was easier to deal with. He listened to what I had to say, then told me both his sons should go and take two of his retainers as well. 'There is no future for you here,' he told them. 'Go off, serve this Emperor loyally and make your fortune away from England.'

And so, we rode on into and through Essex and around East Anglia, up and down the country, always staying with English farmers, men who would have been important under King Edward and King Harold, but who now found their place taken by strangers from the other side of the narrow water, who spoke a different language and used different customs. In many ways, it began to resemble riding through Apulia and Calabria with Richard. Most evenings a new host, most evenings the same topic – and most nights Erik finding himself a new bed-mate. I was getting to a stage where I would have preferred a room of my own. The one difference was that it kept raining. In fact, I was getting rather tired of the rain. I had forgotten how much it could rain in England and how long it would last.

Sometimes it worked, sometimes it didn't. But a small trickle of recruits was sent to Dover, to meet us there on our return.

Near Norwich our questions led us to seek hospitality with a landowner who was not English, but Danish. His name was Nils. Unfortunately, what no one had told us was that he was an old man, with no sons. What he did have was a young wife – a Norman wife. I decided that this was not a good place to bring up our mission and it was clear that Erik agreed. But Nils must have had heard something about us anyway. That was no surprise, since we had been riding around a fairly limited area for close on two weeks now. Once he knew our names, it was clear that he was terrified of having us there. He couldn't very well turn us out, and not only because it was raining. But dinner was a hasty and uncomfortable meal. His wife kept looking at us, saying nothing. If Nils was over 60, she cannot have been more than 22 and I wondered what had convinced her to marry him, particularly since she was very good-looking, with long blonde hair and piercing blue eyes.

Nils, meanwhile, was saying very little, mainly telling us of how he was on excellent terms with the local Norman lords. All the time he was nervously looking over his shoulder at his servants and his wife, as if fearing that any of them would run off to tell the Normans who his guests were. As soon as he could, he bade us good night and said how sorry he was that he would not be able to see us go. Doubtless we wanted to get away early the next morning and at his age and so on and so on. The wife still said nothing.

When we were led away to our room, I could see that Erik was smouldering. As soon as we were alone, I asked him why he was so angry. 'Is it the lack of servant girls?'

He didn't even smile. 'That is a nuisance. But it angers me to see one of my own people having turned so craven in his dotage. In truth did my forefathers say that a man should not cling to life like King Ane of the Swedes until he must be spoon-fed his milk.'

'Well, there is nothing for it. Tomorrow we will leave him and ride to Ely. For now, let us sleep.'

But before we had gone to sleep, there was a quiet knock on our door. When I opened it, one of Nils's servants stood outside.

'What is it?' I growled.

'There is one who would speak with you', he replied.

'Who?'

'I am not allowed to say. But if you were not ready to come, I was bidden to tell you that you are in danger and you should learn of it.'

'Wait here.'

I turned to Erik, who was lying on the side, looking at me. I told him what the man had said and that he should be ready for anything. Then I opened the door again and told the man I would come with him. I did take my sword and made sure he saw me loosen it in its scabbard.

As we walked through the house I tried to question the man, but he refused to say anything. Eventually we came to a door on which he knocked. There was a muffled reply and he opened the door, stood aside and motioned for me to go inside. Once I had come in, the door shut behind me. I swore, drew my sword and turned around, but the door was locked.

Then I heard a voice behind me. 'You won't need that here. The danger doesn't come from here – yet.'

When I whirled around again I realised why the voice was unfamiliar. It was Nils's wife – she who had not said a word during dinner. She was wearing a white shift and precious little else and her long hair was unbraided. She was alone in the room, which contained little apart from a bed and was dimly lit by two tallow candles.

'Then where is the danger?'

'Here, there, everywhere', she replied. 'But not just yet. Tell me, did you not wonder why I am married to this old doddering fool of a Dane? Oh, and put away your silly sword – you won't need it.'

I felt foolish when I realised I was still holding my sword and stuck it back in its scabbard. Then I looked at her again. 'Why don't you tell me.'

'It is simple', she said. 'I have no wealth, even though I come from a noble family. By marrying Nils, who is too old to have children, I will inherit his lands. They are wide enough. As soon as he is dead, I will sell them to William of Warenne, the local lord. That will make me wealthy enough to marry who I want. But meanwhile, I am stuck with Nils, who doesn't amount to much.'

'But what of the danger?'

'All in good time. I will do something for you. Will you do something for me?'

'Of course. You have only to ask. And you will have my gratitude.'

'Very good. As I said, Nils doesn't amount to very much. We have been married for three years. Our marriage has not been consummated. I tire of living alone. But I cannot use his servants or any of the neighbours – too much risk of talk. You, however, are a stranger. Tomorrow, you will disappear. Tonight, you will help me.'

I couldn't believe it. Oh, believed the bit about the unconsummated marriage all right. But I refused to believe that I had been summoned to act the bull to her cow. And why me? Why not Erik?

'My Lady', I said, trying to sound formal. 'I am a married man and – '

'Nonsense', she interrupted. 'Your wife – if you have one – is far away. Look at me.' She tore off her shift and stood naked. 'Am I not beautiful?' She certainly was attractive, with blond hair tumbling down below her shoulders, her big breasts almost pointing straight at me and blue eyes flashing. I could feel my body responding to the sight.

'Now you have two choices, Englishman', she continued. 'You will render me this service and in exchange I will warn you of a danger threatening you. Or else you refuse, in which case I will scream. The servants will come rushing and find you here with your sword and me naked. I will tell them that you threatened to rape me. They will believe me, or at least obey me. They will neither believe, nor obey you. You will die, but first you will suffer. Is the choice clear?'

I nodded. She had me in a bind and she knew it.

'Then come here and begin, I am tired of waiting.'

I dropped the sword, disrobed and went up and took her in my arms. She opened her mouth under mine and bit my lips until they began to bleed. Then we tumbled to her bed. I had, I think, intended this to be a quick, soul-less coupling. But once we began, I couldn't stick to that resolution. She may have looked cold, but she was certainly warm. Her marriage may never have been consummated, but I was clearly not her first man. I don't know how long we coupled, but it felt like hours.

When she was finally tired, I held her in my arms. I was dimly trying to remember that there was a reason I had done this, but I had forgotten it and I was content just to lie there. Meanwhile, the lady had become much less imperious and much more – affectionate, strange as it seemed.

Then she turned her face towards me and kissed me. 'Why don't you stay here?' she murmured. 'Forget your wife and stay with me.'

My wife! Yes, that was one of those things I had forgotten! Not to mention her husband. (I suddenly realised I didn't even know her name.) And what about the danger she had mentioned?

'What about your husband? He might not like that.'

'Of course not, silly. You would have to kill him.' And she kissed me again and nuzzled my neck.

That took me aback. I had cuckolded the man (and enjoyed it, even though I could claim to have been forced into it). But murder did not seem like a bed topic.

She sensed my reaction and looked at me. 'Why would you care? He already seeks your death.'

Now I was wide awake. 'What do you mean?'

'As soon as the morning breaks, he will send a man to William of Warenne to tell him of your presence and ask for help in capturing you. If he fears you will get away first, he will try to have you killed.'

'But why?' As if I didn't know.

She shrugged. 'My husband is a coward. He has lived a long life and now all he can think about is how to prolong his life and live at ease. That means not angering his new overlords. But why are you worried? You can kill him – you are strong. Or do you want it to be an 'accident''? That can easily be done.'

'What about my friend?'

'He will probably have to die as well. The fewer who know, the better.'

This was rapidly turning into a very unpleasant conversation. And I was trying to think of how to extricate myself from the clutches of the naked, beautiful and murderous woman, who was smiling at me and running her fingers through the hair on my chest while plotting God knows how many killings.

'We have to think about this. My friend is a better warrior than I. We may need help with him. And if you fear talk, what about your servants?'

'They will keep quiet. They know the price of crossing me as well as the rewards for obeying.' That probably explained how come she was not a virgin –

although she had said that she could not couple with the servants.

'You are not drawing back, are you?' Although she still lay in my arms, there was a faint touch of steel in her voice. That was exactly what I was doing, but having seen her true nature, she had better not suspect it. 'Of course not, my dearest', I replied and bent down and kissed her. I made sure to put a lot of passion into the kiss. Anything to make her believe me.

But time was short. Nils was supposedly sending someone to alert the Normans at day-break and the sky was already turning lighter. How to get out of this? Preferably without any killing at all. If there was no other way, I might have to kill the woman. I had never killed a woman yet, let alone one with whom I had just coupled. I suppose a priest would find it interesting to discuss which was the greater sin of the two acts. Or would it be the combination? In any case, I did not have the faintest idea how I was going to explain it to anyone if I did have to kill her. To her husband, for instance.

As I was desperately racking my brain, there was a knock on the door. The woman turned towards it and called out a question.

'Your husband, Lady. He is on his way and will be here any second.'

That got her going her. 'Quick', she hissed. 'You must kill him as soon as he comes in the room. No, wait!' She thought for a moment. 'No. He should not find you here. Go, wait outside. I will let you know as soon as he is gone.'

I was only too glad to comply. For a brief second, I had feared that she would grab the opportunity and force me to kill Nils there and then. Perhaps she realised that this would be unlikely to be seen as an accident and she wanted to plan the killing. Whatever the reason, she threw my clothes and sword at me, dragged on her shift, unlocked the door and bundled me out of the room and into another room off the same corridor. 'Wait here!' she commanded, before disappearing back into her own room and closing the door.

As soon as she was away I quickly dressed. Opening the door a crack showed that her servant was still in the corridor, but otherwise it was empty. In my haste to get dressed I hadn't heard if Nils had passed or not, but that could not be allowed to matter. I drew my sword and stepped out in the corridor. The man gave a start and opened his mouth, but before he had time to utter a word, I grasped his throat with my free hand.

'If you make a sound, I will kill you! Do you understand?' I hissed at him. He looked frightened and nodded. 'Good. Now lead me back to my room. And remember, one sound, and you are dead! My sword is right at your back.' To make him realise this, I prodded him with the point. But it didn't seem necessary. The man was clearly in a state of panic already. As quickly as he could, he led me back through the house to my own room.

When I came in I dragged him with me. A quick look showed me that Erik was still there, fast asleep. That was good; I had been worried that the she-devil would already have done away with him. But maybe she hadn't planned that far ahead.

Keeping an eye on the servant, I shook Erik roughly. He quickly woke up and threw a startled look at me and at the manservant. 'What's going on?' he asked.

'No time to explain', I replied. 'Get your things. We've got to get out of here now.'

Fortunately, Erik didn't ask any more questions. While I held the terrified servant, he quickly gathered all our belongings. As soon as he was done, I turned to the man again. 'Now take us to the stables. Hurry up!' Again, I prodded him with the sword, although by now I doubted if it was necessary.

When we came out, dawn was breaking. Some of the servants were out and about, but no one took much notice of us, although we tried to make sure to stay in the shadows. We got to the stables, found our horses and without further ado rode out of Nils's farm. I left the servant in the stables, having threatened to kill him if he told his mistress what had happened. Not that I could have, of course. But I very much doubted if he was prepared to explain to her how we had gotten away. She had left me little doubt that she was not very tolerant of failures, and this would certainly count as one of them.

As we galloped off, I could see that Erik was burning with curiosity. But he was sensible enough to know that if I would tell him, it could wait, while if I would not, questions wouldn't get him anywhere.

For an hour or so we rode on in silence. Then we slowed the horses to a walk and I began to tell Erik the whole story. As I went on I could see him becoming angrier and angrier. By the time I came to the end, he was punching his saddle with his fist.

'You are angry because of the way she treated a fellow Dane?' I asked.

'No. He is an old fool. He deserves it.' I didn't agree with that, but I let it pass. 'No. I am angry because I wonder why she picked you and not me.'

I stared at him, then I started to laugh. Poor Erik! So convinced of his success with women that he'd rather he'd been the one caught in this net. I would have been happier for that to happen as well. We were lucky to have gotten out of this scrap. And although I had enjoyed what I was doing – no use denying that – I felt bad at having been unfaithful to Irene. True, she never would find out. But I would know and that was bad enough.

‘And what would you have done is she had picked you?’

‘Why, I would have shown her how her best choice was to let us – or at least you – go off so that everyone knew we had left the farm. Then, I would have told her, we would come back in the middle of the night and do her bidding. That way, we would have gained a full day’s head start. And I could have stayed with her all night!’ And he preened himself.

‘Maybe. But now things are as they are and we don’t have much of a head start. But somehow, I don’t think she will have men out after us. I am more worried about her husband and his wish to notify the Normans.’

‘Bah, them! But this story – do not tell anyone else she picked you instead of me.’

‘Don’t worry – I won’t tell anyone else about it at all. As far as I am concerned, it never happened.’ And I suddenly realised that this was indeed the best solution Even leaving aside Irene, I somehow doubted that I would confess this sin. I would just have to live with it instead.

CHAPTER 9

Leaving England

Two days later, we finally rode into Ely. The last time I saw Ely had been when I was with Hereward and we still felt free. There was the abbey church where we had heard Mass before we went out for our last fight with the Bastard's knights. When we passed an inn, I told Erik to find us a room – and to try to stay away from the women – while I had a look round. I would meet him at the inn later.

I didn't really need a look around. What I wanted to do was to go to the church and be alone with my memories. I left Erik with the horses and walked to the church.

It was dark inside after the brilliant sunshine outside and it took a few moments for my eyes to get used to the light. The church was much as I remembered it. I sat down in a pew and closed my eyes, thinking back to that day, eleven years ago, when we somehow still hoped that we could drive the Normans back to Normandy. So many of my friends had died and we still hadn't succeeded. But maybe we still could. One day, I thought, one day we *will* be rid of them. I began to pray for the fulfilment of my dreams to restore an English King. Then I suddenly started to laugh; I realised that I was indeed praying for the return of an English King – but my prayer was in Greek and was addressed to a Greek soldier saint, Saint Demetrios! My laughter echoed in the church and I quickly stopped and went back to thinking about the past.

Suddenly I heard a voice. I must have been dozing, because I hadn't heard anyone approaching me. I opened my eyes and looked around.

'I said, 'Is there anything I can help you with, my Lord''. Now I could see the speaker. He was a monk, standing a few feet away, looking quizzically at me.

'No. No thank you. I was just thinking.' It seemed as if he didn't hear me, so I repeated my words.

'May I welcome you to our church, then my Lord. If there is anything I can do for you…' He let the question hang in the air. But something about him nagged at me. It was almost as if I recognised him. As he turned to go, I held him back. The way he spoke –

slightly too loudly, as if he couldn't hear his own voice. And he certainly had trouble hearing mine.

'No, don't go. Wait.'

He stood back. 'My Lord?'

'Who are you? I mean, what's your name? Have you been here long?'

'I am Brother Peter, my Lord. I have been a monk here for ten or eleven years.'

'Peter? Were you here in the days of Hereward?'

'Yes. But I wasn't a monk then. It was before I was called by my God to serve Him.'

I tried to remember. Had I known anyone called Peter? I didn't remember – and yet he *did* seem familiar. As he turned to go, I asked for his blessing. When he put his hand on my head, I noticed that he was missing two fingers. And then I remembered.

'Were you always called Peter?'

'No, my Lord. Before I became a monk, my name was Edward.' And then I remembered!

'Edward. Deaf Edward?'

'How do you know that name, my Lord? No one has called me that for eleven years. Who *are* you?' He looked both surprised and frightened.

'I am not a lord. I am Edmund. You and I fought together for Hereward. You didn't seem very church-like then.'

'Edmund? Little Edmund who had fought at Hastings and in York and everywhere? I thought you were dead. What are you doing dressed like a Norman lord?' 'Little Edmund', indeed! Even then, I had been much bigger than he was.

'I am not dressed like a Norman lord. I live in Constantinopolis, where I serve the Roman Emperor. I thought you were dead too.'

'No, I survived the last battles. And then God called me to give up the trade of arms and to enter His service. Now I cater to all – English and Norman and Dane alike. But you are still a soldier?'

'Yes, I am one of the Emperor's housecarls. We too fight the Normans.'

'You should not fight. Did not our Lord say that we should turn the other cheek? That we should love our enemies? There is too much bloodshed in this world, Edmund.'

'I doubt if the Lord Jesus thought of Normans when he told us to love our enemy. You know what they did to us and to England. They are doing the same in Greece. And I have heard enough to know that they are still doing it here.'

'I know. But the Lord has His reasons and we mustn't question them. Tell me instead what you are doing in England?'

'I am here to recruit more Englishmen to the Emperor's service. Men who do not want to stay here as slaves of the Normans. Men who one day may come back and get rid of the Normans and free England again.'

'Not so loud,' he said nervously. 'Not every monk here is English – there are Normans and French as well, and Germans and Irish too.' Then he looked at me. 'Do you really hope to come back and fight the Normans here? Why?'

'Why not? With an army of battle-trained Englishmen and the Emperor's help. It could work. We could have an English king again. Is that not worth fighting for?'

'Yes. It could work – maybe. But is it worth all the bloodshed it would cause? Think of the dead men, their widows and orphaned children? You would have their blood on your hands, Edmund.' He looked upset.

'I would not! Their blood would be on the hands of the Bastard and his Normans! Who asked them over? Surely there are still English around who feel that their children would be better off under an English King? I know there are – I heard in France that there had been another rising.'

Edward – Brother Peter, I suppose – looked at me. 'Yes, there was. But did it accomplish anything except a lot of deaths? The Normans are too strong, Edmund. But that is not the most important point. Our Lord said to render unto Caesar the things which are Caesar's. Edmund, he meant that we should not set ourselves up against those that God have set up above us. I am sure God has his reasons for sending the Normans here.'

'I cannot believe that I hear you speaking like this', I almost shouted. 'You fought for Hereward! You were as keen as I to get rid of the Bastard. Why are you speaking like this?'

Even though I had had to speak louder previously, I had been quiet enough for no-one to hear us. But now I noticed that heads were turning towards us. So too did Brother Peter. He had looked frightened and stepped back, but now he came closer again.

'Calm down, Edmund', he said. 'You have to be careful about what you say or we are both in danger.' He stopped and was quiet for a moment and then came even closer. I could see that some people were still looking at us, but not as intensely as before.

'Do you really think it is possible, Edmund? An English King, I mean?'

'Truly, I don't know', I replied. 'But we could at least try. Constantinopolis is far away. But it's not too far away. And an army of Englishmen, blooded in Roman service – it would at least stand a chance against the Normans.'

He was quiet for another little while, as if he thought it over. Then he spoke again.

'Maybe you are right. I *did* fight with Hereward, after all. Perhaps it would be worth it if it gave us an English King again. Yes, I think it would – it's just that after so many years, I thought this was no longer possible.' Once again, he was quiet. When he began to speak again, his voice was firmer.

'Yes. This may be why God asked me to his service. To learn about His flock here, so that I could right a wrong. I will help you. And you were right to speak to me. A lot of the people here know about my past. They talk to me about their feelings for our Norman overlords. And they confess rebellious feelings. I always counsel against revolting, but that is because I do not want to see them killed. Your plan could work – at least there will be no killing here and now. I will get some of them together for you. But not now, not here. Outside of town. I need a day to get them together. Tomorrow night. One mile south-west of town. There is a barren field with a few trees. You must have passed it coming in. Meet me there at midnight.'

I felt that he was exaggerating the danger. After all, with the exception of my experience with Nils's wife, I had had no trouble anywhere. And that had been because of her, not because of me. Still, he lived here, and I didn't, and he did seem very wary of anyone overhearing us. So, I agreed, asked him for more detailed instructions about the field and then I left him.

Back at the inn I noticed that Erik had managed to get us two rooms. I took that to mean that he had not listened to my advice about leaving the servant-girls alone. I explained to him what had happened and about the next night's meeting.

Although we had two rooms, the walls of the inn were not particularly thick. It was perfectly clear that Erik did not spend his night alone.

The next day we walked around Ely. I marvelled at how strangely my life had turned since last time I was here. If it weren't for my wife and daughter, it would almost seem like a dream – something already forgotten. Surely this was where I belonged: in England, smelling English flowers and feeling the English drizzling spring rain. If it were not for the Normans, how could I ever leave? But I would be back, back with an English army and the Normans would be sent skulking back to Normandy. Like my ancestors, I and my children after me and their children after them would once again live in England, ruled by an English King.

In the evening, we ate together. Then I got ready, told Erik I'd be back in the morning and about an hour before midnight I set off.

It wasn't particularly difficult to find the field Edward – or Brother Peter, rather – had talked about. For one thing, the nights are not dark in mid-June. For another, there was a fire burning near the trees. When I arrived and dismounted, Brother Peter was standing there, warming his hands.

'Hello Peter. Did you manage to get hold of your friends?'

'Friends? Yes. Yes, I did.' He looked at me. 'I'm sorry Edmund.'

'Why?' And then, even as I asked I began to realise what he meant and grabbed for my sword. Too late. From the shadow of the trees three men appeared: one Norman knight and two men-at-arms. The knight had a drawn sword in his hand, one of his men was aiming a cross-bow at me and the other had a spear. I let my hand fall away from the sword.

'Sorry that an old friend could be so misguided, I suppose.' This was the Norman knight speaking. 'Sorry that he had to do his duty to his King.'

'Why?' It was me again, turning to Peter.

'I told you. There is too much fighting and bloodshed, Edmund. Don't you understand? I don't *like* the Normans. But they have won. William is our King now. He may be hard, but he is not a bad king. And then you come. If you had your way, you would drag away all the young men of England to faraway lands. Many of them will die there, leaving their families without heirs. And with those who survive, you propose to come back and again let the ravages of battle sweep over England. Can't you see I *had* to stop you? Think of your immortal soul! When you do, I know you will forgive me.'

I didn't know what to say. The last thing I had thought would happen was that one of my old comrades-in-arms, and Englishman who had fought for Hereward, would betray me to the Normans. Of course, William was King now. It didn't mean that he had to remain king forever. He had invaded England, killed the king and stolen his throne. Someone could one day make him pay for that and do the same to him. And yet – I couldn't be angry with Peter. Yes, he had betrayed me! But he thought he had done the right thing and I had been misled by my joy in finding someone I knew. So I told him, 'Yes, Peter, I forgive you, but I think you had better go now.'

'So do I.' This was the Norman knight.

Peter looked at me again. 'Good-bye Edmund. God bless you!' And then he disappeared.

Now I turned to the Norman. 'Who are you, and why are you interfering with my business?'

'My name is Humphrey. I serve Robert Malet, Lord of Eye and sometime Sheriff of Suffolk. And when someone travels around the country, preaching sedition, it becomes the King's business. He makes it my lord Robert's business and my lord Robert makes it mine.'

'I am not preaching sedition.' That was technically true: I hadn't tried to get anyone to rise against the Bastard. On the other hand, I had rather freely talked about returning with an army of Englishmen to fight the Normans. Anyway, this was not a court of law, so such niceties probably didn't matter.

'You are enticing the King's subjects to go off and join you in the Emperor's service.'

'So that's what it is about! You don't like the idea of some other Normans getting their just desserts!'

This seemed to surprise and then amuse him.

'Oh that! Do you really think King William cares about what happens with the Hauteville brood in Italy? What are they to him? No, no. In fact, in some ways what you are doing is serving his needs. You are finding malcontents, people who are opposed to the King's rule. If they are well-born, they could lead others. Far better if they disappear from England and leave the country quieter.'

'In that case, just let me go my way.' I didn't think this very likely, but it was worth a try.

'I am afraid not. You see, you *are* talking about coming back with an army of Englishmen and driving the Normans out. Oh yes, we have heard about your progress, not only from that sad monk, but from others as well. There have been other men here from Greece, recruiting soldiers. But no-one else talks about returning. *That* is treason. Also, you are giving the people hope that we can be defeated, and the King can't have that.'

‘So now you are going to kill me?’

‘No. At least, not yet. And probably not at all. We are taking you to my lord Robert’s castle. He will sit in judgment over you. But you need not fear for your life. King William is a gracious lord. He doesn’t believe in killing people. Instead, you will most probably be blinded and gelded.’

That scared me. The Greeks were fond of blinding people as a punishment, usually by holding a red-hot iron in front of their eyes until their sight had burned away. And there were plenty of eunuchs at the Emperor’s court. It was said that being incapable of having a family of their own, they would be loyal to the Emperor. Well, they might not be able to have children, but they could have brothers and they seemed quite loyal to them. It may have suited the Greeks, but it certainly did not suit me. The thought of being gelded like an ox, of living my life like a blind half-man terrified me. I would rather die. Let them kill me here and at least I would die fighting. My hand moved towards my sword again.

‘Don’t!’ Humphrey said. ‘What chance do you think you have? Surrender now and come with us.’

And he held out his hand for my sword and stepped forward to take it.

In so doing, he stepped in front of the crossbowman. And suddenly there was a roar behind him. 'You would geld my friend, would you, Norman cur? Not quite yet, I think.' At the same time, a sword was swung in an arc towards the crossbowman, almost taking his head off. As his body toppled, the bolt fired, hitting Humphrey in the left arm. Because he was so close to the crossbow, it didn't penetrate his mailshirt, but it must have hurt. The shock and the noise from behind made him turn around. That was all the time I needed to whip out my own sword and run towards him. He must have heard me or at least realised what was likely to happen, because he turned around fast enough and brought his own sword up to guard. Meanwhile, Erik – I had recognised the voice but had no idea how he came to be here – was engaging the spearman, who was having trouble fending him off at such close quarters.

But I had no time to think about them. Although Humphrey had been surprised and his arm must hurt, he had recovered quickly. Our swords clashed against each other. At five feet and eight inches tall I was about two inches taller than he, so my reach was longer. But he was wearing mail and I was not. If I was to get out of this alive, I had to finish him off quickly. I hacked at him again, trying to find an opening. He parried and lunged at me, but I jumped to one side and swept his sword away with mine. Then we circled each other, testing the other's defence. I could hear Erik fighting the man-at-arms nearby.

Suddenly Humphrey swung at me again. I parried but had no time to get a blow in.

'Give yourself up,' he said. 'You don't stand a chance. Even if you kill me, you will be found and captured. Give up now and I'll make sure you are not killed.'

He didn't realise that dying was not my main worry. Instead of answering I aimed a blow at his left side. As he moved the sword over to parry, I withdrew my own blade beyond his reach, continued the arc, turned it and struck at his leg. This was a trick I had learned from Oleg, the Russian Varangian. The move caught Humphrey off guard and I felt my sword bite into the leg. Not as deeply as I had hoped, though. It turned out his legs were also encased in chainmail. Although he stumbled, I didn't have time to get another blow in.

Now he turned to the attack, aiming blows at my head, my arm and my body. I parried most of them, but a glancing cut grazed my arm and now I was bleeding. This was getting worrying. Humphrey could sense my insecurity and was pressing his attack. I retreated towards the trees and he was following. I was getting tired and I still hadn't managed to stop him. I was trying to get a tree between us to catch my breath when I stumbled and fell backwards. In the fall, I dropped my sword. Humphrey saw and rushed towards me, hacking with his sword. I tried to find my sword with my right hand and failed. I rolled away and he swung again. I gave up trying to find my sword and I reached for my knife instead. When Humphrey came closer I kicked his leg – the same leg I had hit earlier. I was lucky and caught him on the knee and he stumbled. Before he had time to get up, I scrambled towards him. He tried to raise his sword, but I managed to knock his hand away with my left arm, even though it hurt like fire. And with my right,

I stabbed him in the throat, where there was no mail protecting him. He made a gurgling sound and blood welled up in his mouth. And then he died.

I rolled off him and tried to catch my breath. Then I heard the sound of fighting from the field. Erik! I had completely forgotten him. There was my sword glittering in the light from the dying fire. I grabbed it, got up and stepped out into the field again. But just as I came out, that fight also ended, with Erik's sword biting into the Norman's face and taking away a good part of it. As the man fell, he turned around and limped towards me.

'Are you wounded?' I asked.

'No, just tired. I took longer than I thought. How about you?'

'A cut in the arm. But nothing serious. Now we have to get out of here.'

Erik helped me tie a rag around my arm. Then he disappeared behind the trees. A moment later he reappeared, leading his horse with our packs. My horse was peacefully grazing a short distance away where I had left him. We sat up and then Erik turned to me: 'Where now?'

'Dover. I think we are finished with England – for this time. Next time, it will be different.' And then I suddenly thought of something. 'How come you were here?'

'The girl.' And he smiled broadly again.

'Which girl?'

'The servant girl at the inn. She asked if I knew you. When I asked why, she told me that her sister was married to a Norman soldier, who was supposed to be away but who had suddenly appeared in Ely yesterday evening. When the sister asked him why he was back, he said it was to catch a traitor and that he would be out that night. Then the girl saw you leaving the inn and guessed you were the traitor.' He sighed. 'I think she will not be happy with me.'

'You left her?'

'Yes. But first I tied her up so that she wouldn't warn anyone. Don't worry. I didn't harm her and I left a few coins to pay for our room. This, you owe me.'

'I'll have to pay you in Constantinopolis, my money is beginning to run out. First, we have to get there. That means Dover and meet our recruits.'

So saying, we spurred our horses and rode off. We had 160 miles to go – more if we wanted to avoid London. Five days should do it, maybe six – assuming we didn't run into any trouble.

As for trouble – how could have I let myself be fooled by Edward. As we rode on, I swore at my stupidity in at least four languages. He had been so transparent! His cant about peace and giving unto Caesar and obeying the king. If he had not been an old friend, I would have stopped trying to recruit him there and then. Instead, when it only took him a short while to change his mind and be ready to join me, I immediately believed him. I could only think that I had been so pleased to see an old comrade-in-arms and desperate for him to join the cause, that I would not believe anything else. Deep inside, I still couldn't believe that he had betrayed me. But it was also something to remember for the future; not everyone would be prepared to fight against the bastard. And the longer he remained King, the more difficult it would be to unseat him.

We were lucky. I don't know if anyone was looking for us, but we didn't encounter anyone. On the evening of the sixth day, we rode into Dover and straight to Robert's inn. He didn't seem surprised to see me.

'I thought you would be coming soon,' he said. 'There have been quite a few people coming by, saying you sent them.'

'Where are they all?' Because I saw none of the men who should have been there, waiting for me. By my last count, there should have been 32 recruits here.

'I didn't want them waiting here. Too much trouble can happen when a lot of young men have nothing to do. And I assumed you would be going back to France. So I sent them over with Henri. You owe me a fair amount of money, my Lord.'

'Would our horses be enough to cover it? And can you get Henri to come and pick us up tomorrow.'

'They will. And I can do better than that. Henri's boat is in port and he should be here any moment. In fact, there he is.' And he pointed. I turned around and recognised the French fisherman. He had played a trick on me, but I was glad to see him.

'Henri! How are you? And when can we leave for Boulogne?'

'I am well. And we can leave this evening, if you want. I was planning to wait until tomorrow, but this is fine. But we have too leave right now, in that case, because of the tide. No time for you to imbibe your favourite remedy.' And he laughed. I scowled.

Erik observed our exchange and asked, 'What was that about?'

'A joke – on his part,' I replied. 'I get seasick. Henri told me that I wouldn't get seasick if I was drunk when we sailed. He thought it was funny.'

'That's stupid,' Erik said. 'Everyone knows that seasickness is caused by the sea spirits' – the mermens' – anger as we trespass on their realm. They rock the boat to try to drown us. We must make a sacrifice to them for a good voyage.'

'Why, Erik,' I said, 'I thought you were a good Christian'.

'I am. But the ancients were right about some things. This is one of them.'

'Well, whatever it is, we have to go now. I am not looking forward to it.' And with that we followed

Henri down to the harbour and stepped on board his boat. As we went, Erik poured ale into the water and muttered something in Danish, presumably to appease the mermen.

I don't know what happened. But I do know that I felt fine during the entire crossing. Maybe seasickness was just a question of getting used to the sea.

CHAPTER 10

To Constantinopolis

I had no idea what to expect when we came to Boulogne the next morning. Would the men I had sent – and whom Robert had then sent over to France – still be there? By now some of them would have been there for more than two weeks. They could have tired of waiting, gone back to England, sought hire with French nobles, quarrelled with the people in Boulogne over money, food, wine or girls and gotten killed.

First, though, Erik and I went to pick up my horse. The landlord at the inn was not happy to see me – I think he would have preferred for me to stay away a little while longer, so that he could claim the horse for himself as we had originally agreed. Not that he tried to argue, though, not with two armed men. He even told us where we should be able to find another horse for Erik. As we walked through the narrow streets of Boulogne, Erik looked around with keen interest.

'Have you been to France before?' I asked.

'Yes. My kinsman sent me here first. I was to find out if the nobles of Normandy would assist us against their lord. I spent a few months there.'

'Did you have any luck?'

'Not really. They all feared that if we managed to win and my kinsman became King of England, it would mean William back in Normandy. Too close for comfort. But I met some nice women. Much prettier than these.'

He had a point. What few women we saw were short, ugly and unwashed. That didn't stop them from eyeing my companion. What *did* he have to make them so attracted to him? Yes, he was young, tall, blond and pleasant-looking. But so are lots of men and they still don't have to fight their way through crowds of women dying to share their bed.

Soon enough we emerged through one of the gates in the city wall and set about looking for the farm where we had been told there might be a horse for sale. It wasn't difficult to find. The horse in question was a sorry creature, but as long as he carried Erik through France, I didn't care. While we haggled about the price, I asked if he had heard anything about a group of Englishmen camping somewhere in the vicinity. The question surprised him – the answer surprised me.

'Everybody knows about them. They are camped a mile south-east of here. They say they are Roman soldiers. Everyone thinks they are crazy. But they harm no-one and pay for what they drink.'

That was interesting news. Roman soldiers, indeed. It made me hope that most of the 32 would still be there. Once we had finished buying Erik's horse, we rode slowly in the direction the farmer had indicated. After a short ride, we came to a camp. It was much dirtier and haphazard than an Imperial camp would have been. In fact, if I hadn't been told, I wouldn't have thought it a military camp at all, just a dirty campsite. No guards or look-outs of course, no latrines, no orderly rows of tents. On the other hand, I was flattered that they thought of themselves as soldiers and that they were all still there – assuming they were.

I was even more surprised when we came into the camp. Although there had been no look-out, once they spotted us, there were shouts of welcome and men came rushing from all around. One of them tried to shout some form of command at the rest, but was ignored. Eventually, they fell silent. The one who had shouted commands came forward. It was Wilfred, one of the two brothers I had recruited in Colchester the day I met Erik.

'Welcome to our camp. We are ready to march as soon as you give the command.'

I didn't know what to say. Whatever I had expected, this wasn't it. Still, the men clearly expected something and I was impressed that – as a quick headcount showed – they were all there. I looked around from my lofty horseback position and said:

'Well done. I am proud of you – and I know the Emperor would be proud of his newest recruits as well. Now, we need to get you there for him to inspect you.'

Actually, if the Emperor had seen them like this, he would probably have been appalled and had all his prejudice about barbarians confirmed. Once we came to Constantinopolis, they would need a lot of drill before the Emperor even saw them. On the other hand, there was no denying their enthusiasm. I could only hope that they would keep it until we went into battle. First, I had to get them to Constantinopolis, though.

'Who is in command?' I asked.

'I am.' This was Wilfred. 'And my brother. We thought that since we came first, we would organise the rest as they came along.'

'And Grim?' This was the serf who had been recruited together with the two brothers. Surely he did not have a share in the command.

'He is in charge of the horses.' The brothers were enthusiastic and wanted to tell me everything they had done. So Erik and I dismounted, let one of the others take care of the horses and walked off to their tent.

It soon turned out that the brothers' knowledge of what to do with a troop was considerably less than their enthusiasm. The sum of what they had done was to keep the recruits together in one group, make sure no-one went back home and try to avoid antagonising the local population. The last was unusual and praiseworthy enough. But they had no idea of how to prepare for the kind of journey we now had to make, nor did they – or seemingly anyone else – have more than the haziest concept of where or how far Constantinopolis was.

'Very good', I said when they were done. 'You have done well and – as I said – I am proud of you. Now we have to plan for the next step. We cannot march through France and Provençe like a small army. I think we should make out that we are pilgrims, bound for the Holy Land. There are always small parties – sometimes not so small – of pilgrims passing travelling to Jerusalem and Bethlehem in the east. No one will bother us. How many horses do we have?'

'Fifteen, with your two.'

'We will use the horses to carry our packs. We will need some supplies. I would like us to set out in two days – St John the Baptist's Day.'

Two days later, we did set out. And now, for the first time, I was getting anxious about speed. The last thing I had heard about the war in Greece had been when I was told that Bohemond had defeated us again and taken Kastoria. For all I knew, he could by now be camped outside Constantinopolis itself, or – even worse – have taken the city. It was all very well to have recruited more Varangians, but what if there was no Guard for them to serve in? I only spoke to Erik about my worries. He dismissed them.

'I have heard about the walls of Miklagård, from you and from the stories in my family,' he said. 'If what I heard is true, a child with a slingshot could keep them safe. Stop worrying and tell me more about the Greek girls instead. Do they prefer their own men or would they rather have a handsome Viking?'

And that was all the comfort I could get out of him.

It was almost 700 miles from Boulogne to Marseille. I estimated that it would take us slightly more than two months to get there, and that was if we pushed ourselves and the horses. That meant arriving in early September. Then, assuming we could get hold of a ship to carry us, it would take at the very least another three to four weeks before we arrived in Constantinopolis, and that only if we had perfect weather the whole way. In other words, I wouldn't be back until mid-October at best, almost a year after I had left for Italy with Richard. In fact, it was more likely to be later. But at least I should be able to get some news of the war in Marseille.

In the end, it didn't take quite seventy days to reach Marseille. Three of the horses died on the way. Since we had no money to buy any new, we had to make more frequent rests. I spent some of the time trying to explain to the men what life in Constantinopolis and the Guard was like and about the current war. I don't know how much impression I made on them or how much they understood. One or two – like Edmund, my namesake – still looked on the whole expedition as an exciting adventure.

When we arrived in Marseille, there was a storm. It took another three days before the weather became calm enough for boats to begin to venture out. I spent the days in port selling our horses and didn't get very much for them. Getting transport to Constantinopolis took longer, but I did find out more about the war.

First, it turned out that Richard and I – and others like us – had been quite successful in Italy. Emperor Henry had marched down from the north and again invested Rome and there was open rebellion in

Apulia. Roger Borsa had not been able to cope, so Guiscard had perforce left Greece – with Bohemond in command – and sailed back to Italy. There he had driven the Germans back from Rome itself, but Henry was still with a large army in Tuscany, whose Countess was allied to the Normans. Then Duke Robert had turned back to Apulia to deal with the rebels himself and had apparently defeated them. What was happening in Greece was less clear: some said that Bohemond was rumoured to have defeated the Emperor in one or two battles, killed the Emperor and probably taken Constantinopolis. No, that was wrong, others said: Bohemond was already dead and his army defeated. Others said that yes, he had won many battles, but the Empire was still around. And most people did not really know anything at all. It was difficult to decide who to trust, but it did sound as if the war was still going on and that Bohemond was still not making any headway towards Constantinopolis or even Thessaloniki. If true, that was better than I had hoped, although this news, too, was old.

By virtue of selling the horses and scraping the bottom of my purse, I was able to pay a trader to take us to Constantinopolis. From there, he said, we should have no trouble finding someone else to take us to the Holy Land, which I had given out was our final destination. At least I was not worried about being seasick, as I felt the last journey to France had cured me of that plague.

Or so I thought. It turned out that I was wrong. I don't know why I had not been seasick then, but I certainly was seasick now. Fortunately, so were quite a few of the others, otherwise I think any respect they had for me would have disappeared. It is difficult to respect someone spewing his guts out over the side.

Aside from my seasickness, we made good speed. After about a week we reached Messina, a port in Sicily just opposite the Italian mainland and stopped there to take in fresh water and supplies. Richard had told me that Messina had been conquered by the Normans early on in their wars with the Sicilian Saracens. Despite that, I wasn't particularly worried about being recognised. Richard and I had not come any closer to Sicily than Scalea and that was still some distance away. Also, we were a group of pilgrims travelling from France – no connection with a Norman lord and an English soldier in Greek service. Still, I warned the others not to wander off alone, nor to get into any conversation – and no quarrels! – with Norman soldiers.

Even though we were already in late September, it was much warmer here than it had been in France. I was finally beginning to feel dry again after all the English rain. It felt good to stretch our legs ashore. Messina being a port, we had no trouble finding an inn by the harbour and soon we were sitting in the sun, trying out the local wine.

While the others were looking around, wide-mouthed at the strange city, where even the houses looked different from home – and the girls were very pretty, those you could see – I closed my eyes and began to drift off.

Suddenly I jerked awake. I had recognised a voice and what was more worrying, the voice seemed to be talking about me. Or, rather, about Richard of Matera.

‘…thought he could buy me with his Greek gold,’, the voice was saying, ‘him and that Englishman he was travelling with.’

Whose was the voice? I knew I recognised it, but which one of the Normans we had met in Italy was it? And was it certain that it was Richard and me he was talking about? I knew that we had not been alone in trying to stir up trouble for Guiscard in his backyard. The voice was deep and that nagged something in my mind.

‘Well, what happened? Don’t keep us in suspense,’ another voice said, while two or three others were loudly laughing. ‘Surely you are not the one to say no to gold, are you? When have you ever passed that up?’

‘I told him there was not enough gold in the whole Empire to buy me. Told him, I did.’ The man didn’t sound sober, which probably was good news. But who *was* he?

‘Told him I was Count Roger’s best soldier. No honour fighting Greeks – fight Saracens, that’s a man’s work!’

Now I knew. The deep voice belonged to William, the man we had stayed with one of our first nights in Italy, almost a year ago. I had to get out of here before he recognised me. But how to get the others? I looked around for Erik, but he was – of course – busy talking to one of the servant-girls. The nearest to me was Grim; he was looking at me and I signalled to him to get closer.

'Get one of your masters quickly – but quietly!'

As he went off, I pulled my cloak over my face and tried to listen to what was going on at William's table. He was still boasting about his prowess, but the men with him seemed more interested in Richard's fate. That was bad news, since it would keep his mind on us.

'But why did you let him go on his way if you are so loyal?' one of his friends asked.

'What could I do? I was all alone. But as soon as he had ridden off, I sent a courier to Roger Borsa, warning him. Anyway, I heard he got himself captured by that stuck-up sot Geoffrey of Scalea.'

'And?'

'Oh, Geoffrey couldn't keep him. He broke out. Yes, broke out. Burned Geoffrey's place, too. Serves him right. Thinks he is so great. Always goes on about what a great soldier he is. What does he know of soldiering. I am a great soldier, I am.'

His friends laughed. 'Yes, yes, of course you are? And Richard?'

'He…'

But at that stage, Wilfred slid down next to me by our table and I didn't hear what had happened to Richard.

'What's the matter?' he asked.

'There is a small man with a deep voice at one of the tables here, 'I muttered. 'Can you see him?'

'Yes. He is with four others. They are drunk.'

'I know. But he knows me. If he recognises me, we won't be allowed to leave Messina. Get everyone together and get them back to the ship. I don't care if we don't have all the supplies we need. We leave at once. If we need anything more, we'll have to get it from some other port. Thank God there is no issue with tides in the Inner Sea.'

Wilfred was not stupid. He didn't waste any more time, but started going unobtrusively from table to table, talking to one man at each and getting him to collect that group and lead them out. That left only Erik. Wilfred looked around but couldn't see him. I cursed inwardly. He must have disappeared with the servant. Devil take that randy Dane and his constant preoccupation with girls! I waved at Wilfred to go off and leave it to me.

Fortunately, there weren't that many places he could have gone off to. Also, since he had been standing in front of a curtain, covering an entrance to the inn, it wasn't difficult to guess where he was.

I got up, careful not to turn my face towards William, hunched down to disguise my height, and began to walk towards the curtain. At that moment, one of William's companions noticed that he was out of wine and began calling for the servant. When no one responded, they got up and began to look for her. I managed to slip into the room before them, but they would be coming in any second. I stopped and listened. Sure enough – from behind another curtain I heard the unmistakable noise of Erik and the girl and went over there. As I came into the closet, Erik turned around and begin to say something. The girl looked startled – as well she might – and cried out.

'Get up!' I hissed at Erik. 'We're in danger. Quickly!'

'Why…'

'No time!'

He did get up, closing his breeches as he did so. I dragged him out of the closet but stopped short as I came out. William and his friends had come in and were facing us. My cloak was still covering most of my face, but I moved my right hand toward my sword. Erik looked startled, but reached towards his weapon. I began to move again, trying to sidle by the Normans.

'Hold!' We froze and turned towards them. 'Have you seen the servant wench? We want more wine.'

'In there,' I mumbled and pointed towards the closet.

'Thank you. You must have a mug of wine with us.'

I shook my head and hoped Erik would understand what was going on. Then I thought he had gone mad.

'Gladly will I stay', he said in execrable French. Where on earth had he picked *that* up? 'Let me send servant away.' Turning to me, he continued, 'Go. Make all ready and I will come.' Then he turned to the Normans again and smiled at them. 'Now, brave men, we drink'

I could only hope that he knew what he was doing. Meanwhile, I walked out of the inn and then ran down to the harbour. As I boarded our ship, I could see that Wilfred had done well here too. Everything was ready to set sail. All we now needed was Erik. While we waited for him to arrive, I tried to calm my anxiety by explaining to Wilfred and his brother why we had to leave. They had had some trouble convincing the captain of the need for speed. Eventually he had agreed, but only after saying that he would have to put in for more supplies soon and this would add to the cost. I told him that he would be paid in Constantinopolis, which he didn't like but had to accept.

It must have taken more than an hour before Erik arrived and I was already wondering if I would have to raid a Norman jail to free him, when one of the men suddenly spotted him. He was sauntering down towards the ship as if he didn't have a care in the world. And given how drunk he was, he shouldn't have any cares either. As he approached the ship he wavered around and tried to put his feet carefully on the gangplank. He did manage a few steps, but then with an almighty splash he fell into the water. I was terrified that he would drown, but two of the sailors threw down a rope to him and as he was spluttering around he managed to grab hold of it and they hauled him aboard. As soon as he was safe, I told the captain to set sail. Then I tried to find out what had happened. It was not easy – I had not seen anyone this drunk since my crossing from Boulogne to Dover.

Finally he sobered up enough to explain. 'They drink well, these Normans', he said. 'I could not let them out-drink a Dane who had come to seek his fortune with his kin in Italy, could I? They wanted to take me to Count Roger, wherever he is, they didn't say, as soon as we had finished drinking. I had to wait until they were all asleep. I am glad they had drunk as much as they had before we began.'

That was all we could get out of him before he fell asleep. At least we had gotten away without any incident.

The rest of the journey was uneventful. We stopped more than once to replenish our supplies, but finally we sailed into the Golden Horn and anchored below the walls of Constantinopolis. I had been away for more than a year.

CHAPTER 11

Back into the Field

I would have liked to go to my family, but first I had to arrange for our captain to be paid what he claimed we owed him and also deliver the new recruits to the Varangian Guard. Along the way to our barracks in the Imperial Palace grounds, the men stared around with wide eyes. I remembered how I had felt myself on my arrival so long ago.

When we arrived at the barracks, the first person I saw was Oleg, the Russian who had come with me on the mission to the Norman camp before Dyrrachion.

'Oleg!' I exclaimed. 'You survived the battle as well! That is good.'

'Yes', he replied, 'I survive, thanks be to St. Vladimir of Kiev. And I get promotion, like you. I too am now Komes.'

'Do we have enough soldiers for all these Kometes?'

'Oh yes. You ask Nampites, he will tell you.'

That was good news – and there was more to come. As I reported my results to Nampites, he didn't look too displeased.

'Thirty-two is not bad – but I had hoped for more. Most of the others brought more. But you did good work in Italy, Richard says.'

'He came back?'

'Oh yes. He was very pleased with himself, but found time to put in a good word for you too. I heard his report to the Grand Domestic and when he saw me he mentioned you.'

'I met Oleg; he said we had plenty of Varangians. But I heard about Kastoria.'

Nampites didn't look happy when I mentioned that. Few enough had survived Dyrrachion and most of those had been lost at Kastoria where they had surrendered without a fight.

'He is right. We have had six or seven hundred English join us and six hundred Russians, some more Vikings. All in all, we are back to fifteen hundred again. You will know more in the morning. Now, leave your recruits here. Tomorrow we will start turning them into soldiers. Tonight, go and see your wife.'

But before I could do that, I had to tell Nampites about the captain's money. He promised he would arrange that and then dismissed me.

And then I finally could go home. I had not seen my wife and daughter for almost a year and a half. For all I knew, they didn't even know if I was alive.

We lived on the south side of the city, just west of the Hippodrome. As I approached, a group of children were playing in the street. One of them was a little girl with yellow hair, who would now be two years old. When she saw me turn into the house, she suddenly broke off playing with the others and rushed in, yelling, 'Mama, Mama, there's a strange man here!'

Irene must have guessed, because she came running out. As soon as she saw me, she threw herself in my arms, crying and laughing at the same time.

'Edmund! Oh, Edmund! I prayed to Saint Demetrios of Thessaloniki that you would come back!'

'It's all right,' I said, stroking her hair, 'I'm back now. With both of us praying to the Saint, he could not but let me come home.'

'Mummy, who is he? Why are you hugging that man?' This was the little girl, tugging at Irene's clothes.

'Dora, it's your father. Remember, you've asked about him often enough. I told you he was away fighting. But now he is back and he won't leave us again.'

That was almost certainly not true, but I let it pass. Instead, I knelt down and held out my arms to my daughter.

'Hello Theodora. Don't you want to greet your father?'

At first the little one was shy, but eventually she came and gave me a hug. Once she had done that, she was completely won over. She refused to let me go and insisted on pulling my beard. Although I was now wearing my beard shorter in the Greek fashion, rather than the English, her little hands found enough to wrap around her fingers and pull. It was actually painful, but she thought I was play-acting. And when it came to bedtime, she refused to go to sleep before I had played 'colour game' with her. Although she explained in great detail what this was, I was unable to understand it, except that it had something to do with the colour of the rag her doll was dressed in. Not that it mattered; I was happy enough that she accepted me.

Afterwards, Irene told me about what life had been like in Constantinopolis after I had left. News of the many defeats had worried people, but nobody seriously thought that the Normans would actually besiege the city, let alone conquer it. The war was far away, and although she worried about me, Irene's main concerns had been about Theodora and about their daily life. I then told Irene about all my adventures. I still wasn't sure how much she knew about the world outside the Empire. She knew I came from England and that this was an island in the Oceanic Sea and that the Normans had killed my king. She had heard me tell about France and Provençe. And, of course, her father was a merchant from Thessaloniki, so she had heard about the world from him. But even as I told her I found myself getting confused and I had no doubt she was too.

'All that matters, is that you are back,' she said. 'I knew you didn't die at Dyrrachion; Oleg came and told me. But he didn't know what had happened afterwards or where you were. And how long will you remain?'

'I don't know. I don't know how the war has gone, but I suppose the Emperor is raising a new army and we will march out and fight the Normans as soon as he is done.'

'I know,' she said. 'The Emperor has seized the treasures of the Holy Church to pay for his new army. The monks are very angry.'

'Well, I can promise you that I won't be leaving tomorrow, at least.'

'That's good. And now I would like to really feel that my husband is home again.' And she smiled at me and took my hand and led me to bed.

* * *

The next day, when I left for the barracks, Irene held me back. 'I know you may have to go off again,' she said. 'I want you to wear this when you go.' And she gave me a small icon. 'It's Saint Demetrios,' she said, 'the patron of Thessaloniki. He was a soldier and will look out for you. I know you already pray to him. But this icon was blessed in his own holy Cathedral in Thessaloniki. I asked my mother to send it to me for you.' Then she hung the icon around my neck and kissed me.

As for Dora, she didn't want to let me go at all until I had promised by all the saints to come back the same evening and play with her again.

The Guards barracks were a beehive of activity. Not only Varangians, but men from all kinds of different units were being outfitted and marshalled into different formations. I could see Oleg yelling at a large group of soldiers – presumably his Russian bandon – and other men doing the same.

My own recruits had been assigned to my command, together with almost 70 others, mostly Englishmen as well. My first concern was to get them properly inscribed and registered and then equipped and paid. Once that was achieved, I set to training them as well. I had made Wilfred and Edgar dekarchs among others and I had offered Erik to be one of my pentekontarchs (Oswy was the other) and command fifty men. He just laughed and said that although he did not fancy being a common soldier that was too much for him. So he too became a dekarch.

For the next few months, my life became rather routine. Most of my time was spent training and exercising the new Varangians. In addition, there was our regular duties, guarding the Emperor and other members of the royal family. Occasionally I escorted the Protosebastos Adrianos, but although he always had a friendly and courteous greeting for me, there were no more exciting duties.

I did run into Richard of Matera one day in mid-December. I had been in the Imperial escort to Mass in Saint Sophia and Richard appeared in the Emperor's entourage. He didn't say anything then, but when I was relieved he came and looked me up in the Guards barracks.

'Welcome back, Englishman. I am glad you managed to come back without further dangers.'

'Oh, I did have one or two. One of them was with an old friend of yours – the braggart William.' And I told him what had happened in Messina. He began to laugh.

'What is so funny?'

'You wouldn't know. But I enjoyed hearing William telling people about his loyalty to Robert Guiscard and how he reported us to Roger Borsa. Not enough gold in the whole Empire to buy him, was that it? Well, you'll be amused too, to hear that he has been taking the Emperor's gold for the last six months, and promising to oppose Guiscard at every turn. Sent a messenger here begging for money. And he's sworn allegiance both to Abelard of Hauteville *and* to Jordan of Capua in addition to Guiscard and his brother Count Roger. Probably to Roger Borsa as well. Such loyalty.'

He was right – that did amuse me. I wondered how many more Norman barons were in the Emperor's pay. Probably quite a few.

When I had free time, I spent as much of it as I could with Irene and Dora. It was strange trying to get to know my daughter – and having her get to know me. I took her to our local church, the Church of Saints Sergius and Bacchus, for Mass; I played with her; I took her to the Hippodrome for races; I took her for walks on the long, huge walls of Constantinopolis, walking between the two lines of walls, in and out of towers, where being a Varangian meant I had no problem getting in. Once I even took her across the Golden Horn to Galata. I had told her about the Speaking Towers that guarded the Golden Horn. She didn't understand how you could be heard from one tower to the next without shouting and thought that the towers actually spoke to each other. When we arrived and she found out how it worked, she squealed with delight and insisted on making me stand in one of them and call out something to hear that she would hear in the next one in spite of the distance. Then we walked around in Galata, looking at the churches and at the synagogues of the Jews who lived there. On the way back, I bought her some sweets from a stall which we munched upon as we walked home.

Some early mornings we would go down to the harbour together and buy fresh fish that had just been brought in by the fishermen, tuna or maybe mackerel, and take home where Irene would later prepare it for dinner for us. And once I took her to the Imperial Palace grounds. She had hoped that we would see the Emperor although I had told her that that was unlikely. We were lucky, though: although we didn't see the Emperor, we saw his eldest brother, the Sebastokrator Isaak and their mother Anna Dalassene in the distance. That was enough to send her running to all her friends in the street that afternoon, boasting about the beautiful people she had seen. To hear her talk, you would have thought that they had stopped what they were doing and chatted with her for hours. Irene was grateful and pleased to see us coming together.

I also took Erik home to meet my family. I had told Irene about him and was pleased to see that at least she did not fawn over him like all the other women he met seemed to do. But Dora immediately became enamoured of him and I realised that in not too many years I would have to start worrying about her and boys. That was a strange feeling for the father of a two-year old.

In general, it was a strange period. When Dora and I stood on the walls and looked northwest, everything looked so peaceful. Yet not many days to the west, there was still a war going on. And still not going too well, as far as I could understand. Although Guiscard himself was still back in Italy, putting down rebellions and fighting the German Emperor, Bohemond was pressing the Empire badly. As I had heard, we had indeed lost two battles, at Yanina and at Arta and the Normans now controlled most of Macedonia and Thessaly. Even worse, the two lost battles had cost us even more of a dwindling supply of trained soldiers. True, the Emperor was raising more troops, not least – as Irene had told me – by getting the church to hand over its treasures. Our local priest had not sounded happy about that at Mass. Well, he wasn't the one who had to go out and fight the Normans.

But every week, new units came into the city. In addition to the Greeks and the Varangians, there were Normans like Richard and Slavs from Raška. Then there were seven thousand Turkish horsemen, sent by one of the emirs of Anatolia, who was a friend of the Emperor; and Pechenegs, nomads from the south Russian steppes. Oleg was not pleased to see them and there were constant small fights breaking out between them and the Russian Varangians. The numbers were rising, but no one knew how well they would fight against the Normans when the time for battle finally came. As for the Slavs, they had already betrayed us at Dyrrachion and no one was sure how reliable they or any of the foreign troops – apart from the Varangians – would be next time around.

Yet for all that, life went on. The new Varangian recruits gradually became a unit, rather than just a group of fighting men. Christmas came around and then the New Year and once again I was in the Emperor's escort in Saint Sophia. And I got to know my daughter better and better.

And then one day, the order came to prepare and we were told that we would be marching out three days later. That gave me some time to prepare my family for it as well. Again, I had to promise that I would not be away for as long as last time and Dora also wanted me to bring her a present. Irene was more concerned that I would wear the icon of Saint Demetrios wherever I went.

When we marched out through the Golden Gate and the walls of Constantinopolis fell away behind us, the months spent there fell away as well, almost like a disappearing dream. Once again, I was a soldier at war. Once again, I had that strange feeling that I think all soldiers get; we can't possibly lose, I can't possibly die. Despite the fact that we had been beaten three times by the Normans, I was sure every single one of us was thinking of how he would come marching back through the Golden Gate again in the future, possibly without a few of his comrades but still alive – and unhurt.

CHAPTER 12

Back to War

Although so much seemed similar, there were differences. Last time, I had been a low-ranking dekarch, eager to get to grips with the Normans and marching with an invincible Roman army. Now I was a Komes and knew that commanding a bandon also meant being responsible for my men as well. Also, I was marching with a raw army made up of soldiers from everywhere in the world, English, Russian, even thousands of Turkish cavalry, who had not had much time to train, much less train together. And finally, last time we knew we were going to win. This time we knew that we had lost three large battles already and many smaller skirmishes and a battle was the last thing we wanted. Most important of all, this time I understood why avoiding battle was the right thing to do.

But if I had at last understood something of the Roman way of fighting wars, the newly-arrived soldiers understood as little of it as I once had. I found myself answering questions from people like Wilfred and my namesake Edmund about why we were not marching directly on the Normans and engaging them. The one person that seemed to understand without having to be told, was Erik. But then he had some experience of warfare from his own country. As for the others, I tried to explain as best I could.

Not that there was much time for idle questions. The soldiers might have been new and foreign, but we marched as a Roman army always did, and that meant building a proper camp every night and dismantling it in the morning. And when the camp was up, there was guard duty to mount – not on the camp ramparts – that was for the other soldiers. But the Varangians stood guard over the Emperor's tent in the middle of the camp and the tents of other commanders and members of the Imperial company.

One evening as I was standing guard – yes, even Kometes have to stand guard, in addition to our other duties – I had a pleasant surprise. I was guarding the tent of the Protosebastos Adrianos Komnenos, but I had not seen him. When I took over the guard duty, he was already closeted inside in a meeting. I heard the murmur of voices from inside, but this was none of my business. We had already been on the road for some weeks and were near Thessaloniki. I was wondering where we would go from there. There were rumours that Bohemond was besieging the city of Larissa in Thessaly and that we would try to bring him to battle against its walls. But others were saying that Larissa was likely to keep holding out for ever and instead we were to march west, to Kastoria or even Ohrid and cut him off from any hope of further reinforcements. Two years ago, I would have been just as anxious to find out what we were going to do as any of the others – including Alf who was standing guard with me and who kept bringing it up. Oh, I was still curious. But I also thought that we would find out soon enough and that no amount of talking or guessing would bring us anywhere nearer the truth.

But while we were standing there and talking – or rather, Alf was talking and I was grunting in reply, thinking more of my family in Constantinopolis, the voices behind us suddenly came nearer the tent door. As we stood at attention, the curtain was folded aside and the Protosebastos Adrianos said a few words to a man who stepped out after taking a very respectful farewell. As he stepped out, he turned to Alf – but I had already recognised him even before he opened his mouth.

'Guardsman', he said, 'I am looking for a Kelt named Edmund.'

'Don't bother, Georgios', I replied in Alf's stead. 'He doesn't speak Greek. But I am right here. Tell me, father-in-law, what on Earth are you doing with the Protosebastos Adrianos? And why are you in our camp in any case, since you are not a soldier?'

Georgios turned around as I was speaking. Then he stretched out his arms and embraced me. 'Edmund! It is good to see you. How is my daughter? And my granddaughter? Can we talk here?'

'I cannot talk here and now. But if you wait a short while, I will be relieved of duty and then we can talk.'

It wasn't long before both Alf and I were indeed relieved and replaced by other men from my bandon. And I could go off and talk with my father-in-law.

I had thought of Georgios as we approached Thessaloniki. But I had thought it highly unlikely that

I would see him, so this was a pleasant surprise. He soon explained how come he happened to be in camp. It seemed that the Protosebastos Adrianos had received some tax lands near Thessaloniki and that my father-in-law had bought the right to collect the taxes. I knew that it would make Georgios even richer, so I was pleased for his sake. He also gave me news of the rest of his family. His wife was well, and Theodora, who had gotten married shortly after Irene and I, was by now expecting a second child. And I told him about Irene and about Dora, who he never seemed to hear enough about. He also wanted to know more about the war, but I was unable to tell him anything more than he knew already. In fact, he told me that Bohemond was definitely besieging Larissa and that this was almost certainly where we would be heading. 'The Emperor cannot allow the Normans to take Larissa', he said. 'If they do, they will be able to march south and threaten Athens, or Corinth or Thebes, while the Emperor will be unable to relieve them. All of Hellas might be lost. No, you have to march against him. And soon, I guess. There are rumours that Larissa won't hold out much longer.'

I didn't ask how he knew all this. I assumed he had his sources among his business contacts. But we talked of other things and then I followed him to his horse and he rode off with his guards. But first, he made me promise to come to Thessaloniki as soon as possible and to bring my family. His wife wanted to 'feast her eyes on 'a beautiful mother, and yet more beautiful daughter', as the ancient poet had put it'. I promised, but wondered when I would be able to fulfil my promise. And then I went off to my tent to sleep. I needed it.

The next day, it seemed that the whole camp had acquired a new purpose. I don't know how it came about – I certainly said nothing – but all of a sudden it seemed everybody knew that we were marching to Larissa.

Knowing where we were heading did not speed up the advance. Bohemond may have been at Larissa, but that did not mean that he couldn't move from there and surprise us. So we continued to march carefully, setting proper camps each night and striking camp in the morning. In spite of that, and the marching and the guard duty, there was seemingly always time to talk – and to grumble. Most of the grumbling was about boredom and about the work. Why could we not simply march to where Bohemond was, beat him and go home? And how far off was actually this place Larissa that everyone said we were marching towards? Why did we have to build elaborate camps every evening instead of just pitching tents and sleeping in them? Or just sleep in the fields? And why was the food so bad? Once again, I remembered my own attitude when we were marching towards Dyrrachion. That was only two years ago and by then I had been a Guardsman for almost ten years. A year ago, these men had not even heard of the Varangian Guard a year and despite their training the last few months, they were still not proper soldiers. So I found myself trying to repeat some of the answers Godric had given me about the need to be careful on the march and to preserve the army. Also, that we couldn't fly to Larissa, so the only way to get there was by foot. As for the food, I pointed out that there was usually a market set up wherever we stopped and that anyone could buy whatever food they wanted.

That didn't help. It turned out that the food available was the wrong food. It didn't taste like proper food. Everything tasted rancid. At least I knew what they meant by that. I thought of telling them that in a short while they would find food that did not have the sharp taste of garum bland, but I realised that they would not believe me. Then some of them were unused to dealing with money and Roman coins were strange. But by now I was getting more than a little annoyed.

'If you have problems with the coins, just ask the other Guardsmen. There are enough of them who know what each is worth. We are pitching camp every night because we are a Roman army, not a rabble! Do you know where the enemy is, so that you can guarantee that we won't get attacked at night! And if you have so much time to complain, you obviously have too much time on your hands. Erik?'

'Yes Komes.' I hadn't known exactly where he was, but had just assumed that he was in the vicinity. In fact, it turned out he was standing just behind me.

'These men need some work. Give them something to do.'

'Yes Komes.' His voice sounded unnaturally mild. But he was not very mild with the complainers. I understood that they had spent a considerable time cleaning up the camp latrines and that by the time they were finished, they were too exhausted to do anything but fall asleep. At which point he had 'volunteered' them for extra guard duty.

The grumbling made me realise two things. Well, not the grumbling in itself. All soldiers grumble. Always. It can be very satisfying to grumble, particularly if there is nothing you can do about the reasons for grumbling. No, it was two other points. First, that although I had tried to train my bandon, I had failed in one significant way. I had brought them over with the idea of recruiting an English force that eventually would go back to England and get rid of the Normans. But that had meant that I had had been too lenient with them. Also, I had not made them Roman enough. I still intended to go back to England. But that was for the future. For now, they had to be made to feel part of a Roman army. Otherwise they would not feel any kinship with the rest of the army. And if we lost again, there would be no Englishmen to lead back to England. Second, that Erik was wasted as a dekarch. I had already realised that he must have commanded more than ten soldiers for his cousin the King of Denmark. Now I had a chat with him and – in spite of his objections – arranged for him to be promoted to pentekontarch.

CHAPTER 13

Larissa

As we began to approach Larissa – it is in Thessaly, north of Greece – I started noticing more differences with the march to Dyrrachion. There were more scouts covering our march, for one thing. For another, our pace through the mountains of Thessaly slowed down. Not quite to a crawl, but near enough. It was almost as if we were trying to find out exactly where Bohemond was, so that we could make sure of being somewhere else. Everyone in the army was clearly aware that whenever we had met the Normans in the open field, we had been beaten, usually quite badly.

But that impression changed once we made contact with the Normans. There were reports of skirmishes between our scouts and theirs. It seemed that we did not lose all those encounters and that in itself helped everybody feel better. Now, when we were ordered to prepare for battle, at least we did not feel beaten already before the battle began.

But it turned out that things were not quite so simple. For although most of the army was told to prepare for battle, we were not. I had assumed that the Guard would be in the van again, when Nampites sent a runner over to me and Oleg to come to him at once. When we came over to him, he wasted little time.

'You two and all your men are not taking part in the battle.' He held up his hand to stop our questions. 'You are on special duty – with the Emperor. You will find out more later. But you are to get horses for your banda – mounted duty today.'

It took a moment for his words to sink in. Then I looked back to be sure before I turned to him again. 'What kind of special duty? And why do you say with the Emperor? I can see the Imperial banners in the centre. If we are with the Emperor, shouldn't we be there?' Oleg was nodding vigorously.

'You will go as ordered. I don't even know where you are going. But I can tell you this. The Emperor is not in the van, whatever the Imperial banners say. Also, you are not going to be alone. And finally, you were specially asked for. And there is no time to lose, so hurry up. Report to the Imperial tent at once.' And with that we were dismissed as he turned to give further orders to other Kometes.

Both Oleg and I realised that we weren't going to get any more answers out of Nampites – if in fact he even knew them – and also that an Imperial summons to hurry at the eve of battle meant that you run. Fortunately, the Emperor's tent was not far away. When we arrived, there was quite a crowd there. The Emperor's brothers, of course, including the Protosebastos Adrianos, who smiled briefly at me before turning away. Was that why we (or I) had been specially picked for whatever was happening? There were other senior commanders there, and also some who were more on our level, including the commanders of the Immortals, another guards unit that consisted of heavy cavalry. We joined him to one side, while the emperor was continuing to address the other commanders.

'Last night, Saint Demetrios appeared to me and said, 'Cease tormenting yourself and grieve not; on the morrow you will win.' I have prayed to the blessed Saint and vowed that if it is granted to me to conquer the enemies of Rome, I will visit his shrine in

Thessaloniki. I will dismount outside the city and walk in slowly and on foot to pay homage to the Saint.'

As he spoke, I touched the icon of Saint Demetrios that Irene had given me and that always hung around my neck, inside my tunic. The carved bone felt smooth to touch, but strangely, it also felt wet. I hadn't noticed that before. It wasn't water or sweat, more oily, but not really greasy either.

But before I could think more about that, I heard that the Emperor was talking about the forthcoming battle.

'Is everything clear?' he asked. 'Nikeforos Melissenos and Basil Kurtikios will command the Roman host. You will fly the Imperial standards to make the Kelts believe that I am with you. Advance against their forces with banners flying, trumpets blowing and with loud war-cries; but as soon as you are getting to close quarters with them, break ranks and flee like Parthians towards Lykostomion.'

As he said that, suddenly there was a loud noise from the outside, as if all the horses of the army were neighing in agreement. When the Emperor heard that, he laughed and said, ‘At least the horses understand.’ At which everyone laughed and the meeting broke up.

We remained, together with the Immortal officers. The Emperor now called us over and explained what we were going to do.

‘Three times we have met the Kelts on the field of battle’, he began. ‘Three times they have defeated the Romans. This time, we are doing something different. While the battle is joined, we will teach this Bohemond a lesson in how the Romans really fight.’

As he explained further what we were going to do, I suddenly felt much more cheerful. I wished Godric had been there to see me agree that this was indeed the way we should fight the Normans. As soon as the Emperor had finished, we disappeared to get our men ready. In the evening, just before sunset, we formed up, 200 Varangians and the Immortals, all mounted. But there was a real difference between us and the Immortals. We were on small horses that were supposed to take us from one place to another. The Immortals’ horses were almost as heavily armoured as their riders and were big warhorses, to be used in battle. Then we marched out, the Emperor leading us. We were only a small force, but we all felt that the presence of the Emperor was worth more than a thousand Norman knights. Finally, we would begin to get our revenge.

Although it was already nightfall, it was clear that the emperor and his guides knew exactly where we were headed. We rode quietly through a defile, passed a stream and through a village that seemed almost deserted. At last we came to a dry riverbed where we were told to dismount and stay quiet until we got new instructions.

It was not the most pleasant night of my life. It wasn't very cold, but wearing armour is not particularly warm, nor is it very comfortable to sleep in. And although we were told to be quiet, it isn't very easy for a troop of hundreds of mail-clad soldiers and their horses to keep really quiet. Also, we were eager for dawn to arrive, since that would bring battle – hopefully on our terms for a change. So, while no doubt most of us did manage to snatch some sleep, it was fitful and not very relaxing.

It felt as if it took longer than usual for the sun to rise, but eventually there was a smell of a morning wind and soon after that a thin grey light began to seep in from the east. Whispered commands to wake up but keep extra quiet were passed along the ranks. That is not easy either, since the first thing you do when you wake up is to stretch, and look over your weapons. But the Emperor seemed quite calm, staring fixedly at the ground. However, soon after sunrise we began hearing battle sounds. The Emperor beckoned to an officer of the Immortals and after a quick conversation, the man came back and sent one of his men up ahead to a small hill where he presumably could see what was going on. I think we all would have liked to be that Immortal – lying and just hearing the sounds without knowing what was happening was making all of us tense up.

We remained like this for some time – maybe another hour or so, while the sun was rising. The sounds of the battle had increased at first, but were now beginning to die down – or possibly move off into the distance. Everyone was looking towards the scout. Suddenly he began to crawl back down the hillside and then came running towards the Emperor. As soon he had reported, the Emperor stood up and signalled to the rest of us to do the same. Then he called the officers to him – the commanders of the Immortals and Oleg and me.

'Now my children', he began. 'You have your orders and you know what to do. Remember – destroy all, but no looting. Make sure your men keep their discipline' (this was to Oleg and me). 'Their Emperor will not fail to reward them.'

Each of us returned to our troops and told the men to mount. We formed up, Immortals in the lead, followed by the Emperor with the Varangians. Then we set off, first at a walk and then at a trot. Finally we rounded a hill and saw the Norman camp. It was guarded – but we came from the opposite side, not from the side closest to the ongoing battle and most guards had moved up towards the front of the camp to try to see what was happening on the distant battlefield. There were a few who saw us and who tried to shout an alarm. But their voices could not be heard. On a sign from the Emperor, two buglers sounded the charge and we went from trot to gallop.

The few guards that tried to stand against us outside the camp were scattered by the Immortals' charge and then we all burst into the camp. In contrast to a Roman camp, it was not fortified – just a mass of tents and lean-tos with cooking fires, weapons stands and enclosures for horses and baggage animals. The Immortals began by riding straight through the camp and attacking the guards on the other side, while the Varangians began to spread out in the camp, cutting down tents and setting fire to them. I had been given orders to stay close to the Emperor, and had told Erik to stick by me with half his 50 men. But the Emperor was just as keen as we were to take part in the battle and stormed ahead of us into the camp. He still had his larger horse, which was much faster than our much smaller mounts. Once within the camp, however, horse speed mattered less and we caught up with him. He was fighting a Norman who had had time to mount his horse, but even as we reached them, the Norman fell with most of his head gone. Other Normans were running around in the camp, trying to make a stand wherever they could. Two of them came towards us, armed with spears. I managed to cut off the spear with my sword and then rode down the man who had wielded it, leaving someone else to finish him off as I turned to his companion. He was stabbing at my horse and at the same time trying to stay out of range of my sword. For a brief moment – which seemed like hours – we continued this strange dance of a man against a man and a horse. I even had time to think how ironic it was that I was the horseman, facing a Norman foot-soldier. Usually it was the other way around.

That thought gave me an idea. If they could practice a ruse, so could I. As he pulled back his sword for another stab, I suddenly turned my horse around and began to flee. He gave a hoarse shout and begun to run after me. But after two or three steps, I suddenly turned around and spurred my horse towards him. As I had guessed, he had come to close to ward me off with his spear. I think he realised it too, for he dropped the spear. But instead of drawing his knife – it was only now that I saw that he didn't have a sword – he just held up his hands as if to protect his face or ask for mercy. If it was the latter, I was in no mood to grant it. I hacked at his left arm with the sword and when the pain made him drop it, I stabbed him in the face, below the nose-guard.

I marvel when I read these words. The time it has taken me to write them is far longer than the time the entire event actually took. Truly the Holy Scripture says that there is a time for everything.

When I turned around from the dead soldier, I saw that I was still close to the Emperor. There had been similar fights going on around us, but these were now ending – usually with a dead Norman, sometimes with a Guardsman on the ground. Somewhat further off I could see horsemen coming towards us and I moved closer to the Emperor, as did the other Guardsmen nearby.

We needn't have worried. As the horsemen came closer, we could see that it was some of the Immortals. When they had approached, the Emperor quickly gave a signal and the Recall sounded. As the Guardsmen assembled, together with such Immortals as were within earshot, we were given new orders. Most of the Guardsmen were told to dismount and start destroying the camp – along with Bohemond's store of supplies – in earnest. Everything that could not be killed or destroyed was burnt. Meanwhile, I was told to follow the Emperor and the Immortals out of the camp, towards the battlefield.

As we moved out of the burning camp, the Emperor called over one of the Immortals officers. ‘Send orders to George Pyrrhos’, he said. Tell him to take peltasts and pursue the Kelts. Make sure they aim their arrows at the horses, not at the men.’

Then we continued riding towards Larissa. From time to time we could see messengers riding up to the Emperor with news of the battle. It was impossible to see whether this was good or bad – but at least on our side we had for once been successful against the Normans. And it seemed that the lessons were not only about how to fight. Erik suddenly burst out laughing and moved closer to me.

‘What’s the joke?’

‘I was listening to some of your countrymen. They talked of the battle. I do not think you will ever hear them ask why we fortify our camps. Now all we need is to make them like the food and they will be proper soldiers.’

Well, well, I thought. So it was not only the Romans that could learn something from fighting.

Even my raw English recruits were picking up valuable lessons. And not only them, by the way; after all, I had suddenly thought of fighting like a Norman in the camp. It was nice to know that not all lessons were learnt in defeat.

But not everyone seemed to be able to learn their lessons. As we came closer and were within sight of Larissa, we suddenly saw a line of Norman soldiers on the ridge above the town. And we also saw something else, a line of Roman knights already advancing up the hill. 'Oh, the fools!' I heard the Emperor exclaim. Then he called to an Immortal officer. 'Stop them! You must call them back!'

The officer saluted and rode off. But his horse was clearly tired and he could barely get it to gallop. It was clear that even riding uphill, the attacking Romans would outpace him. And so it proved.

All we could do was watch how the Romans advanced up the hill. And how they were swept away by the Normans charging downhill at them, before they turned back and retreated up the hill and beyond the crest.

But even with this reverse, it had still been a good day. Even better, while we had taken some wounds, none of the English was killed. Once we were back at the camp and had returned our horses, cleaned up our gear and started to prepare food, Erik and some of the other English sat with me outside our tent.

'What do you think of your first battle?' I asked.

'This was nothing', Wilfred replied. 'Is this the best the Normans can do?' Others nodded in agreement. Edgar, his brother, added 'I don't understand why we were afraid of them in England. They must have been lucky to win at Hastings.'

'Yes', someone else chimed in. 'Or else Harold was just a bad general. Can I have some more of the stew? And some of that fish sauce as well? This is delicious.'

Erik and I looked at each other and burst out laughing. The others just looked at us. They probably thought that we were mad. But I wanted to take advantage of the moment to drive home some lessons.

'Harold was not a bad general', I said. 'I fought at Hastings. We were unlucky – but William was a better general. We let ourselves be defeated. Here as well the Normans have won. The beat us at Dyrrachion. I was there too.'

'Maybe you bring bad luck' Wilfred suggested, laughing.

'Maybe. But Bohemond has beaten the Emperor twice large battles in the past two years, and won other victories against the Roman armies.'

'They didn't have us then', Edgar broke in.

'No, they didn't.' I was going to remind them of Kastoria, but stopped and thought for a while. Right now, they were all cock-a-hoop with their success. They had won a victory and an almost bloodless one at that. I wanted to tell them that one victory would not win the war for them. But did I really want to dampen their spirits again? Would they fight better if they thought they could always win? Or if they thought they were bound to lose? I prayed to Saint Demetrios and hoped that I was doing the right thing.

'You are right', I said. 'They didn't have us then. And God made them vain and arrogant and today he chose an army of Englishmen to show them the error of their ways. It is a good sign for the future. But make sure that you do not fall in the same trap. We have won a battle. But don't expect Bohemond to run back to Italy just yet. He may need some more chastisement first.'

'Good. I know just who will provide it.' Wilfred again.

Afterwards, Erik came up to me. 'You did not tell them about Kastoria. Very good. They will find out soon enough that Normans are not so easy to beat.'

'Yes. But I prefer them to go into battle believing that they can win, rather than fearing that they will lose.'

'I thought you would react stronger when he said Harold had been a bad general. I never knew you fought at Hastings. How was it, really?'

I thought for a moment.

'How was it really? It was more than fifteen years ago, for one thing. I was 14 – not an age when you are a very good judge of generals and their craft. A few years ago, I would have reacted much more strongly. But today? I don't know. Looking back, maybe Harold was a bad general after all. He didn't have to fight.'

Erik looked surprised and nodded to make me go on. I didn't know how come I had never told him about Hastings. I suppose I had always assumed he knew I was there.

'Like I said, Harold probably didn't have to fight. We had just fought a large battle in the north, defeating the king's brother Tostig and his Norwegian ally king Harald…'

'I know. Harald Hårdråde. He too had been in the Guard, did you know that?'

'Oh yes, I was told of him when I came here. Anyway, while we fought the Norwegians, the Bastard William landed in southern England, so we marched down as fast as we could to deal with him there. As soon as we reached Hastings, we offered battle. And we lost, as you know.'

'Yes. But why did you lose? And why did you say that Harold need not have fought?'

'We lost, because we were tired and because we let the shield wall be broken. I don't know if we could have withstood the Norman archers, but once the shield wall broke up we didn't stand a chance. Just like at Dyrrachion.'

I paused.

'But as for Harold needing to fight – I don't know. Looking back, I suppose we were all eager to get to grips with the Normans. And Harold hadn't been King for very long, so he probably felt the need to show leadership. But now I wonder if we shouldn't have waited to gather more troops from other parts of the country. We could have waited. Held William at bay but refused battle. He wouldn't have dared to move far from where he landed, since he had no other way of getting supplies or reinforcements of his own. And Harold's fleet could have stopped some of those. Then we could have offered battle when we were rested and reinforced and they were tired and hungry. It could have turned out differently.'

As I was talking, I realised that I had never really thought back to Hastings like this. Previously, it had always been a battle which we fought and lost and that was that. I don't know what suddenly made me look at it differently. Maybe it was because we had finally beaten the Normans – and we had done it, not by fighting on their terms, but on ours, in a way that suited us and not them.

Throughout this story, Erik had listened intently. Now he looked at me, smiled and said ‘Maybe. But then we would not have met and fought together. And you would not have met your wife. So maybe it’s all to the good. Meanwhile, what will happen now?’

‘I don’t know.’ I thought for a while. ‘I wish there was a church around here somewhere. I would like to hear Mass and give thanks to Saint Demetrios.’

‘Mass is said daily and hourly in the camp’

‘Yes. But I prefer a church. Never mind. You asked what will happen. I don’t know. But I think that having won a battle, the Emperor will be wary of losing the next one. I doubt if we will fight soon again. My guess is that he will try to avoid battles, cut off Bohemond’s supplies and probably buy some more Norman nobles with Roman gold. And you and I will get some more time to turn our English hotheads into proper soldiers – even if now they do like the food.’

If we had hoped for some rest after the battle, we were disappointed. One day was spent cleaning up equipment and reorganising units that had suffered casualties. But the very next day we were hot on Bohemond's heels again. He had retreated some distance from Larissa, but not very far. His new camp was next to a marsh on a plain that the locals called the Palace of Domenikos. There were two hills between us and them and a gap between the hills. We drew up on our side of the gap, with Bohemond on the other side.

At first, nothing much seemed to happen. Then we could hear noise coming out of the gap and some of our infantry – mainly lightly armed peltasts and other archers were advancing.

'What are they doing?' muttered Alf.

Before I had time to answer, Erik – who was Alf's commander – replied. 'They are trying to make Bohemond come to us. The archers will try to break his formation and force him to advance and then we will catch him between the two hills.'

'Well, why isn't he coming?'

'Because he knows that we want him to. Now be quiet!'

In truth, we were all wondering and waiting to see what would happen. But Erik was right. It would certainly be better for us to catch Bohemond on a narrow front between the hills, ideally with our archers on the hillsides. But if Bohemond had let himself be fooled the previous day, he was certainly not stupid. His shield-wall would be as good as ours, and he would make sure it didn't break up without good cause. Personally, much as I wanted to defeat the Normans, today I was happy for our archers to rain death on them. They would already be upset by our victory yesterday. This would irritate them further.

For some time, we stood there, waiting for Bohemond to move out – or not. But eventually I noticed that one officer after another came up to our commander – not the Emperor this day, but the Protostrator Michael Doukas, his brother-in-law – to argue with him. I was too far away to hear what was going on, but I could see that they looked angry when they left him, as did he.

A short period later, Erik nudged my arm and pointed out something. 'Look. Our horsemen are moving into the gap.'

He was right. I could see a trickle of Roman knights moving towards the hills and into the gap between them. The Protostrator had already seen them and sent messengers to call them back. But nothing happened except that more knights advanced. The Protostrator spoke a few words with some of his officers. Then he sent of a few messengers. At the same time, the banners signalled for the cavalry to advance.

I was waiting for our signal as well, but a messenger had now reached Nampites, who listened to him and then called the Kometes to him.

'Hold the line. We are not taking part in the advance.'

'Why not?' Oleg asked.

'The original battle plan was for no advance. But the Protostrator can't hold the horsemen back. They are all eager to repeat yesterday's victory. So rather than fritter them away, he is trying to establish a new line. Meanwhile, we are to stand fast in case the

Normans break through. The rest of the footsoldiers are also holding here. Pass the word to all your men. And make sure that they do not move unless ordered!'

We were lucky that day. Twice lucky, in fact. First, that we did not take part in the charge. Because it turned out that as soon as Bohemond saw the mass of Roman horsemen entering the pass between the hills – in other words, getting into exactly the position they had tried to force him to move to – he charged them. Our brave knights, so eager to defeat the Normans, turned as one and fled, with the Normans hot on their heels.

The second lucky break was pure chance and I didn't find out until much later what had happened. All we could see was that all of a sudden, the Norman advance wavered and hesitated. A gap was opening up between the fleeing Romans and the pursuing Normans, who were slowing down. Then, for some reason, they turned and streamed back towards their original position. On our side, meanwhile, the Protostrator Michael was restoring our line. I was glad that we had not moved – I could imagine that he had some strong words to say to those commanders who had started the advance.

Later we found out how come the Normans had stopped their pursuit. It turned out that one of our Turkish soldiers had managed to kill Bohemond's standard-bearer. In the confusion, he had then grabbed the standard, waved it around and pointed it backwards. The Normans who saw it didn't know that the standard-bearer was dead. Instead, they must have thought it was an order from Bohemond to break off the pursuit. Once our line was restored, it was they who were more at risk, so they marched back and eventually left the battlefield.

CHAPTER 14

Mirroring God

After the battles, we remained for a day or two outside Larissa. We were told that Bohemond had retreated towards the west, to a town called Trikala. I assumed that we would pursue him as soon as we had rested for a day, repaired our equipment and reorganised units that had suffered losses. It was still early enough in the summer to see if we could find another opportunity to hurt him.

But the second day after the battle, there was a surprise. Erik and I were sitting in front of our tent, guard duty done, when someone came up to us.

'Hello Englishman. Had enough of fighting for a while?'

'Richard! How are you? Did you fight in any of the battles?'

It was indeed Richard of Matera, whom I had last seen about a year ago in Constantinopolis.

'I am well, thank you. And yes, I did fight. But we had rather the worst of it. The laurels of Larissa mainly belong to those who destroyed Bohemond's camp with the Emperor. The rest of us did what we usually do – practised our running.'

By then I knew that in addition to the encounter at the Palace of Domenikos, where we had at least kept the battlefield, the various skirmishes around Larissa had generally been won by the Normans. That hadn't stopped us from proclaiming a great victory. No doubt that was the story told in all the cities of the Empire. But those of us who were with the army would talk to each other and we knew that although we had had some success – not only destroying the camp, but also in defeating half of Bohemond's army when their horses were brought down by our archers – honours had been much more even.

'I see you managed to run fast.'

'Indeed. But at least I am alive. As is most of our army, this time. But although I am pleased to see you, I did not come by only to pass the time of day. We have work to do.'

'We?'

'You and I. Time to pay a few more visits to my Norman friends and kinsmen.'

‘Not again. I thought we had managed to stir up quite a hornet’s nest in Italy last time. Surely they are not going to let us travel around the country once again and bribe rebels?!’

‘You make it sound so crude. Show our generosity. Or rather, show the Emperor’s generosity, which, after all, mirrors that of God to mankind. But I fear you are right. Going to Italy with Guiscard himself around and on the loose would be a little too risky. Do not worry, however. We are not going to Italy. Instead, we are going to pay a visit to Bohemond’s camp. Or rather, to what’s left of it.’

In fact, I had not been thinking so much about he dangers awaiting us in Italy, as about the dangers of another sea-crossing. I had already done it once, after Dyrrachion. That had been in the winter, but I doubted that the seasons made much difference, and would prefer not to have to find out. But once the thought of seasickness disappeared, the dangers did make themselves felt as well.

‘We stroll into his camp just like that?’

‘Just like that. A parley. A visit to some of my kinsmen. We need to discuss terms, maybe be able to cease fighting. And, if meanwhile I happen to remind them of the fact that Bohemond is not paying them the money he has promised them for fighting, well, that is really something for them to deal with, isn't it?'

I must say that I was beginning to admire Richard of Matera. There must have been plenty of Normans who were ready to kill him on sight now. But here he was, ready to stroll into the lion's den again as if he had no worries at all. Still, I wasn't to keen too come along. For one thing, I now had to look after my bandon of English guardsmen.

But when I began to voice my objections, Richard cut me off. 'Save your breath, Edmund. I asked for you because we worked well together in Italy. You will have your orders tomorrow, but I thought I'd come by and let you know first. You might as well make the best of it, because you are coming. Now, do you have any better food than that stew you are eating and paximadi? Well, I do.'

And at that he whistled and two servants came up, bearing not only food – roast chickens, cheese and olives and rather better bread than the paximadi barley biscuits – but also a nice wine. With a grand gesture, he invited Erik and me to share his dinner.

The food was a far cry from what I would have been served by my father-in-law. But here in camp, it was certainly better than our normal rations. We passed a quite pleasant evening, mainly talking about the past but not at all about the future. While we talked I noticed that something had changed with Richard and how he treated me. He still called me 'Englishman' from time to time, but it was less mocking. But it wasn't only that. When we had travelled through Italy together, it was clear that he was in charge and I was his subordinate. But now, it was clear that he treated me much more as an equal. Whether it was because of my new rank, or because of our shared adventures or for some other reason, I didn't know. But it certainly made it easier to get along with him.

He also treated Erik with considerable respect, so we spent a very pleasant evening. I still didn't trust Richard. He was very clearly still pursuing his own interests above anything else. But, on the other hand, that did not necessarily mean that his actions were a threat to the Empire. After all, my father-in-law – or other merchants or tradesmen for that matter – did not provide the world with his fabrics and other wares out of the goodness of his heart. He wanted to make money – and did so. But the result was that the Romans were better dressed or had more food to eat and so on. Richard would work for himself, but in doing so, he would help the Empire. And that was all that mattered to me right then.

I should not have drunk as much wine as I did. If I had been on regular duty, I would almost certainly have been disciplined. Fortunately, of course, I was not. Erik – whose capacity to cope with wine seemed even to exceed his capacity for women, took over command of my bandon, while I set off to find Richard.

He also seemed rather the worse for wear, at least as far as I could see in the morning light. It didn't help that it as warm, which is always worse for hangovers than cold. As we began to ride off I asked him how we would gain entry to the Norman camp.

'Oh, there are envoys going back and forth constantly between the Normans and the Emperor.

The important thing is knowing who to see – and who not to see. Oh, and that reminds me. Here, take these.' He gave me two or three sealed parchments.

'Make sure you drop them.'

'Surely you mean, make sure I don't drop them? And what are they?'

'No, I mean exactly what I say. Make sure you drop them. But only in the Norman camp. And try not to be too obvious about it.'

'But what are they?'

'They are letters from the Emperor to various Norman counts, confirming that he is agreeing to their terms for defecting from Bohemond – estates in Asia or Greece, sums of money, Imperial titles and so on.'

'But surely, if I drop these in the Norman camp, won't Bohemond find… Wait a moment. You said the Emperor is agreeing to their terms for changing sides. Are they actually changing sides?'

'These particular ones? Not that I know of. But Bohemond doesn't know either. And he is more likely to think they will change sides – even more so after we have had a few talks with other of his leading subordinates.'

'I thought there might be something like that. So when and where do you want me to drop these letters? Any particular spot? In front of Bohemond? In his tent, perhaps?'

He laughed. 'If you get to his tent, you are welcome to drop them there. But I doubt we'll get as far. Just see to it that they are dropped – and that they will be found.'

As we rode off, the camp was beginning to stir around us. It was going to be a fine autumn day. It was still early enough in the autumn, barely September. I began to wonder if we really would let Bohemond off the hook for the rest of the year. When I asked Richard, he seemed surprised at the question.

'Don't they ever tell you anything? The reason we have set off today is because we are in a hurry. The Emperor has returned to the army. They will probably follow us within a day or two. We need to work fast this time. No more leisurely travel. There are 36 miles to Trikala as the eagle flies, and I would like to have at least a day or two to work with.'

‘I think I should have gotten a better horse.’

‘I think so too. But you have what you have. Now, pay attention.’

He paused to take a long drink from a wineskin he was carrying and then passed it to me. This was a different wine from the one we had drunk the night before. It was more resinated and also clearly mixed with quite a lot of water. But it was refreshing.

‘Last time we did this, your role was to say nothing, watch my back and play the part of the English noble who doesn’t like Norman rulers. This time, we will try for something different. Let me see.’

He thought for a while.

‘I think you had best remain an English noble. But this time, you have come to serve the Emperor because you were attracted by his generosity. I think we may have to tell them about your Anatolian estate and your palace in Constantinopolis.’

‘My what?’

‘You do know what a palace is, don’t you?’ It seemed that he was returning to his old self, the condescending one. But I would humour him this time.

'Yes, I believe so. But I wouldn't really call my house that – nice though it is.'

'No matter. Can you describe a palace so that it feels as if you really live there?'

'Oh yes.' That would be easy. My father-in-law's house in Thessaloniki was palatial enough. I could certainly describe that to anyone.

'Good. We may leave your Anatolian estate for the moment, but be prepared in case it becomes necessary to talk about that one too. Mention the hunting. Normans like hunting.'

'As long as I don't have to mention the names of the servants or how many daughters the paroikoi have. And I'd rather not have to invite any of Bohemond's counts to visit the estate, if I can avoid it.'

That made him laugh. 'There may be some who would like to know the daughters of your farmers – and how old they are. But I think we can leave that aside. And I'll remember not to issue any invitations for hunting.'

As we rode on, Richard was telling me more about what he hoped to achieve. But he was also telling me more about himself than he had done in Italy. Once again, he seemed to be treating me much more like an equal than he had done in Italy.

I began to understand more about him. He was still mainly concerned with his own future and the return of his Italian estates. But I no longer believed that he was likely to betray me – or the Emperor. I still remembered the Sangarios River and how we had been betrayed by the Normans there. But on the other hand, Richard had fought loyally against Bohemond, as had other Normans in Imperial service. Also, were not my own plans similar to his? He wanted to reclaim a place of honour in his own country, but to do so he had to return it to what it had been. I wanted to return my country to my own people, but in order to do so I had to serve a foreign ruler, while building up an army of my own people.

Even as I thought this, I began to wonder. If the Emperor was foreign, how come I was thinking all this in Greek, rather than in English? In fact, apart from when speaking with the English Varangians, when did I nowadays either speak or even think in English? My daughter did not even speak the language, because I had never tried to teach her. This would change, as soon as I came back to Constantinopolis. There were English priests serving in the Church of St Nicholas. I would start taking Dora there and see if one of them could teach her English. Thinking of churches made me wonder if there was a church to Saint Demetrios in England. Maybe I could build one when I returned?

Thinking of the Saint made me touch the icon of him that I wore around my neck. Once again, it felt moist. I was going to take it out to find out why, when I noticed that Richard was speaking to me again.

'What? I am sorry, I was thinking about something else.'

'Clearly. Never mind. Do you want to tell me?'

'Not really. No offence, but it was personal.'

He didn't say anything more and for a while we rode on in silence. So far, the going was easy. We rode along the Via Egnatia, the ancient road from Constantinopolis to Dyrrachion. This was the same route that the army had taken on the march to the battle. That was almost exactly three years ago and I tried to see if I could recognise any part of the road.

But mostly I was thinking about how different things had seemed then. Eventually, I was content just to ride and enjoy the countryside. If I hadn't known that we were in the middle of a war and that I was on what could turn out to be quite a dangerous mission, it would have seemed like a late summer ride. The leaves were still green, and although it was hot, the sun was occasionally hidden by clouds which cast a pleasant shade. All of a sudden, I felt really carefree.

This didn't last long. Suddenly I felt a hand grip my left arm. It startled me and my other hand flew to my sword. But as I realised that it was only Richard, I stopped myself.

'What is the matter?'

'I should ask you that', he replied, with a strange look at me. 'You were singing away as if you were a county boy on his way to his lover. Are you all right?'

Had I been singing? I hadn't noticed, but I suppose it was possible. It would certainly explain why Richard had looked so puzzled.

'I am fine. Really. I didn't realise that I was singing.'

'Are you sure? Did you get hit on the head at Larissa or something? You seem very strange.'

'No, I didn't get hit on the head. Or anywhere else, for that matter. And I am truly fine. I'll stop singing if you want me to.'

'Please.' But in spite of my protestations, Richard continued to look strangely at me from time to time.

In this fashion – but without any more singing on my part – we continued to ride through the Greek countryside. Occasionally we rode through small towns, sometimes showing traces of the war, more likely farms, some of them burnt down and looted. We had to exercise some care to make sure that we were not attacked by Norman stragglers or by local bandits. The ride was not very long. Richard was constantly fretting about our need for speed. But my horse really was not such that we could make much faster progress than we already were doing, it did not take us more than two days to approach Trikala. Once there, Bohemond's camp was not difficult to find, by a wood on the north side of the town.

The camp was large, larger than I had thought it would be. It was a reminder that although we had won a skirmish, we were far from having won the war. Bohemond and his Normans were still dangerous opponents. But a large camp also meant that we could move around without arousing much suspicion. At least I hoped so. Of course, it also helped that this camp was not fortified either.

In fact, once we had entered the camp, no one paid us any attention at all. If this had been a Roman camp, we would not even have been let without explaining our business. And we would then have had an escort to make sure that we actually did what we were supposed to do.

As we were slowly making our way around the camp, leading our horses, Richard was looking around, presumably trying to find someone he knew. I was looking around as well, trying to avoid anyone I knew.

Suddenly Richard called out to a younger Norman, standing outside a tent. 'Ranulf! Over here!'

The man looked around and when he saw Richard, his face changed several times. First he smiled, then he looked worried, then angry and finally he smiled again.

'Uncle Richard. You look well. Would you like to have a drink?' And he held open the flap of his tent.

We tethered our horses outside the young man's – Ranulf – tent and entered. Once inside, he turned to Richard again and embraced him.

'How are you, Uncle? And how dare you set foot in our camp? Bohemond will have you killed if he catches you. And not only he. Geoffrey of Scalea is in camp. I think he is upset with you.'

'I would have thought so', Richard answered. 'He thought he had me in his net, but in vain the net is spread in the sight of any bird, as the priests would tell us. I burned down part of his estate.'

'Yes. Don't we all know it. He wants compensation from Peter and me. Not that he is getting it, of course. But I don't think you should let him catch you again.'

'I will do my best. Meanwhile, how is Peter? Is he with you?'

'He is. I will send someone for him at once. But who is your friend?'

I had been standing to one side, looking around the tent. It was much smaller than the one I had visited before Dyrrachion with the Protosebastos Adrianos. But it was still bigger than I would expect for one man unless he was important. Ranulf was wearing expensive-looking clothes and the grip of his sword was inlaid with gold. He looked as if he was about ten years younger than Richard – maybe 25 years old or so.

Richard turned around.

'This', he said 'is my friend Edmund. He is an Englishman. I will tell you more about him anon. First, however, do send someone for Peter. And can you think of anyone else who might be interested in hearing a message of reason? And who will not be seized by the urge to hand over your uncle to Geoffrey of Scalea?'

Ranulf laughed. 'Are you still up to your intrigues? But I won't deny that people are getting less enchanted with Bohemond by the day. I am sure I can find a few. How many do you want?'

‘Not too many.’ Richard thought for a moment. ‘Another two or at most three in addition to yourself and Peter.’

As Ranulf stepped outside the tent, Richard turned to me. ‘My nephew Ranulf. Peter is his brother. I am not sure that they will listen to me, but at least they won’t give me away. Now we will have to see.’

Ranulf returned inside the tent. He pulled a chest to the middle of the tent, put some camp chairs around it and invited us to sit. He was just pouring out some wine, when the tent flap opened again and someone stepped in. I only had to look at him to know that it must be Peter. He looked like a copy of his brother, only two or three years younger. He and Richard embraced each other and for a few minutes they were all speaking at the same time. Richard was asking about various people – friends or family, I supposed – and his nephews were asking about him. I realised that they did not ask about any family in Constantinopolis, though whether that was because he didn’t have any, or because they didn’t know, I had no idea.

Soon enough, more people were drifting into the tent. Once three more had arrived, Ranulf held up one hand to ask for quiet.

'Comrades. This is our Uncle Richard of Matera. You may have heard of him – if nothing else from Geoffrey of Scalea.' Two of the others laughed. Ranulf continued. 'He says he wants to speak with us. I am asking you to listen to him with an open mind.'

The others turned and looked at Richard – and at me – and then sat down. I looked back at them. They were all roughly of an age with Ranulf, all of them clearly of the same rank – nobles, but not the very highest. Then Richard cleared his throat.

'Thank you for coming', he began. 'And thank you for listening. I don't have much to say. I am a man of few words.' That was news to me!

'You have now been fighting against the Emperor of the Romans for two years. When you came, you were told that the Empire was yours for the taking – a ripe fruit that would fall into your hands if you only as much as shook the tree. Wealth and estates would be yours for the asking. Well, here you are. What you have had out of this war so far.

Money? Hardly. Land? Not an inch. Oh, you have defeated the Emperor, not only once but many times. You have become famous. The Emperor himself speaks with respect of the Normans. But haven't you noticed that however many battles you win, victory seems ever further from your grasp. Win a battle – there is another one a few months later. Destroy an Imperial army – the Emperor easily raises a new one.

'Meanwhile, your lands in Italy are being ravaged by the Germans – or even by Guiscard, who sees rebels everywhere he looks and is always happy to increase his own lands at the expense of someone else's.

'How many battles do you think you can win? Did not Larissa show you that the Romans are learning to beat you? And all this so that Guiscard and his son can set themselves up to rule over you!'

'What are you suggesting? That we betray our Duke?' This was one of the other young men asking.

'Not at all. But you should first ask yourself if your Duke has kept his faith with you. As I said, where are your spoils of war? In fact, let me ask something else. Who is paying for your fighting? You were promised pay – but are you not yourselves having to pay for everything?'

I could see the five young men nodding. Richard continued.

'I repeat, the Emperor respects you. He is upset by this fighting between Christians, at a time when Christians are being pressed by the Saracens and Turks within a few days' ride of Constantinopolis. The Emperor would much rather use his armies for the benefit of Christendom. But he must also protect those whom God has put in his charge against the greed of Bohemond.'

'That is easy for him to say.' This was from the same young man. 'But you are still asking us to betray our Duke.'

'Absolutely not. This is what the Emperor proposes. Go to Bohemond. Tell him that you wish to receive the pay that has been promised you for more than three years of fighting. If he cannot pay you himself, ask him to go to his father and procure the money from him. If he is true to you, you should remain true to him. Neither the Emperor, nor I, would want you to break your oath.

'But: If Bohemond cannot pay you, has he not broken his oath to you? Then he is the faithless one. If you then decide that you do not wish to continue to fight in order to raise a faithless man and his father to the Imperial throne, the true Emperor will reward you.'

At this, Ranulf and Peter and two of the other three looked at each other and nodded. Peter asked, 'How?'

'It depends on what you wish to do. If you wish to join the Romans and fight for the True Faith, you shall have honour, wealth and estates. You will be enrolled in the Roman army and you yourself can decide your rewards. If, on the other hand, you would prefer to return home to your own lands, passage will be arranged for you through Hungary.'

'You say that we will be rewarded by the Emperor. How do we know that this is true? And what kind of rewards? It is easy for you to talk about wealth and estates, but what does this really mean?'

'Ask my friend. This is Edmund. He is the son of an English Earl. He left England because he did not want to live under a Norman Duke made King.'

'Who would?' one of the others muttered.

'He came to Constantinopolis more than ten years ago to seek service with the Romans. The Emperor was so pleased to have him, that he was granted an estate in Anatolia, a palace in Constantinopolis itself and was given the tile of Spatharokandidatos, one of the highest ranks in the Emperor's own guard. He is a close friend to the Emperor's brother. You can ask him yourselves.'

The five turned and looked at me. By now I was used to Richard's way of inflating my importance; and he had told me what he was going to say. But it still came as a surprise to hear myself described more or less as a foreign prince, treating with the Emperor as an equal. And I felt slightly uneasy at having to lie to them.

Finally, Ranulf spoke. 'Is this true?'

'Your uncle likes to exaggerate', I replied. 'My father was by no means King Harold's most powerful Earl.' That was certainly true. 'And I am not sure if I would call my house in Constantinopolis a palace. But it certainly is bigger and more comfortable than what I had in England.' Let them interpret that how they wanted.

'What about the rest? Do you really know the Emperor's brother? Have you met the Emperor at all?'

'I certainly know the Protosebastos Adrianos Komnenos.' They all stared blankly. 'The Emperor's brother. But don't take my word for it. Even Bohemond can confirm this. As for the Emperor, which one do you mean? But I can tell you that I have fought shoulder to shoulder both with the previous Emperor, Nikeforos, and with our current Kyr Alexios.'

This seemed to satisfy them. But then another one spoke. 'What do you mean when you say that Bohemond knows that you know the Emperor's brother? Do you know Bohemond as well?'

'We have met. I accompanied the Protosebastos Adrianos in his embassy to your Duke on the eve of the battle at Dyrrachion.' Guarded would have been truer, but would not have sounded as good. But I had not expected the reaction to my words. The five started to laugh. As I looked at them, my surprise must have been obvious – as was Richard's, by the way. Finally, Peter decided to explain.

'Are you the one with the strong hand? The Varangian? Everyone knows that story.'

It took me a few seconds to remember what he was talking about. But he continued, still laughing. 'Bohemond doesn't like to hear this. It seems that you almost broke his arm the day before the battle. The Duke was not happy with him either, because he had behaved stupidly in front of the Greek ambassadors.'

This seemed very much an exaggeration of what had happened in Robert Guiscard's tent that night. But if Bohemond and the Normans wanted to remember it this way, then who was I to enlighten them?

Now Richard took the opportunity to speak again.

'All of you. You have heard what the Emperor offers you. Let me repeat, no-one is suggesting that you betray either Bohemond or your Duke. But you can demand what is rightfully yours. If they do not give it to you, they are the ones betraying you and you are free to decide your own future.'

'How will we let you know?'

'I will be in touch with you. For now –'

But at this moment, we were interrupted. A servant came in and addressed Ranulf.

'Domine, there is a rumour in the camp that you are hosting enemies. Geoffrey of Scalea is coming with a party of his men.'

'I think', Richard said, 'that this is a good time for us to leave. Can I ask one thing more of you, Ranulf?'

'Anything.'

'Edmund's horse is not very fast. We may need some speed. Will you lend him one of yours?'

'Give him, you mean?'

'I am sure you will be amply recompensed. But it is urgent.'

'Don't worry. You', this to the servant – 'bring the brown mare. Saddle it with Kyr Edmund's gear and prepare my uncle's horse as well. Hurry up and let us know as soon as it is done.'

'At once, Domine.'

Kyr Edmund – that had a rather nice ring to it. My mother-in-law would certainly benefit from hearing it.

We waited inside the tent for a short while, which seemed to last forever. Finally, the servant reappeared. 'Both horses are ready, Domine. But Geoffrey and his men are almost outside.'

'Not a moment to lose then', Richard noted. 'Farewell nephews and you others. Think of what we have said.'

And with that we stepped outside the tent. Both horses were indeed waiting for us. The brown mare was a magnificent mount – a true warhorse. I had never ridden anything as powerful. As we sat up, a small group of men rounded a corner – Geoffrey of Scalea foremost among them.

'You there!' he shouted. 'Who are you? Stop there at once!'

I didn't answer or look at them. But Richard gave a cheerful wave and called out to them. 'No time. Maybe some other day.'

'Richard! Stop them! They are enemies. Get horses!'

Geoffrey was shouting more. Richard and I were already riding away and picking up speed. But the shouting attracted other men who came running. I doubt if they knew what they were doing or what the shouting was about, but the mere fact that we were trying to ride out of the camp must have seemed suspicious. As we approached the outskirts of the camp, one man got close enough to grab my saddle bag. I didn't stop to think but drew my knife and cut of the rope tying the bag to my saddle. The Norman soldier fell back and Richard and I managed to get away again. Once we were clear of the camp, we spurred our horses and set off.

As it turned out, there was no pursuit, at least nothing that we saw. After an hour or so, we stopped and dismounted to let the horses rest a little, though we continued to walk along the road. Suddenly Richard turned to me.

'You lost your saddle bag.'

'Yes. But there was nothing really valuable in it. Only some letters – and I rather think they are beginning to reach their intended recipients now.'

We both laughed.

'Well done, Edmund. An excellent day's work. I will be sure to let Nampites know – and the Protosebastos Adrianos.'

'Do you really know him?'

'Oh yes. I fought under his command at Larissa. And he does remember you. Occasionally asks about you. He will be happy with our work and, more importantly, so will the Emperor. Let us just hope that it leads to something. But I am quite confident. Quite confident indeed.'

CHAPTER 15

Kastoria

We did not encounter any adventures on the ride back. But nor did we encounter the Roman army until we had already passed Larissa. Nor was it following Bohemond towards Trikala, but marching northeastwards, back towards Thessaloniki.

Once we reached the army, Richard and I went our separate ways. But this time it was a considerably friendlier parting than the first time in Italy. I made him promise to come and visit us in Constantinopolis and he assured me that we would meet again.

Then I reported back to Nampites, who told me to go and take over command of my bandon from Erik. Before I went, I tried to find out what was happening and why the army was not pursuing Bohemond.

'We are. He broke camp and left Trikala just after you got away. Our scouts tell us that he is marching to Kastoria, where he has a strong garrison.' And with that I was dismissed.

As the army marched northwards again, I found out two more things. First, the Emperor was not with us. He had gone back to Constantinopolis. Second, Bohemond turned out not to be in Kastoria at all. He had turned towards the coast with part of his army, while the rest continued to march to Kastoria. By the time we knew this, the army had already reached Thessaloniki. Although we were unlikely to remain there for long, I took the opportunity to go off and visit my parents-in-law. But first I went to the church of Saint Demetrios to give thanks to the saint. True, I had not been in any major battle. But I was nevertheless grateful to him for looking after me. And it never harmed to show proper respect to God when you did not need Him or His Saints.

When I was announced to Georgios he came out to meet me himself, beaming.

'Edmond. Welcome. As Odysseus returns to Ithaka after ten years, so you return to our home after a long absence. It is true that they say that one man, by delaying, put the state to rights for us. You have, perchance, your thousands slain? Or even, like the son of Jesse, your ten thousands? But, as the poet says, I strive to be brief, and I become obscure. Come, let us go inside and my wife, smiling through her tears, will her news of her beloved daughter and granddaughter.'

As ever, Georgios managed to confuse me with his literary allusions. I was sure that there were at least three in that brief welcome, but there may well have been more. But his feelings were genuine, and my mother-in-law, the stately Eudokia, also seemed pleased to see me. Runners were sent for Theodora, who arrived – heavily pregnant – with her husband, a merchant colleague of my father-in-law, and their daughter Irene.

Over a sumptuous meal of excellent tuna, sucking pig, white bread, a soufflé and a fantastically-smelling smoked sausage with a taste of cumin, pepper, parsley and even fish, with a white wine that Richard would have been singing about for days, I proceeded to tell them of my adventures. Georgios was very anxious to hear what I thought about the possibilities for peace, as was my brother-in-law, Thomas. He seemed a pleasant man, very considerate towards his wife. I had only met him once – at his wedding – so I only knew what Irene had told me about him. He was a wine merchant, and his main business was buying wine from Italy and selling on to Constantinopolis. So he too was hoping for a quick end to the war.

All the time that I was talking, my mother-in-law kept looking at me with a peculiar look in her face. I couldn't make out what it was. When I had finished, she said, 'Are these all the news you have?'

I was none the wiser. 'Yes. Is it not enough?'

'Do you not, then, feel that there is anything else you have to tell me? About my daughter, perhaps?'

I couldn't understand what she was talking about. I had started by telling them everything about Irene and Dora and how they were when I last saw them. Finally, my sister-in-law took pity on me.

'Mother. Can't you see that he doesn't know? Don't torture him like this.'

'But a husband should know', she sniffed. 'Still, I dare say that the Kelts do things differently.'

'Is anything wrong with Irene?' I almost shouted, rising from my chair. What was this woman going on about?

It was Georgios who replied. 'Nothing wrong. But clearly you have not heard from your wife. It seems that Theodora is not the only one who is increasing our family. Irene, too, is with child.'

Irene pregnant again! I was stunned. There was, of course, no reason why she wouldn't be. We certainly had not let the grass grow under our feet when I had been in Constantinopolis. But it must have happened towards the end of my stay there, because nothing had been visible and she had not suffered from any morning sickness before the army marched out. This was wonderful news! I was so taken aback that I embraced my mother-in-law. She was taken aback too, but put up with it, while Theodora and her husband embraced me and slapped my back respectively.

I am afraid that I was rather drunk when I wandered back to the camp late that evening. Things were not improved by my meeting Erik. When he had stopped laughing, he asked what was going on.

'I am going to be a father!' I exclaimed.

'Edmund, I have news for you. You already are a father. Remember Dora?'

‘No, no. You don’t understand. I am going to be a father again!’

‘That is wonderful!’ We must drink to the health of the unborn child. This time, it will be a son – strong and lusty. I shall teach him to fight like a Dane – none of this weakling English or Greek nonsense! But first – a drink!’

And so we moved off to continue to drink, this time the mead that was one of Erik’s many favourite drinks.

The next morning, after we had been mustered and received our orders of the day, Nampites took me aside.

‘If you ever appear again in this state, Edmund, I shall have some of my countrymen carve the blood eagle on your back. Is that understood?’

‘Yes, Akolothous’ I mumbled.

‘Good. You can celebrate your child’s birth when it has happened and you are off duty. Now go back to your soldiers, and never let me see you like this again. You are lucky to keep your rank!’

How on earth did he know about Irene’s pregnancy?

I had picked a bad evening to drink. That day we were given orders to march as rapidly as possibly towards Kastoria. This was a new type of campaign. When we marched towards Larissa, security and watchfulness had constantly shadowed our steps. We had taken every care not to be surprised by the Normans. But on the march to Kastoria we were always told to speed up and move faster. Oh, we still built a proper camp every night. But we were pushed to keep the speed up to 12 miles every day, which meant that the nights were shorter.

When we reached Kastoria, we understood why. The city is on a cliff at the end of a promontory that juts out into a lake. That makes it easy to defend. But it is also easy to cut off. As soon as we arrived, this is what we were ordered to do. We built a wooden palisade that stretched across the peninsula. Then our siege machines were set up and began to pound the Normans inside it.

Sieges are the most boring parts of a soldier's life. At least, that was what I thought after Kastoria. And at that, it wasn't a particularly long siege. But veterans of other sieges told me that it's everywhere the same and later I would realise that they were right.

First, there is the excitement when you reach the place to be besieged. You race to cut it off, making sure that you don't leave any opening where reinforcements or supplies can slip in or the besieged slip out. But once you have done that, all you do is sit around and wait. To be sure, there is guard duty – guarding against an attack by reinforcements or a sally from inside the siege. But all too often, all that happens is a long period of boredom, while your siege machines hammer the walls and houses of the city or fortress under siege. Mind you, it cannot be too long, because although they may be starving inside, you are also finishing your supplies outside, so it's a race who can last longest. Then finally, there is a breach and you storm the place and the battle is over because you won. Or because you lost.

As I said, Kastoria was a short siege. I think the Emperor was in a hurry to take the place before Bohemond could come to its rescue. That suited us fine. Kastoria was important to us – especially so for the English Varangians. After all, this was where 300 of our countrymen had surrendered to Bohemond two years earlier. By now I had told all my new recruits about this and that this was where we had to redeem English honour.

In any case, it didn't take long before breaches opened in the city walls. Nobody was surprised when we were told that there would be an assault the next day – and that we were to lead it.

The next morning the siege machines were still throwing stones at the walls to keep the Normans from manning them as we began to advance. As we came closer, I touched my icon of Saint Demetrios for luck.

For some time as we advanced, we couldn't see any defenders. The walls were high, but there were two or three large breaches in them where the stones had tumbled down and formed a kind of rampart leading into the city. In any case, even the highest and strongest walls cannot defend a city without the soldiers to man them.

As we got closer, however, the siege engines had to stop, for fear of hitting us. Almost as soon as they stopped, banners were raised on the towers and trumpets sounded and soon the walls were bristling with soldiers. We did not halt, of course, but continued on, each man glancing at the ones next to him to make sure that the ranks were kept straight and close. But once we reached the breaches, the lines could not be kept as men stumbled on loose stones or fell down and had to get up again.

We started to clamber up among the fallen stones and mortar, towards the breach. But now the Normans began to strike back. Storms of arrows whistled down on us. This was where I lost the first of my English recruits. Wilfred, so eager to give Bohemond the lesson he deserved, was grazed by an arrow in the cheek. As he looked up to see what had happened, another one hit him in the mouth and he fell down and rolled to the bottom of the hill. He was not the only one, but most of us were protected by our armour and continued to climb. As we came closer to the actual breach, we began to shout and run forward. Now we were too close for the Norman archers. Instead, we came face to face with the soldiers. At least they were not on horseback. But they were above us and this gave them an advantage when they rushed down. One was coming straight at me, pointing a spear. I tried to jump aside but he was too fast and the spear struck straight at my chest. The force of the thrust was so strong that it pushed the rings of my chainmail back, but the spear stopped before it broke through the mail and he dropped it. I grabbed my axe in one hand and tugged the spear out with the other. I barely had time to do that before the Norman jumped me. He didn't have a sword, but he was trying to stab me with a knife. I managed to roll round and get on top of him. I dropped my axe to grab his arm. Then I punched him in the face with my other hand. He spat blood and shouted at me as I punched him again. He tried to grab my free arm and we rolled around again. Now he was on top, but I managed to throw him over my head. He landed with a thud and for a brief moment he didn't move. That was enough for me to manage to get my own knife out and stab him in the throat. I got up again, looked around for my axe, found it and began to look around. I had slipped down from the top of the wall, but I could see fighting going on in the breach and began to run up again.

As I reached the top, I plunged into a knot of men fighting at close quarters. One of them was a tall Varangian. It was Erik, trying to hold off three Normans, with his back to a large stone. I managed to get closer to them and swung my axe into the back of one of the Normans. There was a crunching sound as the axe bit into his shoulder and he fell, dropping his sword and screaming. As I turned to another of the Normans, Erik's sword broke the third man's shield and he began to move away. Then Edgar came up with another group of Varangians and we killed the two Normans. There was a brief pause and then we looked around to see what was happening. There were still small knots of fighting man inside the breach. But now there were far more Normans than Romans. Even as we stood there, we were rushed by another group of Normans. They may only have been eight or nine – but two of them were on horseback. We barely had time to form a line when they hit us. The line held, but another of my Varangians died here. Then there were more Normans coming from the city and without knowing that we were doing it, we began to move down the slope again. The

Normans didn't pursue. Instead, they stood back. I knew what it meant.

'Watch out!' I shouted, as arrows began to rain down on us again. Those who had shields held them up, the rest of us tried to take cover beneath them. But our choices were limited. Either we advanced again – or we retreated out of range from the archers. We probably didn't even think about it. If we had looked around, we would have seen other Romans retreating. We didn't see them – but we did the same. Another Varangian died before we reached the foot of the walls and could get out of range.

Finally, we managed to get back to our camp. We had survived. But we had taken bad losses. I could see the medical corpsmen going round the battlefield, carrying those who were only wounded back to the camp to be treated. The Normans let them do it. I suppose they kept their arrows for the next assault, instead of wasting them on the physicians. Also, the assault on Kastoria had failed. At least I was alive. And I had found out why. After the battle, as I was stripping off my uniform, I found why the Norman spear had not gone further in. It had actually broken some of the rings in my chain mail. But then it got stuck in the icon of Saint Demetrios that I was carrying around my neck. The armour must have broken the force of the thrust, because otherwise it would easily have broken the icon as well. But even so, it felt like a miracle. There was a crack in the icon now, by the saint's spear and I ran my finger across it. Once again, the icon felt moist and cold. I kept meaning to ask someone about this, but always forgot.

In the end, Kastoria did not hold out for long. Two days later there was another attack on the walls. This time it was supported by an assault from the lake. The Norman commander would have fought even now, but even as we approached, there a small troop of riders came out from the city and asked to be conducted to the Emperor.

I happened to be guarding the Imperial tent, where they were taken. To my surprise, two of them were Richard's nephews, Ranulf and Peter. Maybe I shouldn't have been surprised. The Emperor received them outside the tent. After some preliminaries, they came straight to the point.

‘We will no longer fight for someone who has broken faith with us’, they said. ‘We wish to stop the shedding of Christian blood. We beg Your Sacred Majesty to put up two standards. One by the Church of Saint George. Those of us who wish to serve under Your Majesty will go to the standard by the Church. The other standard should be on the road to Avlona. Those who wish to return to our own county will stand by that standard. But everyone shall first take an oath not to take up arms against the Emperor of the Romans.’

‘And your commander?’ the Emperor asked.

‘He will return to our own country, but he too will take the oath.’

And with that, the Battle of Kastoria was over. The Emperor distributed large sums of money, both to those Norman leaders who enrolled under the Imperial banner and to those who went home. Both Ranulf and Peter stayed – I saw them later that day together with Richard.

CHAPTER 16

Bohemond

After the battle, the Emperor returned to Constantinopolis. I had hoped to return with him. But this was not to be. Nampites informed me that I and my bandon were one of the units that would stay behind to continue the fighting.

'Why us?' I asked.

'The army doesn't have enough soldiers to let you go home. Your bandon needs the experience. And it will teach you to remain sober until the war is over!'

That was unfair! I was not the only one who had ever been drunk – even Nampites himself, like his Swedish countrymen, could out-drink most Greeks and frequently did so.

We knew that Bohemond had taken his part of the army back towards the coast, to the city of Avlona. This was in a bay, quite a bit south of Dyrrachion. But although his army was weakened, we were not looking for a battle this time. First, because the Emperor had taken the greater part of our army with him back to the city. Then winter was approaching. But most importantly, because by now I think we all new that this was not the way to defeat Bohemond.

The winter also meant that we moved much slower. For a change, we were all – Varangians and others – mounted. But sitting on a horse, while comfortable, doesn't really mean that you move fast. For one thing, unless there is forage available, the horses have to carry fodder, so they are more heavily laden. In the winter, there is less forage, so that was one strike against us. Of course, you could have pack horses, but they also need fodder, so there comes a point when you need more pack horses simply to provide the pack horses with fodder. Also, the greater your numbers, the slower you move.

So I was not particularly surprised when we eventually split up and moved in smaller groups of a few hundred men. Our task was not particularly difficult. We were to cut off Norman stragglers if possible, but above all to make sure that no supplies reached Bohemond's camps. Oh, he could be supplied from the sea. But there weren't many skippers who would brave the winter storms and if any did, we had been told that there would be Venetian ships patrolling the straits to catch them.

By now it was getting really cold. There was quite a lot of snow on the ground, which made it slippery for the horses. Even though we were wearing thick tunics under our armour the cold made the iron feel icy cold. The only one who seemed unconcerned was Erik. 'This is nothing. In Denmark, this would be a mild winter. And in Sweden, they would think this is the height of summer. In any case, if you are cold, think of a girl and being in her arms. That will make you warm.'

It certainly seemed to work for him. But even for Erik, finding girls in was difficult in the mountains. Not that he had much time for that anyway.

We moved towards Avlona as swiftly as we could. At first, we did not encounter many Normans. There was the odd straggler, who might have been a deserter or who might really be lost. There was never any fight. A lone man or two, suddenly finding themselves surrounded by a dozen or a score of horsemen will think long before he fights. Even longer if he is hungry and tired. If they were nobles, we gave them the choice of serving the Emperor or of going home. In either case, they were disarmed and given an escort of two or three men to take them back to Constantinopolis or to a Roman port where they could sail home. Common soldiers were disarmed and kept under guard for the next time we came to a Roman fortress.

When we came closer to Avlona and began to come down from the mountains, two things happened. First, it got – very slightly – warmer. Second, there was suddenly more to do. Bohemond was still encamped close to Avlona, but some Normans we captured said that he was getting ready to move back to Italy as soon as there were enough ships ready to take him and his army. Until then, his army needed to be fed and Avlona was not going to do it on its own. So there were constant movements of supplies towards his camp. Sometimes it was carts driven by farmers pressed into service; sometimes herds of animals seized from surrounding farms. We managed to stop most of them.

How we did it would vary. Sometimes we would work with other Roman cavalry. Since their horses usually were better and faster than ours, we developed tactics using both. For instance, a large troop of mounted Varangians would appear in the distance where a convoy of cars were being driven along the road. There would always be Normans guarding and escorting the carts. When they saw us approach, they would form up and ride towards us to drive us off. We would continue to advance until they began to charge us properly. Then we would begin to waver and eventually turn to flee, the Normans in hot pursuit. As soon as they were far enough from their charges, the Romans horsemen would appear from another direction, storm down on the cars, kill the Norman footsoldiers who were guarding them, get the drivers to run off and set fire to the carts. Other times we would gather a larger troop and attack a herd of sheep or pigs. This time we would engage the guards ourselves. But since we were far greater in numbers than they, we would manage to kill a few and drive the rest off. Then we would drive the animals away towards the forest and disperse them. I suppose we should have tried to return them to the farmers who had lost them. But how could we have known who it was? And in any case, we did not have enough soldiers to spare going around playing nursemaids to a bunch of sheep or pigs. If we were hungry, we ate some of them, but that was it. I knew there were going to be a lot of hungry farms this winter. But that was the price they would have to pay for avoiding Norman rule. I knew I would not hesitate to pay it.

It wasn't entirely one way, though. Sometimes the Normans would not fall for our trick of the pretended retreat. Sometimes, the number of Normans guarding a line of carts would be too large for us.

By now we were already getting closer to the Norman camp. In addition to the supply transports, there had also been some skirmishes with patrols sent out from the camp, although so far, I and my soldiers had not been involved in any of those. Now we were following a group of Normans driving a flock of sheep along a road. There were only three horsemen and another five guards on foot, so we were quite a small troop as well, fifteen all told. I had left Erik in command of the rest of the bandon, who were stalking a larger prey.

The road was passing through a forest and we were following them as silently as we could on the north side. Not that they could have heard us. They were quite loud, both sheep and humans, with at least the humans looking forward to getting safely into the camp. As we approached the middle of the wood, I judged that we should attack. We couldn't afford to get to near to the camp so that the sound of the fighting alerted them. I swung my horse towards the road and saw the others do the same. Then I raised my arm and we all shouted 'Edward! Edward!' – the battle-cry I had chosen for my English soldiers – and charged the Normans.

The Normans reacted sluggishly, I thought. At first, they looked around, trying to guess where the sound came from. That was soon clear enough, as we crashed through the underbrush. They formed a line between us and the sheep, but didn't try to advance. It didn't make much difference. Within moments we were upon them. My sword was already out. I made straight for one of the mounted Normans. He parried my thrust with his sword. But he couldn't attack me in turn because at the same moment, Oswy was hacking at him from his left. The other two mounted Normans were already down. One was not moving, the other was up so I realised his horse must have been hurt or killed. I barely noticed this, because I was busy with my own foe. He had managed to deflect Oswy's charge and was turning to me instead. We traded blows for a few moments but we were slowly pushing him back. When I took advantage of one of Oswy's attacks to look around, I could see that the fight was all but over. Some of the Normans were down, the rest were beginning to edge away. My own men were splitting up in groups and beginning to herd the sheep away.

When something moved on my left and as I turned around I saw a line of Norman knights almost exploding through the forest, shouting 'St Michael!' at the top of their voices. I had no idea how many of them there were, because, all of a sudden, my own opponent turned to attack me and pressed me hard. It seemed like an eternity, but it was probably only a few seconds before the Norman reinforcements were upon us. I tried to see what was happening, but by now I had three attackers around me. I hacked wildly in all directions with my sword. Once I hit an arm and its owner shouted as he dropped his own sword. But his place was taken by someone else. I tried to back off, but my horse was rearing and waving its front legs. As it came down, it suddenly shuddered and screamed and fell. I couldn't get away and was trapped underneath him. The sounds of the fighting continued, but very shortly they began to die away. As I struggled to get away from my horse, I could see horses coming back. Then someone grabbed me from behind and cut off my helmet. A dagger was held at my throat.

'Stop struggling and you will live. Do you yield?'

I could have wept, but all I did was nod.

'Good. Get him out from under that horse and bring all the prisoners.'

Three men dismounted and dragged the horse away from men. Then they pulled me none too gently to my feet and took my sword and dagger, before they tied my arms. Now I could look around and see what had happened. The first thing my eyes fell on was Oswy, lying on the ground. Poor Oswy! He had been with me ever since I first came to Constantinopolis. Now he was dead, far from England. Another two or three Varangians were also clearly dead, and there were four of us alive – prisoners. I was the only unwounded one. But unless some more of my men had been killed as they fled, this meant that at least some had escaped. That was good to know.

What was less good was that we were obviously not the only ones who learned from our mistakes. The Normans had clearly picked up how to fight our new tactics. This had been a well-planned ambush, from the small escort accompanying the sheep, to the slow retreat when we originally attacked. I could admire it – but I also wished that they hadn't been quite so quick to learn.

'Mount the prisoners. Humphrey, you stay with your men and bring in the sheep. The rest, with me.' This was the Norman commander. We were put back on our horses – or in my case, on somebody else's – and taken in tow.

As we slowly rode back to camp, I began to wonder what was going to happen to us. The Normans were unlikely to be amassing prisoners – not least because they could barely feed themselves, if the rumours were right, much less prisoners. They might be hoping to exchange us for some of their own men that we had taken. But at least they did not seem to want to kill us. If that had been their wish, we would already be dead. In spite of the humiliation of being taken prisoner, I felt that things could have been much worse. No doubt Saint Demetrios would come through and save us. But I did not quite see how.

After about two hours, we approached the Norman camp. This was right by the see. Once again, I was struck by the difference between this and a Roman camp. Oh, there were some fortifications and guards this time – another lesson they had learned – but it was still haphazardly laid out. And much, much dirtier than a Roman camp would have been.

But it wasn't only that. The men looked different. While I had lost this fight, it was clear that our attempts to stop supplies from getting to the Normans were working. The soldiers looked hungry. And given that it was winter, there were far fewer fires lit than there should have been. Some of them were apparently breaking camp as well. I wondered where they were moving to.

As we approached the centre of the camp, a small group of Normans crossed our path. One of them was a tall fellow, with lank hair, wearing shoddy armour and who looked emaciated, almost like a scarecrow. I thought I recognised him and wondered if he had been one of the ones Richard and I had seen in Italy. Then our guards stopped at a sign from their commander.

'Lord Bohemond', he said. The scarecrow turned towards us. I could barely believe it. THIS was Bohemond? The previous time I had seen him, he had been well dressed, wearing expensive armour. But, above all, well fed. This time, his face looked as if the burdens of the entire world were weighing down his shoulders. I knew that he was in his late twenties or at most thirty years old, but now he looked like an old man of forty.

'We have taken some prisoners. What do you wish us to do with them?'

Bohemond looked at us, but it was clear that he was not really interested in what he saw.

'Kill them' he said in a flat voice.

I could not believe it. I could see that our captors were also surprised, but they began tugging at our horses reins again. I had to stop this. But how?

'Bohemond!' I yelled. 'You can't do this!'

He looked up at me. 'Why not?' he said in the same voice.

I shouted back at him. 'Who is this? A Norman count and a war leader? Or a young boy who only knows how to insult ambassadors?'

This got his attention. 'Who are you? Do I know you?' He came closer and peered in my face.

'I am Edmund', I replied. 'I stopped you from doing something stupid once. Now I will do it again.' At least, I thought, I hope that I can do it again.

To my surprise, he began to laugh. 'You?! The Englishman with the strong hand grip? So you have survived as well. And now, pray, tell me why I cannot kill you?'

I didn't know quite what to say. 'Because we have surrendered', I began. 'We were promised our lives.'

'But not for ever. You were probably only promised your lives on the battlefield. Did anyone say that you would have eternal life? I thought not.' Then he stopped and thought for a while. Turning to our captor, he said, 'I don't have time for this. I am leaving for Apulia within the hour. As for the others, do what you wish with them. Once the whole army is onboard, you can let them go, if you want. But for this one, something different.' He paused.

'Take him out of the camp. There is a tall cliff overlooking the sea a short distance south of here. Take him there and hang him over it – by the hand. Let's see how strong his hand really is.' And then he turned and walked off, before I had time to say anything. But even as he walked away, he turned back and came up to me, seizing my hand. 'Good bye, Edmund. I very much doubt that I shall ever see you again.' And then he did disappear. I was too astonished to say a single word.

There was a brief moment of silence. Then the Norman commanding our guard spoke again. ‘You heard Count Bohemond’, he said. ‘You –’ indicating some of his men – ‘take the others away and tie them with the other prisoners. You two, come with me and this prisoner.’

I was still stunned when the two Norman soldiers and their officer began to drag me away. Once we were some distance away, I finally had recovered my senses enough to begin to argue. But the Norman officer cut me short.

‘Save your breath – I daresay you’ll need it. I have no reason to disobey Count Bohemond and I don’t intend to. Now either be quiet or I will have you gagged.’

‘I’ll be quiet’, I muttered. I preferred to not be gagged – although I couldn’t really see what difference it was going to make. As we rode on towards the outskirts of the camp, the Norman began to whistle. I found that really annoying, but decided that it would do no good to say anything.

I hadn’t really taken notice of the time, but it suddenly struck me that we were getting quite far from the camp and there were still no cliffs around. I tried to look back and found that we were almost out of sight from the Norman army. Finally, we began to climb and shortly afterwards we were standing on the top of a cliff overlooking the sea. It wasn't much of a cliff – maybe 10-15 paces down to the sea. I could smell the salt of the water. But as far as I was concerned, it could have been endless.

The whistling Norman now turned to the two soldiers and ordered them to take me down from my horse. Then he walked up to the cliff and peered down. He looked around at some stunted trees that were growing by the cliff-side, and stroked his chin. Eventually, he turned around and came back to us, taking a rope that was hanging from his saddle.

At a word, my two guards brought me up to the cliff. As I looked down, I could see the sea breaking on some very evil-looking rocks.

The Norman now began to unwind his rope. Until now I had not resisted, but I realised that if I didn't do anything, my time would run out. However, as I began to struggle against my guards, the commander drew his sword and put the point under my chin. ‘None of that’, he said. ‘I’d as soon kill you here and now anyway. You –’ pointing at one of his soldiers – ‘tie the rope around his waist and ready to tighten it when I say the word.’

The soldier obeyed as his commander stepped up to me. Then suddenly he shouted ‘Now!’ and struck me a hard blow in my midriff. As the air rushed out of my lungs and I doubled over, the soldier quickly tightened the rope around me. Then they tied one arm behind my back and also tied my legs together. I was beginning to feel like one of the worms that Irene had told me about that eventually produced silk, but first tied themselves up in a cocoon. That made me think about Irene and I missed what the Norman was saying next. He didn’t repeat it, he just grabbed my left arm and began to tie the rope to that Finally, he walked over to one of the bigger trees and tied the rope around its trunk.

I did not let all this pass. But every time I struggled, either he or one of the two soldiers would prick me with a sword or dagger. When he was finally done, he gave another order and the two soldiers began to let me down the cliff. The rope did not go far – maybe four or five paces, or about one-third down the cliff. But that was far enough. Almost the moment I started hanging there, there was a terrifying pain in my arm. I thought it was going to be wrenched out of its socket. Every time my body moved with the wind, there was another wrench. Never in my life had I felt such pain! I really did not think that I could last long. Nor, I think, did the Norman. He leaned over the cliff and said 'I would advise you not to struggle. If you do, the rope may break or come untied. Although come to think of it, maybe that is exactly what you ought to do. In any case, good night. I shall return in the morning – but I don't think that is much comfort to you. I will leave you with some company, though.' And I heard him order the two soldiers to stay and guard me until the morning.

Then he began to whistle again and as he rode off, the whistling grew fainter.

I was in agony! I couldn't even move to try to climb up. Even if I had been able to swing to the cliff, my arm and my legs were tied up so that I would not have been able to do anything. In any case, the two

Norman soldiers left on guard were standing at the top of the cliff. From time to time one of them would come up to the edge and toss a stone down; occasionally they would do it from further away. I don't know if they were trying to hit me or not, but I was getting to a stage where I didn't care about anything except the pain in my arm.

Actually, there was one more thing. Or rather, three. I thought of my family. I thought of Irene and of Dora and realised that I would never see them again. Nor would I see my new son. Damn that Nampites for a Paulician heretic! If it hadn't been for him, I would now be home in Constantinopolis, instead of hanging here. Then I almost burst out laughing – I had cursed Nampites in Greek and using a Greek oath, instead of in English. Did I really not know any more English curses?

But then I thought of Irene again. I could see her face in front of me. It felt as if she was trying to say something. I was trying to understand what it was, but I couldn't hear and the pain in my arm was getting worse. Then suddenly I felt something cool on my chest and Irene's face appeared again. 'Pray', she was saying. ‘Pray to Saint Demetrios of Thessaloniki. He will help you. Pray Edmund.’ I almost thought that I could hear Dora as well, calling ‘Pray, Baba, pray!’

And so I prayed to Saint Demetrios and promised that if, somehow, I was saved from death, I would give money to the monks in the Saint’s cathedral in Thessaloniki to sing an annual mass in remembrance of my salvation. As I prayed, I could feel the cool icon against my chest. Once again, I imagined that it also felt wet. And then I must have fainted.

I don’t know for how long I was out. I had already been dark when I prayed, but then, darkness comes early in the winter. But I knew that I had been roused by a noise of some kind. I was trying to ignore the pain and understand what was going on. Then something fell down beside me and splashed into the sea. It was too big to be a stone, but I hoped the Normans were not getting bored and throwing large rocks down at me.

I heard something. It was a whistle. We must be near the morning, in that case. I must have been out for far longer than I thought. I was amazed that my arm still held.

Suddenly a face looked over the cliff. I couldn't see who it was – it was still too dark – but I could make out a silhouette. For a moment, the Norman looked down at me. Then he said:

'Hello, little friend. How are you feeling?'

I almost fainted again. It was Erik! I had no idea how he came to be there, but I knew that there was no time to lose, not with two Norman soldiers there and more maybe on their way.

'Get me up, you fool! But gently or you'll tear my arm off.'

'Are you sure? You look very peaceful hanging there.'

'Hurry up! There is no time to lose. There are two Norman soldiers around and their commander is coming back soon enough.'

'Don't worry about your guards. They are feeding the fishes. Didn't you notice them passing by on their way down?' So that was what had fallen. I should have guessed that Erik would take care of the guards. But I was still hanging here. 'Hurry up!' I repeated.

Now Erik turned away and called out to someone else. I could hear more men come running. Now that I all of a sudden was not certain of dying after all, I felt tears running down my cheeks. But I wished they would hurry. I had little or no feeling left in my arm except the pain.

Soon things were happening. I could see a man being lowered down the cliff, with a rope around his waist. When he came closer, I saw that it was Grim – the one-time serf. As soon as he was alongside me he called up to the others to shift until he was close enough to grab me around my waist.

'I've got him! Now pull!'

Slowly, the men on the top of the cliff began to pull and drag us up. It took forever, but at last we actually reached the top of the cliff. As soon as we were past the edge, someone cut the rope that tied my arm to the tree. I couldn't stand up but as I lay on the ground, someone else cut the ropes around my legs and around my waist.

'Can you stand?' This was Erik.

'Not yet. Give me some time. And something to drink. What time is it?'

Someone opened my mouth and poured wine down my throat. That made me feel a little better. Meanwhile, Erik was busy rubbing my arm, trying to get the blood flowing again. Someone else answered – Edgar, I think.

'Not late. You have been hanging there for less than an hour. We couldn't come earlier – we had to wait until we were sure there was no one else around except your guards, and dark enough so that we could not be seen.'

'But how come you are here at all?'

'The survivors from your ambush ran into us. We hoped that you had survived and been taken to Bohemond's camp, so we made straight for it. Then we waited outside in hiding and saw you and your escort coming up here. We followed them and waited again.'

By now I was beginning to regain some feeling in my arm. Mainly more pain, but now that was a good thing. I sat up and tried not to feel nauseous.

'How many are you? Is it the whole bandon?'

Now Erik took over. 'Twenty-five. The rest have returned to last night's camp. I didn't think it would help to bring more.'

'You are right. But we have to get away from here. The Norman camp is still too close. They may send someone up here.'

'Oh, I don't think so', Erik replied. 'Most of them are gone anyway.'

'What do you mean gone? Gone where?'

'Back to Italy, I suppose.'

'What are you talking about?'

'Last thing we saw before it got too dark were ships setting sail from the camp. There wasn't much movement in the camp afterwards. I think all those who could have gone on board and sailed back home.'

Now I remembered that Bohemond had spoken about sailing to Apulia within the hour. But if the whole army – or at least most of it – was gone then this was important news. We needed to get it back to the commanders of our own army as quickly as possible.

They had to tie me to the saddle of a horse and Grim kept riding next to me to make sure I did not fall off. But we managed to ride off and after a while I began to feel somewhat more alive. My arm was still in pain, but that was a good sign. Meanwhile, I slowly began to be able to control my legs and eventually I could ride on my own.

It was already well into midday by the time we reached the rest of the bandon at the camp. Erik had apparently given orders to be ready for departure, because the camp was already struck and they were all waiting. When they saw us, they cheered. We stopped there for a brief rest. Before we set off again, I detached two units of ten with extra horses to return to the Norman campsite. They were to observe the camp carefully. If it was abandoned, they were then to try and find whatever Roman or Varangian prisoners that had been kept and bring them back.

The rest of us rode on, up into the mountains and towards Kastoria. But it took us six days to get there, thanks to the cold and the snow and the need to let the horses rest. There we were told that the Grand Domestic who now commanded the army had gone into winter quarters in Thessaloniki, so we continued there after informing the local commander.

It was another six days before we got to Thessaloniki. Once we finally got there, I was feeling normal again – if frozen to the bone – but our horses were much the worse for wear. At last we could report to the army that the Normans had sailed off – only to find that the Grand Domestic already knew. How he knew, I did not know, nor did he see fit to tell me.

We were ordered to proceed back to Constantinopolis the next morning. I should have gone to see my parents-in-law, but I had something more important to do.

I went to the Cathedral of Saint Demetrios. First, I went into the ciborium, the silver-covered roofed structure to the side of the nave. This is not a shrine, because there are no relics. But there is a couch inside, symbolising a tomb. I lay down on the couch first and thought of what I had gone through. Then I went down into the crypt, the site of the Saint's martyrdom and prayed in thanks for my deliverance. I stayed there for a long time after I had finished praying. What a strange year it had been – I had been back in England for the first time in more than ten years. I had fought the Normans numerous times. I had almost died, and would have, but for the Saint's intervention. But most of all I thought of Irene and of Dora. I wondered how big Dora now was and if she still played the colour game. And I thought of my son whom I now would see in a very short time. And then I also once again thought of how strange it was that I was thinking all of this in Greek. When had I last actually prayed or thought or cursed in English?

Before I left the Cathedral, I went to see one of the priests to arrange for the masses I had promised the Saint if he saved me. It was not going to be cheap – but it was certainly well worth it.

CHAPTER 17

My Son

When I returned to the barracks, I was told that there had been a change. We would not ride on to Constantinopolis. Although it was the middle of winter, the Grand Domestic was sending dispatches to the Emperor by sea. There were another two ships going along, and we were to board them and sail back.

I think this was the worst journey I had ever made. The winds were against us all the time and we had to tack back and forth. As a result, it took us almost three weeks to get to Constantinopolis. I spent most of my time by the ship's side being sick. It was so bad that at one stage I almost wished myself back to Avlona, hanging from the tree. There at least it had only been my arm that was hurting. Here, my whole body was in pain. Erik's attempt to 'console' me by spending time next to me and talking about storms he had sailed through and the monsters of the deep he had battled did not make things any better.

When we finally arrived in Constantinopolis, I had once again been away for almost a year. I badly wished to see my family, but, as ever, duty came first. I gathered my bandon – or what remained of it – from the three ships and marched them off to the Guards barracks. Then I went off to report to Nampites.

'You took your time', he growled.

'I am sorry. We kept being delayed. Normans, snow, bad winds. Those sorts of things. I will make greater haste next time.'

'I hope so. Have you learned your lesson about being drunk on duty?'

'Yes, Akolothous. I believe so.'

He smiled briefly. 'Good. Well done. We already knew that the Normans had sailed away. You may like to know that we had retaken Dyrrachion even before Bohemond left. But what you could tell us about his last camp is still interesting. Don't assume that the war is over. The last thing we have heard from Italy is that Duke Robert is defeating his opponents there. Once that is done, he will no doubt be back. Meanwhile, I wonder if you would like to see your family?'

‘Very much.’

‘Off you go, then. You have one week of leave. Dismissed.’

As I walked home through the streets, I could not really believe that I was back at home and safe. Although, as Nampites had made clear, that safety was temporary. We were certainly going to go to war again. But fighting is what soldiers do. The only thing was that I now had an even bigger family to think about.

As I turned into our street, it was already late afternoon and quite dark. The street was empty, but there were lights from some windows that faced outwards. I walked up to our house and stood silently outside for a moment. There were sounds from the other side of the door and a smell – I think of fish cooked in one pot, the monokythron, with cheese and garlic and some sweet wine.

Once again, I felt tears in my eyes. Then I knocked on the door.

It took a while, before I heard steps on the other side of the door. The little peephole in the door was opened and whoever was on the other side looked out.

Then the door was flung open and my wife flew in my arms, covering my face with kisses and crying and laughing at the same time. The kissing was not one-sided. I held her so hard that I thought she would break. Finally, she stopped kissing me and said, 'Let me go, I can't breathe.'

I relaxed my embrace a little, but still kissed her. Then I put her down and looked at her. I started to speak, but she cut me off.

'Oh Edmund! I was so afraid that you were dead. I had a vision of you. It was terrible. You were somewhere by the sea and you were in pain. It was dark. I couldn't see what was happening, but I knew you were in deadly peril. I tried to call out to you, to pray to Saint Demetrios. Dora too – she woke up when I cried out and said she'd had the same dream. What happened?'

My mouth fell open when I heard this. I could barely believe that it was true. But how else could she have known. 'Irene, I heard you', I said. 'I saw you too. Both of you. I heard you tell me to pray and I did. And the Saint did save me. Although he chose a most unlikely intermediary in Erik.'

Then I put her down and looked at her. 'You look well – for a woman who has just given birth!' now it was her turn to gasp. 'How did you know?'

'Your mother told me that you were pregnant. Given how long ago we saw each other, it was bound to have happened. Now let me see my children. Where are my daughter and my son?'

Irene smiled. As we went inside – all of a sudden I realised that we had been standing outside all this time – she called Dora. Who, as it turned out, had been hiding behind the door. Now she too came running into my arms, squealing 'Baba! Baba!' I gathered her up and kissed her and she kissed my face and began to pull at my beard as she had done a year earlier. As I held her up (to free my beard – it was really rather painful) she began to chatter at me. 'Baba! We have a –' 'Baby', Irene interrupted. 'Your father knows. Do you want to show him the baby?'

'Yes. Put me down.' This was said with all the commanding voice of a three-year old. I put her down and she began to run in front of me. She went into our bedroom and stopped in front of a little cot. Inside, there was a little baby fast asleep. What little hair I could see on his head was dark and curly. There were soft noises coming out of his mouth as he snored. He smelled of milk.

'Baba; this is my baby sister Anna.'

A girl! Ever since Erik had talked of a boy I had been so convinced that it would be one that I hadn't even thought of another girl. Damn that Erik and his visions of teaching him how to fight like a Dane.

Irene was watching me all this time. When she looked at my face, she burst out laughing.

'Why were you so sure that it was a boy?'

'It was Erik', I explained. 'He was convinced that it would be a boy and was telling me how he would teach him how to fight and drink and become attractive to girls. And since we already have a girl, I just thought it would be a boy this time.'

She looked a little worried. 'Does it bother you?'

'No. Not at all. Maybe there will be a boy next time. Or another girl. It just takes time to adjust, that's all. But she looks lovely.' And she did. I picked up my baby girl and kissed her gently, careful not to wake her.

'I want to hold her!' This from Dora. I held out the baby to her and she held her – with some help – and kissed her face. Then I put her back in her cot.

'Why call her Anna?' I asked Irene.

'She was born on 1st December. The Empress gave birth to a girl on the same day. She was called Anna. I thought it was a good name and it could be lucky for her to be named after a purple-born. Would you have preferred another name?'

'No, Anna is fine. By the way, I thought I could smell some food being cooked in this house?'

'There is. And I think it is time for our meal. Dora, come with us. It is time to eat.'

'Yes Mama.'

As we sat down to eat, I looked again at my wife and – eldest – daughter and thought to myself how strange it was that I had ended up in this city, so far away from England, and found a family here. That made me remember something.

'Irene, I want Dora to learn English. You too, if you would like to. I will speak with one of the English priests at the Varangian church and see if he can teach you.'

'If you want us to. It is your language. But why now?'

I had never really explained to Irene my dream of leading an English army back to drive out the Normans. Somehow, this did not really seem to be the right moment either. I still did not know how she would take to living in another country. I would have to bring it up someday. But not now, when I was just back. So I just said something about wanting my child to speak my native language and let it go at that.

Instead, I told them about what had happened to me in the war. When I spoke of Bohemond and of knowing him, Irene looked frightened. Apparently, the tales of Bohemond and his cruelty were beginning to circulate and his reputation was getting to be even worse than his father's. I tried to explain that he wasn't actually cruel.

'You like him!' Irene exclaimed. 'He is your enemy and you like him.'

'Well, not really. I mean, I don't like him and if I meet him on he battlefield I will try to kill him. But he does have something that makes you want to like him – or at least respect him. And he didn't kill me, after all.'

'He wanted to. He hoped you would die an agonising death!'

'Maybe. But I didn't – thanks to the two of you and to Saint Demetrios. And to Erik. Also, he didn't kill my men, and that was because he recognised me. So he cannot be all that bad.'

'Humph.' And that was all I could get out of her. Instead, Dora now wanted to hear everything about her cousin Irene. She sat on my lap and told her about Irene and what she was wearing and what she was saying and what her doll had looked like. She kept me talking and repeating everything and then slowly her eyelids began to droop and then her head began to nod and my little daughter was fast asleep in my arms. I held on to her and Irene looked at us with a smile.

'This was a much easier return to her than last time', I said.

'You should only know how much she has been talking about you. Did you know that you are the most important soldier in all the Emperor's armies?

That's what she told a friend a few days ago. And before that, it was how you are the Emperor's best friend.'

'Oh dear. I can see that I will have much to live up to. Do you think that knowing the Emperor's brother will be a good substitute?'

'I am sure it will be. You will have to try. Meanwhile, you said something about a son 'next time'. Did you mean that?'

'Yes, of course. Why do you ask?'

'Because there certainly are not going to be any sons coming as long as you just sit here, husband of mine.' And with those words my wonderful wife stood up and held out her hands to me. I gave her one hand and then carried my daughter to her bed and gently deposited her there. And then we started working on our son.

Afterwards, when we were lying side by side, I suddenly remembered something. 'I have to send some money to Thessaloniki.'

'Why?'

'I promised to endow masses at the Cathedral of Saint Demetrios if the Saint saved me. I spoke to one of the priests, but I need to draw up the deed and send the money. But I don't quite know how.'

Irene turned to me and rested her head on her arm. 'Silly you. As for the deed, we will get a taboullarios to do it. They do this all the time, so that is easy. And as for money, you don't have to send any to Thessaloniki at all.'

'But I promised -'

'Wait. You don't need to send any money. What you will do is go to my father's cousin Loukas. You will give him the money and explain what it is for. He will write to my father and tell him what you have done and that he now owes my father this money. My father will take money he holds belonging to Loukas and go to the priests and give them the money, together with your deed.'

Loukas was the cousin with whom Georgios and his family had been staying when I saved them from the mob so many years ago. I knew Irene was working with him as her father's representative in Constantinopolis. I had met him a few times since. But this I did not quite understand.

'But surely I need to send the money?'

‘Are you not listening? Look here: Loukas holds money in Constantinopolis belonging to my father. My father holds money in Thessaloniki belonging to Loukas. All they need to do is to let each other know if there is any change in the amounts. This is much safer than sending gold or silver.’

‘But you still have to send it elsewhere. To Dyrrachion, say, or Larissa or Nikaia.’

‘Not if they have someone there with whom they do business. Only if there is no one at all. And that is very unusual. If there isn’t, it is usually because they do not trade with that place. Honestly, darling, you may be the most important soldier in all the Emperor’s armies, but I don’t think you know anything about trade.’

‘Well, I know that you do. How is your own business doing?’

‘Very well. There are 34 weavers employed now and I think I have to take on some more. And get more space. I will show you tomorrow.’

That was an expansion. I knew that when I left for the last campaign, there had been less than 25 women working for her. Clearly, although there was a war on, the people of Constantinopolis were still doing well and had money to spend on buying fabrics and clothes.

I leaned over and kissed my wife on the nose. She turned her face up towards me and kissed my mouth instead and embraced me. We decided we had had enough of business and should spend some more time working on our son.

I made the most of my week's leave, spending as much time as I could with my family. Once again, I walked with Dora – but now I sometimes also carried Anna – around in the neighbourhood. We went to the markets and looked at the food sellers and to the harbour where the fishing boats still came in despite the winter. I went to see Georgios' cousin, who assured me that it was absolutely no trouble and who made a careful note of how much money I gave him and what it was for. Irene and I wrote a letter to her father, explaining as well, and paid a taboullarios to draw up the deed for an annual mass. We included that in the letter to Georgios.

And all too soon, my leave was up and I went back to duty. My bandon had shrunk somewhat, and was now down to 80 men. But when I asked Nampites if we should try to bring it up to full strength, he said no.

'Eighty is plenty. You are still a Komes. It's a good idea to have units at different strength. Then an enemy who counts the banners will still not be able to figure out how many we are.'

Over the next few months, as winter turned to spring and then to early summer, I quickly returned to the routine of duties in the capital. Training the men of my bandon was much easier now. They were no longer raw recruits, once they had seen a season of campaigning. But they still had much to learn and if you do not keep training, you soon grow sloppy. Then there was guard duty, at the Great Palace or the Blachernai Palace when the Emperor occasionally moved his family there. Guarding the Emperor or members of the Imperial family on functions, either in one of the churches or in the Hippodrome. Once or twice I guarded the Protosebastos Adrianos, who always greeted me with a kind word for me. Once I was on guard duty when the entire imperial family went to Saint Sophia. This was the first time I had really seen the Empress Irene. But for me, what was more interesting was seeing the Emperor's daughter, the Porphyrogenita Anna. This child, who shared my daughter's name and date of birth. I wondered if it really did mean something. Or were there hundreds of girls born on the same day, all named Anna, whose mothers desperately hoped that this would help them in their future life? Was there any chance of any of them seeing this hope fulfilled?

We also heard from Thessaloniki. Theodora had given birth to a son, who was named Nicholas, apparently after her mother's father. Georgios wrote back saying that he had arranged everything with the Cathedral of Saint Demetrios. I also got a letter from one of the priests there that was so full of mystical allusions that Irene and I gave up and a simply noted it as 'the thank you letter'. It did include a blessing on me and my entire household, which always came in handy.

And whenever I could, I spent time with my family. Once again, Erik became a regular visitor as well. Dora loved him and Irene liked him too. And I think he liked coming away from being a soldier sometimes. Irene kept telling him that he should find himself a wife, and offered to introduce him to any number of her friends. But he kept fending her off. Sometimes he hinted that he was already married in Denmark, which sounded unlikely. At other times, he said that he couldn't marry without his King's permission, since he was the King's kin. Since I knew how little he respected his royal relative, that was not a very plausible reply either.

I did not get involved. Let Irene play at this if she wanted. Erik would find himself a wife if he wanted. Or else he wouldn't. But he would do it on his own, without either Irene or anyone else getting involved.

CHAPTER 18

The Return of Robert Guiscard

As summer approached all sorts of rumours were spreading. Guiscard was dead in Apulia and Bohemond and Roger Borsa and Guy, their brother, were fighting over the inheritance. No, that was not true. Robert Guiscard was still very much alive, but he was caught up in fighting in Rome against the King of the Germans. No, that was also not true. The Germans were defeated and Guiscard was gathering his army to attack the Empire again. No, Guiscard was facing a full rebellion in Apulia, fuelled by Imperial gold. In addition, every rumour fuelled dozens of sub-rumours, all carefully elucidated by beer- or wine-lubricated throats wherever any group of soldiers managed to meet and have a drink.

Whatever the truth of the rumours, however, it was clear that the Emperor was preparing for the worst. There were more soldiers around than ever before, and more war material was being produced and bought.

The Imperial army had changed yet again. For one thing, there were more Turks than before. Godric had once told me that they were not supposed to drink beer or ale, of course, as it was against their faith. But I already knew that they certainly did drink something, because they were clearly capable of getting as drunk as even the Swedish Varangians. I finally asked one of them about this. He replied that their faith only forbade them to drink fermented grapes – that is to say wine – and that he and his friends were drinking mead, made of honey, or beer. But he was quite drunk when he said this and had a large goblet of wine in front of him, so I was not quite sure how much he was joking. Once I also encountered another encountered another group of Turkish soldiers in one of the inns. They made me try one of their drinks, based on fermented dates. It was not bad, but very strong. That night, I slept on a couch in the home. In the morning, Irene did not ask me where I had been, simply commented that my snoring had reminded her of being out in the countryside as a child and watching a farmer drive his pigs to the market.

There were also quite a few more Normans serving with us. These were people like Richard's nephews, who had switched sides at Kastoria; and others who did it in Avlona. I took the opportunity of meeting up with some of them, to try to find out more about our enemies. This was strange to me. After the betrayal of the Normans at the Zompos Bridge, I had sworn never to trust them again. Yet here I was, sitting down with Norman commanders in Imperial service, paying for their wine – or they paying for mine – and talking about past battles as if we had fought on the same side. Of course, sometimes we had – but mostly not.

They told me much about Duke Robert and about his rule in southern Italy. Some of this I already knew. Richard had explained to me how Guiscard had attempted to set himself up as ruler over the other Normans; and how many of those resented it. This was an important difference between the Normans in Italy and the ones in England. When William conquered England, he did so as Duke of Normandy and their unrivalled leader. But the Normans in Italy had never had any single leader. Quite a few of them were convinced that they themselves were called upon to rule. It was true that most of them were ready to accept the leadership of the Hautevilles – Duke Robert's family. But even the Hautevilles were split among themselves as to who of them was the leader. And there were enough other families, including the Princes of Aversa, who did not accept the Hauteville leadership at all, except under duress.

As for Robert Guiscard himself, they said that although a very old man – he was 68 or 69 years old, they though – he was still full of vigour. He had managed to impose a tenuous rule, but at any time this was open to challenge, as we knew. He was also tenacious. Unless he was killed, he would clearly return to attack the Empire. Not a single Norman I spoke to was prepared to consider anything else.

'It is his destiny', one of them told me. 'He will conquer the Roman Empire for himself, and then he will conquer Jerusalem. It has been foretold.'

Then he explained that a soothsayer had told Guiscard that he would not die until he had seen Jerusalem. Since the only way to Jerusalem ran through the Empire, he was convinced that he would vanquish us first. I wasn't too sure of that, but my Norman friend was absolutely convinced that it was true.

'Look', I said, 'I will toss this coin in the air. Can you predict which side it will fall on? I know I can't. How can someone then foretell what Robert Guiscard will or will not manage to do?'

He shook his head.

'Because you are not a true soothsayer. A true soothsayer would be able to call the coin's fall. For you and I, the best thing to do with a coin is to buy more wine.'

So, I bought more wine.

But when I told Irene about this later that night, she was quite shaken. She clearly believed in the prophecy and now she was worried that all of us would be killed by the Normans. I did my best to reassure her that we were not quite dead yet. As I cradled her in my arms, she touched the icon of Saint Demetrios that I was still wearing around my neck and ran her finger along the crack. This suddenly reminded me of something I had meant to ask and always forgotten.

'My icon – it always feels wet. I don't understand why.'

'It's the myron, silly.'

'Don't call me silly. And what is myron?'

'Don't you know? It's a holy oil that comes from the icon. You should take care of it. It can heal wounds.'

'Really? Can it cure a sore throat as well?'

'Don't laugh. Any priest will tell you that the myron of Saint Demetrios has performed lots of miracles. It also smells nice.'

That was true; I had noticed the smell myself, without being sure of where it came from. Whether the myron really could heal wounds I had no idea. But Irene clearly believed it did, and the Saint had saved me before, so why not. But now, I took the icon off and smelled my wife instead. 'You smell much nicer', I told her. She giggled.

Towards the middle of summer, here were fewer rumours and more facts. Nampites called in his senior commanders and told us to start preparing for an autumn campaign. Guiscard had really subdued all the opposition and was calling a grand muster of his army for September. Come October, we were likely to find ourselves back in the west, to our old fighting grounds of Ohrid, Dyrrachion and Avlona.

The prospect of another campaign in late autumn or winter was not welcomed by everyone. Oleg looked very annoyed.

'What is with this Duke?' he exclaimed. 'Why he not fight in summer, like civilised persons do? Is he some kind of barbarian?' Everybody laughed.

Nampites didn't even reply. Instead he repeated his orders to make sure all the banda were ready to march by late August. The army was to assemble at Thessaloniki, where we would presumably await further developments.

And so, it came to pass that for the third time in four years I marched out through the Golden Gate and onto the Via Egnatia. The first time, we had been certain of victory, but defeated. The second time we were worried about defeat, but eventually victorious. This time, the army was larger than a year earlier. But what was more important was that this time we were once again confident of victory. Not like the first time, four years ago. Then it had been because we thought that no-one could defeat the Roman Empire and because we were anxious to get our revenge on the Normans. But this time around, we knew that we had defeated them. They might be back, but we had learned how to fight them. Also (and I never thought that I ever would say this) our army was strengthened by the presence of a large body of Normans. I still didn't like them. But every Norman that abandoned Guiscard for the Emperor meant one Norman less to fight – always assuming they stayed loyal.

Because we did not know what the Normans would do, the march to Thessaloniki was only a shift towards a more forward base. So we kept a good, but not rushed pace of about 20 miles per day. Including rest days, it took us forty days to cover the distance. It helped that instead of carrying supplies, there were markets established where we stopped for the night. Or else supplies had been stored in the vicinity. Our speedy march meant that when we arrived, it was still summer.

The army spread out in different camps around Thessaloniki. Since we were likely to remain there for some time, I applied for leave, not only for myself, but for Erik as well.

We went into town together. First, we went to the Cathedral of Saint Demetrios and listened to mass there. I spoke with the priests and explained that I was the Edmund who had endowed some masses recently. The expressed their thanks and blessed Erik and me with hopes of success in our forthcoming war.

Afterwards, Erik asked me if I really believed in the protection of Saint Demetrios. I didn't tell him about my vision of Irene, nor how she had apparently had a similar vision of me at the same time. Instead, I said that I personally felt that yes, the Saint did look out for me. Erik was sceptical. The saints no doubt had many good qualities, he thought, and no doubt you could sway them with your prayers – sometimes. But they were probably all too busy with other things to really look after single individuals. I just said that everyone had to reach the truth in his own way.

When we arrived at my parents-in-law's house, Erik looked impressed. He had heard of Irene's father's wealth, but I think he always thought our stories somewhat exaggerated. If Georgios was so rich, why were we living so modestly? I had explained that I did not want Irene to pay for everything we did and that this put a limit on our life. But he always dismissed this, asking what was the point of marrying someone rich, if you couldn't enjoy the money?

I had sent a note to my parents-in-law, so they were expecting us. Georgios greeted Erik, nothing that thanks to him, he was a 'debtor both to the Greeks and to the Barbarians'. Then he brought us in and introduced Erik to my mother-in-law, as well as to Theodora and her family, who had also come over.

'I bring you not only our kinsman Edmund, but also his Tauro-Scythian friend, a veritable Patroklos to his Akilles, the chief admirer of my grand-daughter Theodora, the King's kinsman Erik Orm's Son.'

We had an exquisite meal, where I think Georgios' kitchen staff surpassed themselves. There was lamb and hare, served with honey vinegar, green olives, also in honey vinegar as well as in brine, asparagus, white bread of course, some excellent light white wine and heaps of fruit, apples, pears and cherries. There were also some delicious cheeses that

Georgios said came from Crete. He insisted that we should take some with us back to the camp to improve our diet.

I don't know how Erik did it, but my mother-in-law, who had taken years before she actually smiled at me (although after Dora's birth I found her even regarding me with some warmth) started laughing within moments of meeting him. Towards the end of the meal, she half removed her veil and exchanged barbed comments with him that alternatively had Georgios laughing, me open-mouthed and Theodora blushing furiously. I had certainly never believed this of the normally so proper and strict Eudokia.

As we left, Eudokia suddenly asked Erik 'Are you under the protection of any of the Saints?'

He looked a bit uncomfortable at that. 'I pray, of course', he said. 'But a Dane also remembers the gods of his fathers. Thor, the God of Thunder, and Tyr, the God of War. They still have power.'

'Nonsense', she interrupted him. 'The heathen gods may have power in the barbarous north. But you are a Christian soldier, fighting for God's vice-gerent on Earth. You must have the protection of an important saint. Let me think. Theodora, bring me the small icon of Saint Theodore Tiron from your father's study.'

As Theodora disappeared, Eudokia turned back to Erik and explained that Saint Theodore Tiron was one of the most important military saints and a great hero. 'He slew a dragon, you know. It is best to be protected by one of the greatest saints.'

Then Theodora returned with the icon. Like my icon of Saint Demetrios, it had a ribbon so that it could be worn around one's neck. Theodora gave it to her mother, who hung it around Erik's neck – he had to stoop to allow her to reach. Erik looked embarrassed, particularly when she kissed him loudly on both cheeks. He actually blushed. Georgios shook his hand and said something – no doubt with a great many literary allusions, I didn't hear it – as did Thomas, while Theodora also kissed him.

As we left, Erik was unusually subdued. He kept looking at his icon. 'Who was Saint Theodore Tiron?' he finally asked.

'I don't know. A soldier, though, that I am sure. You'll have to ask a priest.'

'Is there a church in his name?'

'I know there is one in Constantinopolis. Why?'

'No, here. In Thessaloniki.'

'Don't know. Why?'

He looked abashed. 'I just felt I should go and ask for his protection.'

I did not laugh – although given our words earlier that day, I well could have. That Erik of all people would suddenly put his faith in a saint – even a warrior – was indeed a surprise.

Less surprising was the orders that greeted us the next day. The day was to be spent preparing everything and in the morning, we were breaking camp and marching off. At the moment, it was not quite clear where we were marching, only that it was towards the west. Some guessed Dyrrachion, others Avlona or even further south. But clearly, the Emperor had heard something that made him want to move even closer to the coast. But we marched slowly and it was only in October that we had advanced as far as Kastoria. There we waited again.

We all began to realise that once again we would be fighting through the winter.

Finally, new orders were issued and we began a series of force marches – southwards. It turned out that Guiscard had finally crossed the narrows between Italy and Greece and landed on the island of Kerkyra. This was quite a bit south of Avlona and due west of Larissa. As we pushed on through the mountains, all sorts of rumours began to circulate again. The Norman fleet had landed a huge army on Kerkyra. No, it had been sunk by the Venetian and Roman fleets in a great battle. No, there had been two battles – with all the Norman fleet sunk in each one of them, however that could be. No, there were three battles – the Norman fleet may have been sunk twice over, but it still defeated the Venetians in the third battle. Guiscard was dead. No, he had survived, but one of his sons was dead. No, that wasn't true either.

As we approached Kerkyra, there were more reliable reports and finally Nampites called in his Kometes to explain what was going on.

As far as the Emperor knew, we were told, this had happened. Guiscard had crossed the sea with 150 ships and landed on Kerkyra. There had been three sea battles. Unfortunately, the Norman fleet was not sunk in any of them. They were defeated twice and the Duke's son – Roger Borsa, not Bohemond, I was disappointed to hear – had been wounded in the second battle. But as the Roman and Venetian ships sailed away, the Normans had suddenly sallied out and attacked them and won a large victory. Then part of the Norman fleet had sailed south and conquered Kephallonia, another island.

'This is what we know so far. The Emperor thinks that the Normans will have to move into winter quarters soon. They won't be able to sail across the Adriatic again. That means we go back to what we did a year ago. Make sure there are no supplies reaching them, but stay out of battle.'

In fact, it turned out that the Varangians were not called upon to do much fighting or even raiding. Instead, we were kept in camp with the Emperor, while the Turkish horsemen were used to make sure that the Normans had nothing to eat. By this time, it was already winter. Duke Robert had moved onto the mainland and stormed the city of Vonitsa, where he made his winter quarters. This city was inside a bay, on the south side of the Ambrakian Gulf. The entrance to the Gulf was quite narrow, but I suppose it didn't matter as he did not expect to receive any reinforcements by sea.

Our army was camped some days away, while the Turks raided the countryside, occasionally bringing in herds of animals. They always said that they had taken these from the Normans. Sometimes they brought Norman prisoners to prove it. But other times they would be followed a day or two later by the headman from some village who claimed that the Turks had stolen the villagers' sheep or pigs.

But wherever the animals came from, it was clear that they did not reach the Normans, and that was the most important thing.

As the winter wore on, our duties began to change. Now it was not only the Turks who were harassing the Normans. The rest of us began to get involved as well. Once again, we were issued with horses and began to scour the countryside for Norman stragglers and foragers. On the Norman side, the less food they had, the more they sent out raiding parties of their own, trying to find supplies from ever further a field. We would clash with these, with mixed results.

Even so, I was glad at the activity. So too was Erik. 'What is the use of being protected by a saint if he has nothing to protect me from?' he would grumble. But soon enough there was plenty of work, both for Saint Demetrios and for Saint Theodore Tiron. But there was a difference this time, compared with the previous year. This time, we never took prisoners. If we defeated them, we took their food and their weapons and armour and let them go again. If they deserted, well and good. If they returned to their camp, even better, since they would just add to the pressure for food and drink.

On our side, we were kept well supplied with everything. Occasionally, a Norman noble or count would come to our camp and throw himself at the Emperor's mercy. Whenever this happened – I know, because I stood guard on the Emperor's tent often enough – he and his followers would be invited to a banquet with the Emperor. They would be given rich gifts of gold, silver and silk clothes, before they were either sent home, or, if they wanted to enter the Emperor's service, to Constantinopolis.

But towards the end of January, this trickle dried up and there were no more Norman deserters. We also noticed that there were far fewer foraging parties. At first, we did not know why. Then a Turkish troop returned in haste from a raid, with some of the riders looking terrified. Soon afterwards, rumours began to spread in the camp that the plague had broken out in the Norman camp. The same evening, Nampites called us in again and told us that this was true. He also told us that we would have to be more careful and avoid getting too close to the Normans. And then he said that we would be closing in on the Norman camp, trying to pen them in even more. Nobody asked how we would manage to avoid getting to close to them while at the same time closing in.

For the next few weeks we therefore started to ride closer to the Norman camp. Not too close. Plague or no plague, we had a healthy respect for the Norman knights. One group of Roman soldiers had been braver – or less careful – and a troop of mounted

Normans had sallied out, killed a good number and scattered the rest.

Towards the end of the winter, I was out on one patrol to the west of Vonitsa. There is a peninsula that juts out to the north a short distance from the town. We were riding along the western side of the peninsula, when Erik stopped and looked further out towards the bay.

'Look. There is a ship beached up ahead. Just beyond the trees.'

I looked where he was pointing and saw something. He was sure that it was a ship, so I gave orders to spread out and approach carefully. As we came closer, we could see that Erik was right. It was a ship, but more importantly, it was beached. The crew was working hard to try to float it. A small group stood to the side, watching and directing the work. They were all so intent on their work that, and the noise of the surf pounding the rocky beach so loud that they didn't notice us until we almost were upon them.

There were some startled shouts and some of them tried to grab weapons and form a line. But they were outnumbered and disorganised and they knew it. Part of the bandon surrounded them, while I kept another part in reserve in case more Normans approached. Then I told Erik to bring up the little group that seemed to contain the leaders.

There were five of them. Two were almost carrying a third. When they came up, the man being supported looked up. I gasped as I saw his face.

'Bohemond!'

He peered up at me and in a voice that was almost a whisper, he said 'Who are you? The Englishman! Edmund, yes. So you didn't die in Avlona? How come? Well, it doesn't matter. How is your hand?'

I dismounted and stood in front of him.

'My hand is fine. But why are you here? Are you deserting your father? That doesn't show much filial duty.'

His face showed that he resented that.

'Don't be impudent. My father the Duke has ordered me to go to Salerno. There are doctors there who can cure the plague.'

At the word 'plague', Erik and the two guards with him moved off. I would have liked to move off as well, but I was not going to give Bohemond the satisfaction of seeing me afraid.

'So Duke Robert is still alive?'

'Alive and well. As are my brothers Roger and Guy. And most of the army.'

'But not you.'

'But not I. Not that it matters anymore. I am in your power. What are you going to do? Kill me? Or hand me over to the Emperor so that he can do it instead?'

I had been thinking about the same thing. What to do. Oh, my duty was clear enough. He was the Emperor's enemy. I need not kill him, but I must certainly bring him back to the Emperor. With Bohemond in his hands, who knew what he could force Guiscard to do. But even as I was thinking that, I thought of other things. He had not killed me when he had the chance. Nor my men – they had eventually been saved. And there was something with him that made me not want to kill him – a sense of, I don't know. Not friendship, but maybe fellowship. Yes, we had fought against each other, but soldiers everywhere were also comrades – even on opposing sides. But there was something that was even more important. When Richard and I had travelled around in Italy, I remembered how most of the people we met had spoken about Bohemond. They had talked about his ambition, some of them with admiration, others with loathing. There was certainly no love lost between him and his half-brother Roger Borsa, this much I knew. Bringing Bohemond to the Emperor might upset Robert Guiscard, but there were probably quite a few Normans who would be happy to see him gone. On the other hand, what if Bohemond was on the loose back in Italy? The war against the Empire had been very much for his sake, this was clear. How eager would the other Norman leaders be to leave him at large in Italy, while they were toiling away in a campaign that no longer seemed so certain of victory?

I could see him looking at me while these thoughts crossed my mind. I don't know how much of them he could guess, but he must have realised that I was unsure. Not for long. I made up my mind.

'Neither', I said. 'You are free to go to Salerno.'

I could hear gasps of surprise from Erik and from one of the other Normans. Bohemond himself did not say anything. He just looked at me. Then he nodded. 'A life for a life', he said. 'But what happens next time?'

'I don't know. How do you know that there will be a next time?'

'Oh, I am sure there will. You are not rid of Bohemond yet, Englishman – Edmund', he corrected himself.

Erik opened his mouth to say something, but I interrupted him.

'Pentekontarch. Tell the bandon to mount up. We are returning to camp.'

Then I held out my hand to Bohemond. 'Good bye. And good luck.'

'Good bye. And thank you', he replied, gripping my hand.

As we rode off, I could see the men talking about what had just happened. But apart from Erik, none of them knew who the Norman had been – although some of them may have guessed. But Erik had plenty to say.

‘Are you possessed? By all the gods – by all the saints, I mean – how could you let him go? The Emperor would have granted your every wish if you had brought him Bohemond. You could have been a noble, had a palace – anything! And you let him go.’

‘I couldn’t kill him.’

‘But you didn’t have to. The Emperor would not have. You just had to take him prisoner. It was your duty!’

‘I owed him a life.’

‘No, you didn’t. Don’t you remember hanging off a cliff over the sea by Avlona? Did he spare you then?’

‘He didn’t kill me. Look Erik – he has the plague.’

‘Yes – and you are lucky if you don’t, having almost embraced him.’

I hadn’t thought of that.

‘He is going home to Italy to die. He is no danger to us – or to the Emperor – anymore. Would you kill a dying man? You saw how he could barely stand up alone.’

‘Well, I think you will live to regret this. He is not dead yet. What do you do if he survives?’

‘Even better. If he survives, the fact that he is in Italy will do more than anything else to make the Normans go back.’

‘What will Nampites say?’

That was a good question. The Emperor might actually understand what I had done. But somehow, I doubted if Nampites would look as kindly upon my action.

‘It might be best if Nampites did not know exactly what happened.’

‘You want me to lie?’ Erik sounded outraged.

‘No. It will only get you in trouble. I will tell him myself.’

Suddenly he laughed. ‘Don’t worry. Of course, I will lie for you. Saint Theodore Tiron will forgive me. And I will make sure that the others keep their mouths shut. Mind you, I still think that you are mad. And I know that you will live to regret this day. I only hope that I won’t be there to regret it with you. Or maybe that I will be there to save you from your folly.’

I didn't say anything. I just held out my hand to him and he took it in his. He was a true friend – my first real friend since Godric died outside Dyrrachion.

But as we came back to camp I decided that I was going to report the whole story anyway. Not because I was worried about it coming out, but because I had thought more about it and had was convinced that I had done the right thing.

I went to Nampites and reported the result of our patrol

'Oh, and we came upon a beached Norman ship. Bohemond was on board. He has the plague and was going back to Italy for a cure. I decided to let him go.'

'You did what?! Are you completely insane? How could you let one of our greatest enemies go when he was in your power?' He stood up and clenched his fists and his face turned red. For a brief moment, I thought that he would hit me.

'I let him go, first because he was sick. He will probably die.'

'Oh, so you are a great physician, are you? How do you even know that he was really sick and not play-acting?'

‘He was sick all right – ask anyone of my men. Ask Erik.’

‘That is neither here, nor there. How could you let him go? How can I tell the Emperor? You will be dismissed and blinded, probably even have your nose cut off. I’ll do it myself if nobody else does!’

‘Wait. Listen. The plague is rife in the Norman camp. This we know. Guiscard is an old man. He may well catch it – the old often do. If he does, having Bohemond free in Italy is a far greater threat to Roger Borsa’s inheritance, than it would serve us to have Bohemond in Constantinople. He will never do the Emperor’s bidding. But he may do the Emperor’s work anyway. If Guiscard dies, the Normans will rush back to Italy. The war will be over.’

‘And what if Guiscard doesn’t die?’

’Then his men will force him to go back. The last thing they will want is Bohemond in Italy, free to take over their lands and building up his own powerbase. Even Guiscard’s other sons will want to go back.’

Nampites did not seem convinced. But he sat down again and thought for a while. Then he said ‘I will tell the Emperor. He will decide. But you are confined under guard until I have heard his decision.'

I hadn't counted on that. But there was nothing I could do. He called two Russian Varangians to come over and lead me away. I was not treated badly, but I was kept locked up and guarded while I thought about what would happen if the Emperor agreed with Nampites. It was not a nice thought, so I tried to think about my family instead.

Two days later, I was brought to Nampites again. His face revealed nothing as he started speaking.

'You are lucky. I have spoken with the Emperor. He was taken aback at first, but then thought very carefully about it. His brothers were there as well. The Sebastokrator Isaak thinks that you should be discharged and mutilated.'

I said nothing.

'But the Protosebastos Adrianos spoke up for you. He said that if Bohemond died, it didn't matter. And if he didn't, it might well work to our advantage to have him in Italy, stirring up mischief for his brother and forcing them to keep an eye on what was happening at home. He argued very strongly in your favour.'

The Protosebastos Adrianos again. I touched my icon of Saint Demetrios and breathed a quick prayer of thanks.

Nampites was still talking. 'It seems that he convinced the Emperor. It is official – you did the right thing. But in the future, will you please sometimes do the wrong thing? For instance, if you ever get your hands on Bohemond again, cut his head off?'

'I will. Thank you for letting me know.'

CHAPTER 19

The Anglo-Saxon Revenge

Now the days began to move faster. Winter turned to spring and the days got both warmer and longer. The Normans were still penned in their camp, but scouts reported that they were getting their ships ready. We were kept in constant readiness to break camp in case the Normans moved away and threatened some other part of the Empire.

By April and May, it was clear that such Normans as had survived the plague were ready to move out. We kept getting reports from our scouts that they were working on their ships to get them in shape. On our side, we were also told to get ready to move out on short notice. Then in June we were told that the Normans had sailed off. The question was now, where?

It turned out that they had not sailed very far. Only across a small stretch of sea to Kephallonia. Then they remained there for some weeks, while our army moved closer to the shore. This was a very strange kind of campaign.

We hadn't really done much fighting for a long time. Yet it did not feel bad. The Normans had not managed to make any headway against us. Four years ago, I would have wondered why we did not force a battle. By now I knew that if we did nothing, we were actually winning.

There was a constant stream of people going back and forth between the two armies. I bumped into Richard again. He was in a hurry, but told me that he had just been to Kephallonia on what he called 'our usual business – making my fellow Normans see the light'. Geoffrey of Scalea was not there, he told me. This year he was fighting with Count Roger in Sicily.

In early July things suddenly began to happen. It turned out that the Emperor was once again trying to end the war. He was sending another delegation to the Norman Duke. The delegation was headed by the Protosebastos Adrianos, who as, Nampites informed me with a scowl, had specifically asked for me to head his escort.

'Try to be careful. The Emperor's brother may like to have you around, but I like to have my

Kometes back here, in command of their banda. There may still be a battle.'

I promised to do my best. Then I picked out a dozen men, left the rest of my bandon in Erik's care and reported to the Protosebastos. He was surrounded by courtiers and priests who were trying to get his attention, but when he saw me, he made a sign to them to leave and came up to me.

I bowed deeply, but he held out his hand to me. 'Edmund the Kelt. Once again we are going on adventures together.'

'Kyr is most kind.'

'Nonsense. You were very helpful the last time we saw Duke Robert. Are you ready to leave?'

'As soon as Kyr gives the order.'

'In that case, let us leave. Do you have horses?'

'Yes Kyr.'

'Let's go, then.'

The Protosebastos, like his brother the Emperor rode a large warhorse. But for once, I was not on one of the smaller horses. I still had the brown mare I had been given, or lent, by Richard's nephews, and towered over the Protosebastos. He did not speak very much. But he mentioned that he was very pleased with my father-in-law's work. I made a note to remember to tell Georgios – preferably in my mother-in-law's presence.

Suddenly I remembered something. The Normans were on an island. The only way to get to an island was by sea. I really did not want to be seasick and the mere thought made my stomach turn. But there was nothing doing. I could hardly turn around and beg to be excused on account of seasickness. I would have to bear it and hope for the best.

When we came down to the shore, there was a large Venetian ship waiting for us. The captain greeted the Protosebastos respectfully and led us on board his ship. This was the biggest ship I had ever been on. They even took our horses on board.

It was not a pleasant journey, even if it was short. I started to get seasick and was lurching towards the railing, when one of the Venetian sailors grabbed me. He shouted something at me, but I couldn't understand what he was saying. So instead he dragged me to the front of the ship, and showed me that I was to stand there and look straight ahead. It helped – a little. I was still feeling terrible, but at least I wasn't sick. I suppose it helped that even I could understand that the sea was calm. But even so, the journey to Kephallonia took the better part of a day. I could not have lasted another day like this.

We had set out just after dawn, so when we arrived, although it was still quite light, it was already evening. But we were apparently expected, because we were met by a group of Norman nobles with a guard of soldiers. As soon as we and our horses were ashore, we sat up and followed them towards their camp. I was riding behind the Protosebastos and a Norman Count whose name I had not heard. I noticed that the Protosebastos was trying to engage the Norman in conversation, but he was only getting short answers and eventually gave up.

The Normans had taken over one of the towns on the island. As we entered the town, we were told to dismount and were taken to a large house in the town centre. It was a nice house, not as large as Georgios', but still showing signs of a wealthy owner. As we entered through a gate in the wall, we were led through two rooms and into a garden. There was another group of Normans there, gathered around a bed. As we approached, they stood aside and showed a figure lying on the bed.

As I looked at him, I suddenly realised that it was Robert Guiscard himself. But I did not have time to start reflecting on this. The Protosebastos signalled to me to wait with my men and then walked up to the bed alone. He greeted the duke respectfully and then stood there for a while talking with him. Eventually one of the Normans brought him a chair and he sat down; and something to drink.

As they continued talking to each other, I looked around. The Norman nobles stood to one side, except one of them who was now sitting down next to the bed as well. But there were some common soldiers standing near us – guarding us, I suppose. I turned to one of them, who seemed to be their commander, and asked what was going on.

'The fever', he said. 'The Duke is dying. It is as it was foretold, that he would die here.' He looked mournful.

'Here?' I asked. 'I thought it was foretold that he would only die when he reached Jerusalem.'

He stared at me. ‘Don’t you know?’

‘Know what?’

‘Look over there.’ He pointed towards another island, barely visible in the dusk. ‘See that.’

‘Yes.’

‘Well, that’s called Ithaka. There is a ruined town there. When we came here, the Duke caught a fever. He asked for some cold water. One of the men of this island told us that the best water around was to be found on Ithaka in that ruined town. When we asked what the town was called, he said that it used to be called Jerusalem. Someone told the Duke and the moment he heard, his face turned grey and he was unable to get out of bed. Do you not know the full prophecy?’

‘No. I just heard about Jerusalem.’

‘Well, it seems the Duke was once told that as far as Atheras, he will conquer everything, but when he gets to Jerusalem, he will die. Now do you see?’

‘Not really. I mean, I understand about Jerusalem. But what is Atheras?’

‘Atheras is a peninsula on this island.’

Now I did understand. Clearly, Robert Guiscard himself expected to die here. That was important news. I had to tell the Protosebastos at once. But how?

That question was easily answered. Even as I was thinking this, the Protosebastos stood up and bowed to the prostrate Norman. The other Norman also stood up and they exchanged a few words. Then the Protosebastos came over to us and signalled for us to follow him.

We moved quietly through the town and were taken to a smaller house nearby. As the Protosebastos began to leave, I spoke up.

'Kyr.'

'What is it?'

I explained what the Norman soldier had told me, as well as how I had heard the prophecy earlier. He seemed interested, but when I had finished, he said 'I didn't know this, but it doesn't matter. My mother is very skilled in all matters of health. I already knew that he is dying as soon as I saw him. The important thing is to let my brother know. But we cannot get off the island tonight. This will have to wait until morning.'

But the next morning, when we walked back to Guiscard's house, we were told that it was already too late. The Norman who had been sitting with the Protosebastos received us. 'Count Guy', the Protosebastos said. So this was Guiscard's third son. He looked slightly like his father, but nothing like Bohemond. I remembered Richard once having mentioned that Guy of Hauteville had toyed with entering Imperial service.

'Protosebastos', he replied. 'Your mission here is ended. My father, Duke Robert, died this morning. I have sent for my brother Roger. If you have anything to say, it will have to wait until this afternoon, when he is back.'

It was a strange meeting. The Protosebastos expressed his sadness that such a noble warrior should have died in this way and Count Guy thanked him. The fact that the late Duke was a bitter enemy of the Protosebastos' brother the Emperor was somehow never mentioned. After some further comments, we returned to our house, where we had nothing to do.

The Protosebastos stayed in his room, and I had no idea what he was thinking.

The next day we were summoned back to he late Duke's house. This time we were received by Count Guy and someone a few years older but so like him that he had to be his brother Roger. I had heard much about Roger Borsa when Richard and I had been in Italy, so I looked curiously at him. I knew that he did not have a good reputation. He was supposed to be lazy and too concerned with money. He looked weak-willed, with vacant eyes which showed signs of tears.

He asked the Protosebastos to step into a smaller room. To my surprise, the Protosebastos asked me to join them.

Once the Protosebastos had repeated his sadness at the death of Roger's father, he quickly came to the point.

'This sad war was very much your late father's plan', he said. 'And you know that it was very much to further the ambitions of your brother Bohemond.'

'Half-brother', Count Roger interjected with a scowl. There didn't seem to be much brotherly love lost there.

'But things have now changed. Your Duke is dead. Much of your army has been killed by the plague. The Roman weapons have been victorious everywhere. You have lost all your footholds in Greece, except these few islands. The Emperor's Venetian fleet can stop you from going home and starve you here.'

The two brothers looked at him.

'But the Emperor does not want to shed any more Christian blood. He prefers to be a friend of the Normans, whose bravery and loyalty he admires. You know that many of them are already serving the Empire. Other simply accept the friendship of the Emperor of the Romans. Those who do, know that the Emperor's generosity indeed mirrors that of God.'

I had heard that before, but where?

'My brother the Emperor would be proud to count the Duke of the Normans, a powerful lord in Italy, as his friend. Such a friend would also bask in the Imperial bounty.'

I could see that Roger Borsa was taking in every word. Guy seemed less convinced. But the Protosebastos went on.

‘Of course, this assumes that there is indeed a Duke of the Normans. Surely, Duke Roger’ – I saw a gleam in Roger Borsa’s eyes. Was this the first time someone had addressed him as Duke? ‘Surely you are certain of the loyalties of your father’s vassals – and your own family.’

‘I have already sworn fealty to my brother!’ This was from Count Guy.

‘Of course. I did not mean to impugn your loyalty.’

I knew what he meant. So, too, did the two brothers, who looked at each other. Bohemond was on the loose in Italy. How loyal was he?

Now Roger Borsa spoke. His words belied my impression of him. He really sounded firm and determined.

‘Tell your brother this. The Duke of the Normans is ready to be his friend. We should indeed no longer shed Christian blood. I will return with my father’s coffin to Italy and bury him there. My vassals will join me. Afterwards, I will send an emissary to the Emperor to discuss our friendship further. And now I ask you to go. I have matters to attend to.’

And with that we left. But we could not leave Kephallonia yet. The Venetian captain told us that the winds were against us. So we stayed for another day.

That afternoon, Roger Borsa called a general meeting of all Norman nobles and a great part of the army. He spoke to them about his father's death, reminded them hat he was his father's chosen heir, and made them all swear fealty to him – beginning with his brother Guy. Then he told them that they would return to Italy to bury his father. As for the war, they would return to that later. When the Protosebastos heard the last words, he smiled. I understood him. With Roger Borsa and Bohemond fighting each other in Italy, and other Normans joining in, there was not going to be any war on the Empire for some time – whatever they were being told now.

The next day we were able to board our ship and sail back to the mainland. This time, standing at the prow and looking ahead did not help. Once again, I was seasick during the whole voyage. It didn't help that the wind turned halfway across and the journey took even longer back.

Once we had landed, we returned to our camp. The Protosebastos Adrianos thanked me – although I had not done anything – and went to report to the Emperor. I went to Nampites to tell him that I was back – and that the war most likely was over. He seemed pleased to see me and even more pleased with the news. Erik was also pleased when I told him and the rest of the bandon, although one or two of the others claimed to be disappointed that we were not given an opportunity to defeat the Normans in battle.

Two days later we received word that we were breaking camp and returning to Constantinopolis. Once again rumours began to spread, but Nampites quickly set us straight. Our scouts had reported that the Normans were beginning to sail home. The war really was over.

As we began the march back, Erik rode up next to me.

'Are you sorry?' he asked.

'Sorry? For what?'

'You did not get your revenge. For Hastings.'

I thought about that. In one sense, he was right. I used to dream about a big battle, fields running red with Norman blood and fleeing Normans being cut down by victorious Englishmen – or Romans. That had not happened. But, on the other hand, we had beaten them. The Normans had tried to conquer the Empire and they had failed. We had won and, in the process, I hope I had learned a few things about how to fight them. This would come in handy when I began to train my Englishmen for our return to England and the final battle against the Bastard.

Erik was still looking at me.

'I am sorry. I was thinking about your question. The final reckoning for Hastings will still come. But meanwhile, I am not disappointed. I have had part of my revenge.'

'They will be back, you know.'

'Probably. But this time we will be ready. We know how to fight them – and how to beat them.'

'And Bohemond?'

'I don't know. But I don't think that we have seen the last of him. Roger Borsa did not strike me as the man who could control his brother. No, Bohemond will definitely be back. But I am not going to worry about that until it happens.'

The march back to Constantinopolis took many weeks. But for me, the time seemed to fly by. When we stopped in Thessaloniki, Erik joined me in visiting the Cathedral of Saint Demetrios to give thanks to the Saint. We also visited my parents-in-law, and my mother-in-law told everyone that it was the power of Saint Theodore Tiron that had preserved Erik.

And finally, in the autumn, we marched in through the Golden Gate again. The Guard marched to our barracks in the Great Palace. There we were mustered and inspected once again. Finally, we were dismissed.

I left as quickly as I could and hurried home. For once, I was not coming home late in the evening.

As I walked through the door, two shapes, one larger and one smaller threw themselves at me, while a very small one looked on with wide open eyes. And I suddenly, strangely, found myself thinking of Bohemond again. Yes, he would no doubt be back. But I hoped it would take a very long time.

First published in 2018 by Rhomphaia Books

25483935R00280

Printed in Poland
by Amazon Fulfillment
Poland Sp. z o.o., Wrocław